a Man loves a Boy -3- our quickly growing flock

Copyright © 2011 by Aad Aandacht

All rights reserved.

No part of this book may be used or reproduced by any means, graphic, electronic, or mechanical, including photocopying, recording, taping, or by any information storage retrieval system, without the written permission of the publisher, except in the case of brief quotations embodied in critical articles and reviews.

AandachtPreSS books may be ordered through regular booksellers, or by visiting the appropriate homepages or contacting:

www.aandachtpress.com
www.gypsyseries.com

First print, December 2011

ISBN 978-90-79092-06-2

NUR 341

www.gypsyseries.com
gypsy@gypsyseries.com

a Man loves a Boy
-3- *our quickly growing flock*

Another famous 'Gypsy Series' book
- **Written by Aad Aandacht** -
Dutch psychotherapist and writer
www.gypsyseries.com

*

Inspirational Fantasy
Age: 12 and older

*

AandachtPreSS
"Books with a message"

Our famous ongoing 'Gypsy Series' consists of:

a Man loves a Boy -1- my little Gypsy Soul Mate
a Man loves a Boy -2- a little upcoming Shaman
a Man loves a Boy -3- our quickly growing flock
a Man loves a Boy -4- my boy gets a new face
a Man loves a Boy -5- claiming our Gypsy roots

a Boy loves a Man -1- Gypsy Heir to the Throne
a Boy loves a Man -2- training my Shaman skills
a Boy loves a Man -3- becoming a Real Trapper
a Boy loves a Man -4- our caravan burns down
a Boy loves a Man -5- recognizing my new Dad

Throw-away-kid -1- born as a halfblood Shaman

Please visit www.gypsyseries.com to stay informed.

Table of contents:

1. My happy threesome, planning to go out..........7
2. Visiting a zoo and meeting our ancestors. 15
3. My little soul mate vanishes into thin air. 23
4. The zoo's security guards, and the police. 31
5. John feels Harry's energy; he is still alive. 39
6. We have little Harry back, lost and found. 47
7. Anti-anthropoid; and teasing each other. 55
8. My boy's face clinic and our 'face doctor'. 63
9. Harry goes outside and gets a new friend. 73
10. What is a 'homo'; and Jason is in trouble. 81
11. I am Davy's new Dad; and meeting BJ. 91
12. Nicky sleeps over; two little whisperers. 101
13. Eat, the Magic Word for Growing Kids. 109
14. Supermarket; and I am angry with John. 117
15. We are buying a beautiful Golden Van. 125
16. Buying a big inflatable swimming pool. 133
17. Dinner with Mary; my boys' sleepover. 141
18. Birthday suit; tree house; meeting Jason. 149
19. Jason still misses his former 'boyfriend'. 157
20. Two detached 'soul mates' are reunited. 167
21. Road restaurant; Carl's beautiful dream. 179
22. A Moby Dick is a whale; BJ apologizes. 189
23. BJ makes up with Jason and with Carl. 199
24. A new tree house; and BJ will survive. 209
---. You've reached the end of our third book. 219

I want to thank my precious friends, Henk and Marja, for their invaluable help. You helped me tremendously, by staying with me and patiently offering me your much appreciated comments and advice.
I will commend you in my prayers!

AandachtPreSS
www.aandachtpress.com
aad@aandachtpress.com
www.gypsyseries.com
gypsy@gypsyseries.com
"Books with a Message"

Aad Aandacht is a Dutch psychotherapist who loves writing 'books with a message'

1. My happy threesome, planning to go out.

"Dad or John, could you please help me? I want to set up the first chapter of my first 'Gypsy Series' book about myself."

Sitting in front of our computer screen, my little soul mate looked at John and me with eager eyes, while waiting for our response. Feeling full of tender loving care, I looked at my adopted son, my eight-year-old little Gypsy Crown Prince and only Heir to the Throne, 'Harold Janovski Romani'. Usually, we called him 'little Harry', to distinguish him from me, 'Big Harry', and also because his tiny frame still was a bit too small for his age. However, his extremely intelligent spirit full of sunshine and happiness certainly was not too small!

John, who was my thirteen-year-old 'young friend' and also little Harry's 'big brother', chuckled at seeing his little brother's eager face, while he went to our computer to help him start up a word processor. For the time being, John was our houseguest; because his mother, Trudy, had a fight with her husband, Eric, and she had left our small village to escape his wrath. Her youngest children, Mark and Marrie, had wanted to join her; but John had wanted to stay here, where he had his own friends, his 'little brother', and me.

Helpfully, John explained how his little brother should start our word processor first, before he could set up the first chapter of his own book. Yesterday evening, our 'Spirit Guide', Jack, who was the deceased former owner of my newly bought house, had asked us to start writing two different 'Gypsy Series' of books. My little Gypsy Prince would start writing his own series of books, about growing up in his secluded Gypsy camp in the Rumanian mountains. Then, I would start writing my own series of several books, about taking a severely burnt little Gypsy boy into my house, and raising him until he would be old enough to be 'Gypsy King Harold the Second'.

Eagerly looking from the empty computer screen to the patiently waiting keyboard, my boy's deep baritone voice asked John:

"Shall I now type the title of my first book about myself? I want to call it 'a Boy loves a Man - book 1 - Gypsy Heir to the Throne'."

Looking a bit unsure, John hesitatingly responded:

"To be honest, I am not sure... Dad? Could you please help Harry set up the first page of his first 'Gypsy series' book about himself?"

Still feeling full of love with my two 'adopted sons', I answered:

"Well, I suppose that typing the title of your own book will be an excellent start to begin with. Then, you could go on from there."

With a happy smile, my little soul mate returned to the computer keyboard and started to look for the first key he needed, the 'a'. After he had found the correct key and pushed it, he looked at the screen to verify its correctness, before he started searching for the next key.

It was a funny sight to see my boy like this, typing character after character, now and then using the backspace to correct an error. His little tongue hung out of his mouth, while he searched for key after key, sometimes reacting a bit frustrated because he knew that John and I could type much faster, but he didn't want to give up too soon.

After a lot more searching, typing, and correcting, my more and more frustrated looking boy finally stopped and asked:

"Dad or John, could you please help me spell those difficult words in your language? Spelling my own Gypsy words in my own Gypsy language always was a lot easier..."

Despite his extraordinary intelligence and extremely bright brain, our little Gypsy Prince never went to school. Up to his sixth year, he had lived in Rumania, in a secluded Gypsy camp that was surrounded by huge mountains and vast forests. Two years ago, the Royal family had to flee from a witch-hunt, because the Rumanian police wanted to have a scapegoat and accused them falsely of robbing a 'gadjo'.

After driving through several foreign countries, while pretending to be on a sightseeing vacation, they stopped in this small village, felt tired of all the traveling, and planned to go home the next morning. Only, that same night, their caravan was set ablaze! Both the Gypsy King and his Queen perished in the fire. Only their six-year-old son and Heir to the Throne, their little Royal Crown Prince, survived; but he was severely burnt all over his body and face.

That same night, the former owner of my newly bought house, Jack, couldn't sleep, and left his house to take a walk through the neighborhood. Just in time, he arrived at the already burning caravan; where he rescued the suddenly appearing little Gypsy boy, by rolling him around in some wet grass. Jack accompanied the burnt little boy to a hospital, where he visited him every day, bought him everything that he needed, paid his many skin surgeries for him, comforted him with the loss of his parents, and taught him our language.

After several months and many skin operations, the burnt little Gypsy boy finally left the hospital and started living with Jack. Here, in what is now my house, he had his own room, upstairs, second door to the left. Until two months ago, when Jack suddenly died and his house went up for sale; while little Harry had to share John's bedroom and his possessions were stowed away in their garage.

A few days ago, I bought Jack's former house, hoping to live here in peace and quiet for the rest of my life, as a retired psychotherapist. Within a few hours, I met my best friend from several past lives who had reincarnated as John, and I met my burnt 'little soul mate' from even more past lives who soon got his 'own' room back in my house and started to live here again. Yesterday, my boy's own Gypsy people found their disappeared little Crown Prince; and they asked me to adopt him, because their Wise Woman recognized me as being the next incarnation of their famous 'Gypsy Monarch Harold the Great'...

Looking a bit frustrated, my little soul mate left our computer, climbed onto my lap, and tried to melt away in my enveloping aura, as he always did when he needed some tender loving care or craved a cuddle. Happily, I folded my arms around his tiny frame and held him close to my chest, while enjoying his 'pleasant company' very much.

I already loved my boy with all my heart, mind, and soul; and I would do everything that I could to help him feel happier! Tomorrow, I would take him to what he called his 'face clinic', where his 'face doctors' would cultivate some healthy skin and transplant it onto his burnt face and body. For the time being, I had bought him a flexible rubber mask, to hide his 'freaky' face from any pestering or nasty name-calling kids, whenever he wanted to join us outside.

While my little soul mate snuggled up under my chin, he sighed:

"Dad? As soon as I have my new face, I want to join John to a real school, because I don't want to feel stupid any more."

Feeling a bit surprised about his sudden pessimism, I responded:

"Please, my dear son, don't ever think you could be stupid! You only never learned to write those words in our language, that's all."

"I know, Dad. While I lived with Jack, he always tutored me for a few hours a day. Sometimes, Jack called me his 'linguistic miracle', because I seem to have a knack for languages and pick up foreign words very fast; but Jack also told me I tend to write phonetici... err... as I speak the words or hear them in my mind. Even after two years of speaking your language, writing it is still difficult. Unfortunately, Jack died before he could teach me your complicated spelling rules."

Still wanting to help my boy feel a bit better, I proposed:

"Perhaps, John could help you, by teaching you our spelling rules so that you can stop writing phonetically?"

"Then, John will be my tutor! Are you going to pay him for his work? I am sure he can use some larger allowances."

My chuckling imp offered me a warm kiss and a broad smile, before he hopped off my lap and returned to the still waiting computer keyboard. For a few seconds, he again tried to type a difficult word.

Then, he beckoned John to come over and help him:

"Come on John; let's start your tutoring me! First, teach me please how to use those strange 'capitals' correctly."

Immediately, both boys sat glued to the computer screen, where John showed his little brother how to start every new sentence with a capital, and how he should write 'boy' instead of 'boi' although both words were sounding the same. Feeling full of love and very happy with my two young friends, I went to our kitchen; to brew a cup of coffee for myself, and fetch colas and cookies for my boys. After I returned into my living room, I sat down on my couch, sipped my coffee, and started to look back upon my own life...

As a freelance psychotherapist, I had been working with troubled children and their often desperate parents, until I retired and divorced. Having some money to spend, I soon bought this 'nice house with a surrounding garden' in this small village. Within a few hours, I befriended five nice neighborhood children, including John. Two years before, as an agreement with CPS, John's parents had taken a badly burnt little Gypsy boy into their custody; but, in reality, little Harry lived here with Jack and had his own room in Jack's house.

Two months ago, Jack suddenly died, and little Harry was sent to John's house; where he had to share John's bedroom, while Jack's house was put up for sale. Now, my boy was living again in his old

Chapter 1. That first day of the rest of my retirement.

house, I had given him his own room back, and his own Gypsy people had allowed me to adopt him, to raise and educate him until he would be old enough to be their next Gypsy Leader and start reigning.

My boy interrupted my train of thoughts, by telling me:

"Thanks a lot, Dad, for letting John tutor me! Finally, I understand how to use those capitals. In my own language, we never use any, and we always write every word down exactly as we speak it. For now, John and I want to stop and get some more colas and cookies."

My two boys left the computer and went to our kitchen, while bumping into each other on purpose. Soon, they reappeared, carrying a tray with another cup of coffee, two glasses of cola, and the refilled cookie jar. Sitting together on our couch, both boys leaned into me and very much enjoyed our close companionship, our drinks, and our tasty cookies. Sitting together like this, and feeling our mutual love radiating between us, felt wonderful, despite our differences in age.

A few seconds later, little Harry tilted his head as if he had sensed something unexpected. As a little Shaman, he had developed a 'sixth sense' that let him feel the preceding aura of any known visitor, at least ten seconds before they actually showed up at our front door.

With a suddenly beaming face, my little Shaman announced:

"Here comes Davy!"

Happily, he hopped off our couch and raced to the front door, to welcome our thirteen-year-old mutual friend; while I rose from my couch to greet my 'third son'. My boy's extraordinary 'gift' was only one of his many Shaman surprises. Now and then, he picked up our thoughts, he could read our minds with ease, and he sometimes talked with our 'Beloved Ancestors' and 'Spirit Guides' from 'the beyond'. Now, John and I heard him open our front door and greet Davy.

My 'third son' had been abused by his own 'father' from his early youth; until, a year ago, his mother found out what was going on, because Davy started to bleed from his anus. Now, his 'father' was in jail for a very long time, and Davy had adopted me as his 'new Dad', with the consent and happy blessings of Mary, his mother.

John went to our kitchen to fetch a third glass of cola, while Davy and little Harry entered our living room. Davy immediately stormed towards me and trustfully jumped up at me, to let me catch his rather heavy frame in midair. I could catch my enthusiastic third son just in time, while he threw his strong arms around my neck, attached himself against my chest, and offered me a big kiss.

Happily cuddling up to me, Davy told me:

"Hi Dad! Sorry for being this early, but I started to feel a bit bored at home. Did you have any plans for today? This morning, I woke up and thought... Well, today is a beautiful day, and it looks like an excellent day to pay our ancestors a visit! Can we do that, please?"

"Hello son, hi to you too; and yes, today is a beautiful day. Only, what do you mean by 'pay our ancestors a visit'?"

"Of course, our ancestors are the apes, where we human beings originate from. School should have taught you that! They are living in a new zoo, about an hour drive from here; so I thought, if you didn't have any other plans for today... Could we go to that new zoo, please? I've already asked my Mom, and she agrees when you agree, but I have to be back home around nine o'clock this evening."

Smilingly, I thought that taking a 'day off' certainly sounded good! Especially after yesterday, when we had lived through our powerful emotions around meeting little Harry's own Gypsy people, and they had allowed me to adopt their little Crown Prince as my own son.

Trying to tease my enthusiastic 'third son' first, I asked him:

"What happens if that new zoo makes a mistake and accidentally keeps you in an ape cage, with your monkey looks?"

Chuckling at seeing my teasing face, Davy responded:

"You better look out for yourself, with such a monkey beard! But, can we? Oops... Sorry, I mean, please Dad, may we go to that new zoo and greet our ancestors the apes?"

Chuckling at seeing Davy's more and more pleading face and dark brown puppy doe eyes, I asked my other monkeys:

"John and Harry, what do you think? Shall we take the risk that this new zoo accidentally puts our young monkey in their ape cage?"

My little soul mate reacted enthusiastic at the thought of going out for a whole day, and he almost lost his head in vigorously nodding 'yes'! Seeing him this happy, I thought this probably was the first time my Gypsy Prince visited such a zoo. Fortunately, he now had a rubber mask to hide his severely burnt face, so that nobody in that zoo would feel shocked or call him a 'freak' or an 'alien'.

12   Aad Aandacht is a Dutch psychotherapist who loves writing 'books with a message'

With a suddenly naughty face, John chuckled:

"Dad, I hope this new zoo doesn't want to put YOU in an ape cage, thinking you are an escaped old beard-ape."

Then, he quickly dived away, before I could grab him. Therefore, I just started to tickle Davy's ribs, in an effort to free myself from my limpet-monkey, who immediately started to squeal while trying to tickle me back. Unfortunately, this triggered my two other monkeys. Working closely together, they floored me and mercilessly started to tickle my 'old' ribs, wherever they could find a sensitive spot.

Soon, their tickling became too much for me, and I panted:

"Stop please, because I'm nearly wetting my pants."

Teasingly, John responded:

"We will ask Kees from The Netherlands to put diapers on you."

"Stop NOW, or we aren't going ANYWHERE!"

Surprisingly, my threat worked on them, because they quickly pulled me upright and promised to be good boys for the rest of the day! Chuckling inwardly, I thought I had trained my monkeys very well, in such a short amount of time. Or, was I now flattering myself?

Together, my three monkeys raced to our kitchen, to prepare a wagonload of sandwiches; while I got my old cooler from the hallway closet, opened our refrigerator, and piled some ice and lemonade cans into it. Davy started to boil a couple of eggs, while John dissected half a head of lettuce; and my boy demonstrated another extraordinary gift, by fetching some spicy plants from his own small herbs garden in our backyard. In his own Gypsy camp, he had been their little Chief Cook, because he always searched their surrounding woods for spicy plants or tasty pods, to spice their roasting meat and other food.

Again, my little cookie provided our sandwiches with exquisite flavors. Next to being a prolific Shaman, mind reader, and medium, he also was an amazing cook and an excellent chef! When our sandwiches were ready, we packed them into a few plastic bags; and I put them into my cooler on top of the lemonade cans.

Now, my boy took his rubber mask from its green model, and made its inside sticky with some brown fluid from a bottle. Wearing his skin-colored mask, nobody would see his burnt face and make fun of him. He put the sticky mask onto his face and went to our mirror, where he rubbed his mask to all sides until it fit perfectly around his mouth, nose, and eyes. Suddenly, my burnt little Prince looked just like every other eight-year-old boy, except for a couple of still visible scars and colored stains on his unclad arms.

John snatched my wallet and my keys from my desk and put them into his own pockets, before we went outside and trotted to our car. John opened its doors and dived onto the front seat, while little Harry and Davy buckled up in the rear seat. I got my keys from John, gunned the engine; and we drove off, while Davy helpfully told me where I had to go to find his new zoo and our 'ancestors'.

Soon, John scanned our stereo for a cheerful song, found one on some regional radio station, and we all started to sing along with the happy music, now and then clapping our hands and stamping our feet while trying to raise the roof of our old car. It felt marvelous to have an unexpected day off; and I suddenly started to feel like a little boy myself, going out on an unexpected holiday.

2. Visiting a zoo and meeting our ancestors.

For quite some time, we sang along with the happy songs from our car stereo, while John had fun searching for even more nice music. At last, my threesome started to get a bit bored, until Davy told us a funny joke. From now on, my boys filled the rest of our driving time concocting all sorts of silly riddles, laughing and joking while trying to outdo each other. By listening to their happy bantering, I found out that Davy was our always-happy comedian, while John proposed his clever ideas, and my little soul mate came up with all sorts of funny remarks. Silently, I very much enjoyed the happy feeling of being the 'old Dad' of my three fine young men, while I listened to their happy antics and basked in our mutual love. In the meantime, I tried to keep my eyes on the long and boring road.

Now and then, Davy again told me the way; until, after almost an hour of driving, an enormous zoo suddenly showed up. My boys started to cheer, while I drove our car into its parking lot and joined the many already parked cars. Obviously, we weren't the only ones who thought this would be an excellent day to visit this new zoo.

My three boys left our car and already raced towards the entrance, while I first locked our car doors before I followed them at a slower pace, while chuckling at their eagerness. At the entrance, my three musketeers were impatiently waiting for me to buy our tickets, but we first had to join one of the waiting lines. Slowly and step by step, we shuffled forward, until it would be my turn to pay for being allowed to park our car in their lot and to enter their zoo.

When we finally arrived at the front of our slowly moving line, I ordered four tickets and a parking coupon. The casher told me the price, and I put my hand into my pocket to get my wallet. Only, much to my surprise, my pocket turned out to be empty! Where could I have left my wallet? Had I been the innocent victim of one of those light-fingered pickpockets the newspapers always warned us for? Or, had I forgotten to take my wallet from my desk, because I was only a 'forgetful old man'? I was sure I had seen it this morning, lying on my desk in our living room. Again, I searched my pockets, but to no avail. Obviously, I really was becoming more and more forgetful...

Feeling ashamed of my obvious forgetfulness, I turned around, to tell my impatiently waiting boys we had to go back home... Then, I saw John, looking at me from a way too innocent face, but with little fun lights in his deep brown eyes. Suddenly, I remembered that John had snatched my keys and my wallet from my desk, just before we left our house! The impish young monkey... Again, he had me.

When John saw that I remembered his misdeed, he first offered me a broad smile. Then, he fished my wallet out of his own pocket, opened it, and paid for our tickets, while Davy and little Harry started to snicker and told each other 'funny' stories about a certain 'forgetful ancient grandpa'. Yeah, well, just wait until they are sixty-five-years old and becoming forgetful! Then, it will be MY time to guffaw and snicker at them, supposed I am still alive by then.

Immediately after John bought our tickets, little Harry and Davy started to drag me towards the zoo's gate, where a gatekeeper already waited for us. The man smiled at my impatient boys and teasingly slowly clipped our tickets, making John grumble aloud while Davy and little Harry threatened to tickle-torture the chuckling man. Trying to look impressed, the man smilingly handed our clipped tickets back to John. Finally, we could enter this zoo and look at our 'ancestors'.

My impatient threesome already raced inside, in their eagerness to start looking around nearly tripping over their own feet. Before I followed them, I first put our tickets and my parking coupon away in my wallet and stuffed the wallet into my pocket, next to my keys. In the meantime, my three boys were already racing around in the over-crowded zoo, trying to look everywhere at the same time, while now and then beckoning each other to come over and look HERE!

Much to my delight, the zoo turned out to be really nice-looking and animal-friendly. Everywhere we looked, we saw animals behind nearly invisible bars, in huge water pools, in roomy cages, or walking around free. The neatly maintained walkways were over-crowded with hundreds of enthusiastic children, and with their less enthusiastic parents who desperately tried to tame their little monkeys.

Smiling at the funny sight, I waited until my monkeys had tamed themselves and returned to me voluntarily, as they always did. Within a few minutes, they had seen everything around here; and came back to me with enthusiastically beaming faces. Impatiently, they took my hands and started to drag me towards the next spectacle that looked even more promising in their eyes.

Aad Aandacht is a Dutch psychotherapist who loves writing 'books with a message'

A smiling man with a professional looking camera approached us and politely asked my busy boys and me:

"Sir, may I please take some pictures of you and your three sons? Boys, say 'cheese' to the camera, please."

Quickly, the man took his camera and started to take a couple of pictures. Within a few hours, he would pin our developed and printed photographs onto a board at the entrance, where we could buy them before we left the zoo and went home.

However, soon after the man started to take his pictures, he asked my boys to behave more naturally, without sticking out their tongues at his camera! Only, my boys weren't impressed at all, and again made silly faces towards the frustrated looking man, while John told him they were already behaving naturally and just wanted to go on.

The very moment the photographer was ready and left us alone, my happy threesome dragged me towards a building that, to their utmost delight, turned out to be the ape house! Cheering loudly, they bolted through the door, to take their first look at our 'ancestors'.

At a bit slower pace, I followed them into a dark and smelly hallway; where my boys raced up to the first brightly illuminated cage, stopped, and stared at its inhabitants in obvious awe. All of us felt a bit entranced; while looking at several huge and impressive gorillas, sitting on their straw-covered floor or walking around. A few gorillas scratched their behinds and stared back at us with bored faces.

"Are we looking at them, or are they looking at us?" Davy chuckled, while making silly faces at the bored looking apes.

"Of course, they are looking at YOU and wondering what kind of a monkey you are!" John snickered, while poking Davy's ribs.

"I think they recognize you, because the resemblance is striking!" little Harry teased Davy, while poking his ribs from the other side.

Davy quickly turned around and stormed towards little Harry, as if trying to teach him a lesson. However, our smallest monkey saw him coming and was already prepared for the attack. At full speed, he dived away into the crowd and ran towards me, with Davy close on his heels. Jumping up at me at full speed, to let me catch his tiny frame in midair, my boy shouted:

"Dad, please help me, because monkey-ancestor Davy is picking only on the smallest kid..."

While I tried to loosen my boy's suffocating arms around my neck, I looked at Davy. My 'third son' showed me a broad smile from ear to ear on his beaming face, although he also seemed to expect me to tell him he shouldn't pick on the smallest kid any more.

Chuckling at seeing his happily sparkling eyes, I told him:

"Davy, please try to be more careful with our smallest kid, as he is still such a little baby monkey."

"Dad, you are no fun!" my 'little baby monkey' shouted, with a frustrated sounding baritone voice. With a surprising agility, he wrestled free from my arms and quickly slid down onto the floor, immediately chased again by a snickering Davy.

Two seconds later, they totally forgot their quarrel and again stared at the bored looking gorillas, with their arms around each other's shoulders like sworn brothers. This time, two smaller gorillas were chasing after each other, loudly screeching while trying to avoid bumping into the still bored looking others.

Chuckling, my boy's deep baritone voice told Davy:

"That one is you, and this is me; and you are chasing after me."

"Look HERE!" John suddenly shouted from the next cage, already bellowing with laughter.

Of course, we raced towards the next cage; to find out what John thought could be funny. A mother ape tried to hold her child in her extremely long arms, while rolling around in the straw. Every time her screeching child tried to escape, she pulled it close to her breasts again. Now and then, her little baby escaped and ran away; but it returned immediately, to restart its game of being caught and trying to escape. Both playing apes were extremely ugly, at least to our prejudiced standards. Laughing at the funny sight, we never thought that monkeys could behave as certain human beings usually do.

With a naughty look in his sparkling eyes, John told us:

"Look, here are Big Harry and little Harry, behaving as usual!"

For a moment, my little soul mate and I only stared at each other. Then, we turned around at the same time and went after John!

Of course, John saw us coming and easily escaped into the crowd, on the way sticking out his tongue towards us, while Davy bellowed with laughter and plainly refused to help us.

Faking an upcoming anger, I told my snickering young friend:

"As soon as we get home, we will tickle-torture you to death!"

Again sticking out his tongue towards us, John retorted:

"You, and Harry, and who else's army of ugly monkeys?"

A few onlookers started to laugh, and my little soul mate and I couldn't keep straight faces either. Laughing, we left our still playing 'ugly ancestors', and decided to leave John for now and to go on.

Suddenly, Davy pointed to another cage and shouted:

"Look at THIS! Have you ever seen such beautiful buttocks?"

All of us joined Davy, and stared in total surprise at a screeching bunch of smaller monkeys. All the female monkeys were showing off their bright violet and pink colored behinds that were protruded and wrinkled. Surprisingly, the male monkeys seemed to be attracted to the females with the hugest and most colorful protrusions, because they constantly ran after them and tried to catch them.

John and Davy started to roar with laughter, slapping their knees and nearly hiccupping with fun! Together, they turned around and showed their own behinds to the monkeys, who weren't interested at all. Only my little soul mate fell silent, while he looked at the heavily protruded female apes with suddenly saddening eyes.

Plucking at my arm, he asked me with concern in his voice:

"Dad? How come their butts look like this? Are they ill?"

Still chuckling at the funny sight, I explained that Mother Nature tries to make the female monkeys more attractive to the males. In some way, our own females are doing the same thing, by putting lipstick onto their faces to look more attractive to the men.

Suddenly shaking his head in obvious disbelief, my boy's indignant sounding deep baritone voice chuckled:

"If my girlfriend ever tries to make herself attractive like this, I will force her to wear a rubber mask over her BUTT!"

This time, John and Davy fell down onto the concrete floor and started to roll around in the thick dust, while bellowing with laughter! Still laughing and snickering, we left our colored 'lipstick monkeys' and went on with our visit. Walking together, we went through another double door, and suddenly entered the zoo's reptile house.

Looking at an enormous anaconda in a glass cage, Davy chuckled:

"Look, here is the Harry Potter snake! Let's try to talk to it..."

All three boys tried to arouse the snake, by pounding its cage with their fists, but the animal didn't react. It just stared back at us with unblinking eyes, as if it felt extremely bored and couldn't care less.

After a couple more tries, John shook his head and chuckled:

"Of course, we will have to use 'snake language' to talk to it! Unfortunately, I forgot my magic wand and my broomstick."

Soon, we left the motionless animal; and shuffled to the next cage that contained a bunch of wriggling smaller snakes. Little Harry knocked its glass, but they didn't react and just went on wriggling. Impatiently, he left the snakes to us and raced through the next door.

With a surprised baritone voice, my boy shouted:

"Look at this. They have REAL alligators!"

All of us followed our little leader into the next reptile room, where we saw an enormous crocodile, lying outstretched on the grass under a warming lamp. A second crocodile swam around in a muddy water pool, with its mouth slightly opened. For a second, I thought about teaching my boys the differences between an alligator and a crocodile. Then, I discarded the idea of trying to be a good parent, and decided to wait with my lectures until we returned home, or to leave their lessons to their schoolteachers, once their vacation ended.

Yet, my boys seemed to be very impressed, and Davy exclaimed:

"Wow, what dangerous teeth! Look at those mean eyes! Did you know they can eat small elephants, next to little boys like Harry?"

Although my little soul mate started to shiver at the unwelcome thought, he cleverly kept his mouth shut. Soon, we left the crocodiles and went through the next double door...

All of a sudden, we stepped outside, and squinted at the suddenly way too bright sunlight!

For quite some time, we continued our strolling through the huge zoological garden. We stared at all the different animals in their cages, in vain trying to get them react to us. We talked to the parrots, and a couple of them talked back to us. We visited a smaller building that contained all kinds of small fish, bats, rodents, and creepy insects. We bought a bag of peanuts and fed them to the prancing peacocks, trying to get them to show off their beautiful feathers. We looked at the seals, the sea lions, the bears, the elephants, the zebra's, the tigers, and at all the other exotic animals this enormous new zoo had on display.

At last, my old feet started to feel a bit tired, and I told my three monkeys to look for a place to sit down and take a rest and a drink. Like magic, my three monkeys immediately found a playground, and enthusiastically dragged me towards it! A microsecond later, they had left me alone and disappeared into the loudly shouting crowd.

Feeling really tired, I sat down at a small table on a terrace with some nice shadow, called a waiter, and ordered a cup of coffee. Stealthily, I reached down under the table, untied my shoes, and kicked them off. That felt a lot better, sigh...

Strangely, I suddenly felt alone, although I was still surrounded by a huge crowd of enthusiastically playing and loudly shouting kids. Now and then, one of my boys showed up amongst the other kids, enthusiastically racing around while having lots of fun. All three boys seemed to have the time of their lives, coursing from swing to slide, to climbing rope, to conning tower, to labyrinth, to waterfall.

Feeling happy to be able to sit down and take some rest, I heaved a deep sigh of content, sipped my lukewarm coffee, and looked at the playing and shouting children around me, suddenly feeling old. How long ago was the last time I had visited a zoo? I couldn't remember...

Half an hour later, John showed up, rubbed his belly, and asked:

"Dad, could we please eat now? We are starved!"

I took my cooler from under my table and opened it; and, at that same moment, all three boys surrounded me like magic! Chuckling at seeing their hungry faces, I distributed our sandwiches and our cans of lemonade, and told them to sit down and enjoy our meal.

Quickly, my boys sat down on hastily gathered chairs, and started to chew and drink. Thirty seconds later, they were ready, and again disappeared into the loudly yelling and shouting crowd.

Chuckling at seeing their happy eagerness, I sipped the remainder of my coffee, and started to nibble on the only remaining sandwich I had been able to rescue for myself. Now and then, one of my happy looking boys reappeared, to take a quick sip of their lemonade before giving me a quick kiss and disappearing again.

One time, Davy suddenly hugged me, and told me with a heated face and happily sparking eyes:

"Thank you very much, Dad, for taking me to this new zoo. We are having lots of fun, and you are the best Dad in the whole world! I only wish you were my Dad for real, so that I could be with you and John and Harry all the time..."

Davy offered me a quick kiss, turned around, and disappeared through the loudly shouting crowd towards the children's labyrinth. In a far distance, little Harry and John seemed to wait for him; and I thought they could be playing 'hide and seek', the usual game they often played in and around their own backyards at home.

Soon, my three boys disappeared into the labyrinth, and I didn't see them back for a long time. After some time, I closed my eyes, and slowly dozed off in the joyful sounds of happily playing children.

3. My little soul mate vanishes into thin air.

"Dad? Do you know where Harry is? We've already looked for him everywhere, but we just cannot find him anymore..."

Slowly, I woke up from a happy dream, rubbed my eyes, and squinted at the too bright sunlight that initially dazzled my vision. Where was I, in this crowded area full of shouting children's voices? Oh yeah, I remembered. My boys and I were visiting a new zoo, and I had wanted to take some rest and kicked my shoes off to feel more comfortable, before I drank my coffee and slowly dozed off.

Still feeling sleepy, I looked up and stared at the worried faces of John and Davy. They were looking around anxiously, as if searching the playground for their disappeared little friend.

When they saw that I woke up, John explained:

"We were playing hide and seek around the children's labyrinth, until Harry suddenly disappeared and we cannot find him any more. Have you seen him around here, or do you know where he is?"

"Well, let me think... Around half an hour ago, Harry showed up here, emptied his lemonade can, and disappeared again. Since then, I haven't seen him any more, and I don't know where he went from here. Where did you see him the last time?"

"While we were playing hide and seek around the labyrinth, about fifteen minutes ago."

First, I stretched my stiffening old muscles, before I ducked under the table and put on my shoes. Grunting with the effort, I slowly rose from my chair and followed John and Davy through the playground towards the small children's labyrinth at its backside.

For now, I didn't worry too much about my little soul mate not showing up, because nothing serious could have happened to my boy, in the relative safety of this over-crowded zoo. Besides, my little Shaman had already proven to be mature enough to be able to fend for himself, if necessary. In his own Gypsy clan, he had been their youngest 'recognized Real Trapper', and their Wise Woman had allowed him to stroll through their outstretched forests all on his own!

Besides, my little Shaman once told me he only had to concentrate on where he wanted to be, and follow its energy that pulled at his aura. Beyond any doubt, his outstanding Trapper abilities would flawlessly bring him back to us or to my small table, in no time. Therefore, I didn't worry too much, and just followed John and Davy.

Impatiently, both boys dragged me towards the small children's labyrinth that was located at the backside of the zoo's playground. Here, John stopped next to a big tree, and explained:

"Behind this tree, I closed my eyes and counted to twenty, while Davy and Harry ran away to hide. First, I tagged Davy who hid behind that big tree over there; but I couldn't find Harry. Then, Davy started to help me because he hadn't seen where Harry went, but he too couldn't find him. Together, we looked in all our usual hiding places and yelled for Harry to show up because he had won, but he didn't answer and seemed to have vanished into thin air. At last, we decided to give up, and went to you to ask for help."

At the small children's labyrinth, we first had to duck under a low wooden bar to get in. Groaning, I followed both boys, crawling on my hands and knees, while complaining about my too old joints that already started to protest. Of course, John and Davy also knew the way out, and they took my hands and quickly dragged me through the meandering labyrinth towards its cleverly hidden exit.

On our way out, all three of us looked into all the blind paths and yelled our little deserter's name everywhere, while trying to shout beyond the loud playground sounds. Everywhere we looked, we saw other young children, happily playing around or chasing after each other through the labyrinth, but not OUR boy.

At the back of the labyrinth, we entered an oblong square that was surrounded by heavily overgrown fences. Well, this square certainly didn't allow any hiding, being at the back border of the zoo and having an iron gate that was secured with a huge padlock. We also peeked through the abundantly growing vegetation into its secluded yard. However, the only thing we saw was a tiny storage barn, at a small distance from the locked gate, with its door closed. Little Harry couldn't possibly be hiding here, because the gate was padlocked, so we turned around and went back to the playground.

This time, I started to feel a little bit worried. This wasn't my boy's normal behavior! Up to now, he never disappeared like this before. Could he be trying to tease us, by hiding in some thick bush and

Chapter 3. A little spy, my nightmare, and pondering.

waiting for us to give up so he could show up in triumph? John once told me that his little brother was extremely good at hiding, due to his Gypsy nature and growing up in their surrounding woods while hunting small animals to roast them over their campfire. Could my boy be staring at us, at this very moment, chuckling inwardly while waiting for us to give up and break into tears?

However, I couldn't believe that my little soul mate would tease us like this, without showing any consideration. This totally contradicted his caring nature of always reckoning with other people's feelings. Therefore, I could come up with only one logical conclusion: something unexpected had happened to my suddenly disappeared boy!

Could he be trapped somewhere and unable to free himself, now waiting for his friends to rescue him? Or, had he gotten lost while looking for another hiding place, despite his brightness and amazing Real Trapper skills? Ultimately, my little Trapper boy was only eight years old and still a bit too small for his age...

Starting to feel more and more worried; I turned towards the still searching John and Davy and asked them:

"Do you know where the children's restrooms are?"

With sad faces, they took me across the crowded playground towards what turned out to be a small children's restroom. Inside the smelly building, I opened all the stall doors, hoping to find some trace of our suddenly vanished boy. Only one stall was occupied by a small boy, looking at us with a bewildered look on his face while hastily pulling up his trousers. All the other stalls were empty.

After leaving the foul-smelling restroom, I asked John and Davy:

"Boys, do you have ANY idea where Harry could be now?"

Davy looked back at me with sad eyes and only shook his head; but John stared at me as if he thought I could be the dumbest human being on our planet. Of course, if he had only the faintest idea where little Harry could be now; he would have looked in that place at least a century ago! How dim-witted did I think they could be?

At last, we returned to my small table, where we tried to decide what we should do now. Firstly, from this very moment on, at least one of us had to stay here all the time, in case our disappeared little friend unexpectedly showed up. What other options did we have?

To read all our famous 'Gypsy Series' books, please visit www.gypsyseries.com

John thought I could best go to the zoo's office and ask their security guards to help us find Harry... Of course, Davy and I immediately agreed. This certainly was the best thing we could think of for now. The zoo's own security guards would undoubtedly know where to look for our lost boy, being familiar with every nook and cranny of their outstretched zoo and its surroundings.

I thanked John for his clever idea and rose from my chair to go to the zoo's office, but first told both boys:

"Please, stay around this table until I return, because I don't want you two to get lost as well."

Looking a bit affronted, John curtly rebutted:

"DAAAD! How dim-witted do you think we are?"

"Yeah, well... Harry too is a clever boy, but where is he now?"

Despite my growing sense of despair, I chuckled at seeing John's indignant face. Of course, I could always trust my mature and reliable young friend, and I was sure that Davy would stay at his side.

After promising to return as soon as possible, I walked away, and headed for where I thought I could find the ape house and the zoo's entrance, hoping its office would be there too, as the most likely place that I could think of. Besides, I would soon stumble upon one of the many zoo's security guards my boys and I had seen during the day...

Much to my dismay, within a minute, I felt totally lost and looked around in despair, because I didn't recognize anything any more. All at once, all those heavily overgrown walkways started looking the same, meandering around and spreading out into different directions. Obviously, I totally lacked any sense of my little Shaman's useful Real Trapper gift of always knowing his way home!

What should I do now? From where I was now, I couldn't even find my way back to the playground, were John and Davy waited for me and for my disappeared little soul mate! Feeling more and more uneasy, I started to look around for one of the zoo's security guards. Only, where were they, now that I needed them to find their office? Were they all taking their coffee breaks at the same time? Desperately, I tried to remember my own past life as a powerful Shaman, but I was too nervous to remember anything at all. How would my own little Shaman do that, always finding his way by just concentrating on where he wanted to be until he sensed its energy?

Hesitatingly, I closed my eyes and tried to concentrate on the zoo's entrance. Nothing happened, and I tried to force my enveloping aura to stretch out and contact the zoo's office, but the only thing that happened now was an upcoming headache. This clearly didn't work!

Would I be able to orient myself, by looking at where my shadow was pointing to the ground and trying to keep the sun to the same side of my body? Only, because all those overgrown walkways were twisting and meandering, the overgrown and very heavy vegetation obscured the sunlight nearly everywhere.

Much to my delight, I suddenly saw the ape house tower, showing up in a far distance! Well, the ape house had been near the entrance where I supposed the zoo's office would be! Feeling relieved, I started to walk towards the again disappearing tower, while trying to remember its direction. Without looking where I went, I rounded the next corner, while craning my neck to see the ape house tower again...

OUCH! Because I didn't look out where I went, my head suddenly collided with a bright yellow signpost that stood in my way. Much to my delight, I saw that it carried several colored arrows that pointed to the entrance, the restaurant, the nearest restroom, the snack bar, the playground, and the zoo's office... Now, I also saw that the zoo had placed quite a lot of these helpful signposts, on every crossing!

Really feeling like a too old and too absent-minded grandpa, I started to follow the colored arrows that pointed towards the office. Within a minute, I arrived at a brick building with the word 'OFFICE' over its entrance, and went inside with mixed feelings. Would really somebody inside this zoo's office be able to help me find my missing little soul mate? Hesitantly, I went to a small counter that carried the word 'information', and pushed a tiny bell.

A smiling woman showed up and politely greeted me:

"Good afternoon sir! How may I help you?"

Still hoping for the best, I told the smiling woman:

"My boys were playing hide and seek around the playground's labyrinth, until my youngest boy suddenly disappeared. Since then, we have looked for him everywhere, even in the children's restroom, but he seems to have vanished into thin air. My two older boys are waiting at our table on the playground's terrace, still hoping their little brother will show up, while I am here to ask for help..."

Smiling professionally, the woman reassured me:

"Don't worry, sir, this happens here all the time. Could you please describe your youngest boy, and what is his first name? As soon as I've informed our security guards, everybody will start looking for your lost boy, and you will have him back in no time."

Feeling relieved, I tried to describe little Harry for as far as I could, although I wasn't sure about the clothes he was wearing:

"My son Harry is an eight-year-old small boy with unruly blond hair, bright blue eyes, slightly stuffed cheeks, and a funny pug nose. I think he dressed this morning in a yellow T-shirt, blue denim pants, and white or grayish sneakers, but I am not sure. Besides, my boy has a severely burnt face and therefore wears a rubber mask to hide his scars, so that only a few colored fire marks on his unclad arms will be visible. And I suppose that, by now, a couple of our pictures will be pinned onto the photographer's board at the entrance."

Without any more questions, the woman took her mobile phone and started to call several security officers. She described little Harry, told them about our pictures on the photographer's pin board, and asked them to report to the playground's terrace where the boy's Dad and two older brothers would be waiting.

After ending her calls, the no longer smiling woman told me:

"This is all I can do for now, sir. From now on, all our security guards in our zoo will be looking for your boy. In no time, you will have him back in good health! Please, return to the playground's terrace, and wait there until one of our guards shows up."

Although I thanked the woman for her help, my inside has started to feel even more worried than before. Would really the zoo's security guards be able to find my boy? Why hadn't my little soul mate found us on his own, by using his outstanding Real Trapper abilities? He once told me he only had to 'tune in' into some place he knew, to feel its energy and walk towards it in a beeline...

Why hadn't my boy 'tuned in' into our own small table at the playground's terrace; that is, IF he got lost and really couldn't find his way back to us? To me, it was now clear that something different had happened to my suddenly lost boy, which prevented him from showing up at our table or contacting one of the many security guards. Only, what could have happened to my boy?

Chapter 3. A little spy, my nightmare, and pondering.

A very disturbing thought crossed my mind, making me shudder with its implications. What if someone else knew that my little soul mate was a Gypsy Crown Prince, and had decided to kidnap him? Perhaps, they had the wrong idea about Royal Gypsies being rich, and wanted a ransom? Or, what if somebody loathed little Gypsy boys and had decided to abduct one in this crowded zoo?

Although I was sure that my proud Gypsy Prince would rather fight himself to death instead of surrendering, he was only eight years old. Could the same people that once set their caravan ablaze, around two years ago, have arrived here to finish their job? The police never found them. Only, how would any stranger know we were here today, in this particular zoo? Could they have followed us towards here?

After leaving the zoo's office, I first waited until my eyes got used to the suddenly dazzling sunlight. Then, I started to follow the colored arrows that lead me back to the playground and my waiting boys. Within three minutes, I reentered the playground's terrace, while secretly hoping to see my little soul mate running towards me.

Alas, only a worried looking John greeted me, while I slumped down at my table and hid my head in my hands, trying to hide my concern and my suddenly welling tears from my young friend.

Whilst trying to hide his own tears, John asked me:

"Hi Dad... Are the zoo's security guards now looking for Harry? I hope they will find him and bring him back soon. While you were away, Davy and I have taken turns searching, so that always one of us would be here in case Harry suddenly showed up."

Clever boys! I complimented John with is inventiveness, while I took my handkerchief out of my pocket and dried his and my tears. Then, I told John about my visit to the office, and assured him that every security guard in the zoo would be looking for our lost little friend. Soon, we would have him back, happy and healthy...

At that moment, Davy showed up, looking sad and disappointed. With a slightly trembling voice, my third son explained:

"Hi Dad... I've again looked everywhere, but I still cannot find Harry. Are the zoo's security officers of any help?"

Already sobbing, Davy climbed onto my lap, seemingly oblivious to the surrounding crowd, and started to cry earnestly.

While trying to comfort my third son, I dried his teary eyes for him and held him close to my chest, while John leaned into me from the other side. In no time, my handkerchief was soaking wet, because it now served all three of us. Why hadn't I thought of bringing a few packets of tissues? Yet, it felt good to support and comfort each other like this. I only wished that my little soul mate could be here as well, to join our shared cuddle as usual...

4. The zoo's security guards, and the police.

After a few minutes of sitting together and waiting, a uniformed man entered our terrace, wearing a clearly visible 'security' badge. He looked around at all the chattering customers, until he saw my two sad looking boys and me and quickly approached our table.

With very much compassion in his voice, he asked us:

"I suppose you are the lost little boy's family, and your boy hasn't shown up yet? We are still looking for him. In the meantime, could you please tell me some more about how he suddenly disappeared?"

With again welling tears in his eyes, John told the guard what had happened, now and then filled in by Davy:

After first trying out the playground's facilities and having very much fun, they had started to play their usual game of 'hide and seek' around the children's labyrinth. Again, they had lots of fun finding more and more good hiding places, until it was John's turn to tag his friends. Soon, John tagged Davy who cleverly hid behind a big tree, but he couldn't find Harry. Because Davy hadn't seen where Harry was hiding, he started to help John. Working together, they looked in all their known hiding places, until they had searched every nook and cranny at least three times. Now, they decided to give up, and walked around the labyrinth while shouting Harry's name and telling him to show up in triumph. However, Harry still didn't show up; and they started to feel a bit worried and went to Dad for help.

The security guard thanked both boys for their detailed description, took his mobile phone, and asked their headquarters for any news about the lost little boy. After listening to their answer, he seemed to feel a bit disappointed, but tried to smile anyway.

While tousling John's and Davy's hair, he told them:

"Don't worry too much, because I am sure your little brother will show up in no time. I think he just went too far away and couldn't find his way back, because that happens here all the time. In the meantime, all our security guards are still looking for him. And, please, don't leave this playground without informing us first, even if your lost boy suddenly shows up and you want to go home..."

Of course, we promised the security guard to keep him informed in case Harry unexpectedly showed up and we wanted to go home. He promised to keep us informed, and walked away to have another look at the playground while talking into his mobile phone.

At seeing the guard using his mobile phone, I suddenly cursed myself for being shortsighted! Although I once thought about buying such a cell phone for myself, I had discarded the idea. Why should I buy such a modern thing? At home, I had my own telephone, and my answering machine would answer any unexpected calls in case I was away, unless I forgot to switch it on. Now, I wished that my boys and I had our own cell phones, so that we could call each other in case something unexpected happened. I was now responsible for three growing young boys, and I had to live up to that standard!

Feeling angry with myself, I made a mental note to buy a couple of cell phones immediately after we had little Harry back and returned home. Then, each of us would have our own phones, to carry with us all the time. That way, nobody would ever again get lost without the possibility of letting the others know what had happened. Why hadn't I thought of this before? Today, I finally started to feel the full weight of my grownup responsibilities resting on my shoulders, and the heavy burden almost crushed me!

In the meantime, John and Davy still fidgeted around our table, until John leaned against my side and told me:

"Dad, I want to start searching for Harry again! Davy and I just cannot sit still and wait, while my little brother might be in trouble. Of course, we will return here and report to you every few minutes."

Because I didn't want to lose John and Davy as well, I answered:

"Please, be very careful not to get lost yourself!"

Looking a bit offended, John responded:

"DAAAD! You really seem to forget that Davy and I are already thirteen years old and very mature for our age! Of course, getting lost in this secluded zoo will be totally impossible for us, especially with all those searching security guards around us."

"Yeah, well, Harry is very mature for his age too, but where is he now? Besides, did you see these bright yellow signposts at every corner? Please, don't forget to use them if needed, as they also point to the office and to this playground."

Chapter 4. A talk with John; remembering past lives. 33

This time, both boys only stared me down, with indignant faces. Again, I seemed to forget they were big boys and not little babies. Of course, they had seen and used those yellow signposts at least a century ago! Never underestimate youth... After offering me a quick hug and a kiss, they turned around and disappeared into the crowd.

Suddenly feeling a little bit abandoned, I sat back on my chair with a sad feeling. Would really John and Davy be able to find their little brother, while even the zoo's trained security guards seemed to fail? Where could my little soul mate be now? What could have happened to him while playing hide and seek around the labyrinth?

Had my boy really lost his way, despite his outstanding Shaman abilities and Real Trapper gifts? Or, had some kidnapper abducted him, knowing I had some money to spend and hoping to get a good ransom? What else could have happened to my boy? I was sure he would fight any attackers with all of his might; probably screaming at the top of his lungs and raising hell and the devil, whilst kicking and punching his assailants wherever he could! With his enormous amount of Inner Power and Royal pride, he would never surrender, unless they had surprised him and immediately gagged him.

Or, had my boy bumped his head against something unexpected and lost consciousness with a concussion? Only, why hadn't one of the zoo's many security guards found him and brought him to me? I thought and thought, but nothing seemed to make sense...

Suddenly, an idea popped up in my mind that made me wonder. As a reincarnated Shaman, would I be able to send a message to my boy, by concentrating on his aura and sending him my Love? I was sure he could pick up my thoughts effortlessly, by concentrating on me and reading my mind. On the other hand, I also knew that most sensitive people tend to protect their too vulnerable auras against any 'energy intruders'. Would my little soul mate recognize my personal energy and be open to what I wanted to tell him?

As a psychotherapist, if one of my clients started to feel uneasy, I always concentrated on their auras and sent them my Universal Love, to help them calm down and feel more at ease. Although I didn't understand why it worked, sending them my Love always helped. Would I be able to contact my little soul mate by using my Universal Love? To try it out, I sank back on my chair, closed my eyes, and visualized my little soul mate in front of me. Next, I opened my Inner Self towards my lost boy, and concentrated on his feelings...

To read all our famous 'Gypsy Series' books, please visit www.gypsyseries.com

Immediately, an enormous wave of panic and distress tried to overwhelm me! Feeling shocked into my deepest core, I quickly opened my eyes. Had I really contacted my little soul mate's feelings, or had I felt only my own despair? Unfortunately, I wasn't sure, but at least something very unusual had happened.

Now, another idea popped up in my mind. What would happen if I did the same thing again, but without opening my aura and making myself too vulnerable? Would I be able to look at my boy's energy field from within a so-called 'guided meditation', or perhaps through an 'induced daydream'? Although I didn't know where those unusual thoughts came from, they sounded reasonable.

Again, I closed my eyes; but, this time, I let myself drift off into a controlled trance, as I had done many times before. Next, I went into a guided daydream, and tried to 'remember' what had happened to my suddenly disappeared little soul mate. This way, I could look at my boy from a short distance, without getting too involved...

Feeling fascinated, I stared at my little soul mate who was playing hide and seek around the labyrinth, while looking for an appropriate place to hide. At the backside of the labyrinth, he entered an oblong square that was surrounded by overgrown fences. This square didn't seem to be a proper place to hide, but what interesting secrets could be hidden behind its overgrown fences? Feeling curious, he peeked through the heavy vegetation, and saw a small barn with an open door. What could be hidden in that open barn?

After some searching, he found a small gap in the fence where its iron netting had rusted away. Being only a tiny boy, he worked his lithe little body through the gap and tiptoed towards the open door. Inside the barn, he saw a huge pile of food bags. What would be in those bags, and what animals would eat this particular food?

Curiously, my boy entered the small barn through its open door, and tried to read the labels... Suddenly, the door closed behind him, with a loud click. Everything inside the barn went pitch dark, and my boy was trapped in a small barn and unable to free himself!

Hurriedly, I left my controlled daydream, because my brain was starting to panic. My lungs were wheezing like an overworked horse, and my overstrained heart tried to pound out of my throat. While I slowly woke up some more, I immediately started to think. Could this be for real? Was this what had happened to my little soul mate?

Chapter 4. A talk with John; remembering past lives.

Was my boy trapped in a small barn behind an overgrown fence; and was this why even the zoo's trained security guards couldn't find him? I knew I had seen such a small barn before, behind a fence in an oblong square, with its door closed... Only, I couldn't leave my table to take a closer look at that barn, because John and Davy expected me to be here when they returned from their next search. I also had to stay here, in case my little soul mate showed up unexpectedly...

A second later, I started to laugh at my own silly expectations. Everybody knows that daydreams are only a product of your own imagination, and certainly nothing more! Of course, my daydream had shown me only a few recent pictures from my own memories, as dreams always do. Besides, by now, the zoo's security guards would have looked in all their hidden barns and behind all their overgrown fences! There was no way they wouldn't have found my lost boy, IF he had been trapped in some barn and couldn't free himself. Of course, he also would have screamed and pounded the closed door, until one of the searching security guards heard him and freed him.

Still trying to get rid of my feelings of panic, I asked a waiter to bring me a glass of water and another cup of coffee. All the time, the panicking face of my little soul mate continued to waver in front of me, looking at me with fear and desperation in his bright blue eyes. Could this be genuine, and was really my boy thinking of me? Well, even if he was desperate, this proved he was still alive and kicking!

Now, I thought of Jack, our 'Spirit Guide', who had promised to be there for us and help us when and wherever he could and was allowed. Only, where was Jack now that we really needed him? Why didn't Jack help me find my boy, by pulling me into his 'induced trance' and showing me where I could find him? I tried to call Jack in my mind, but my inside felt too nervous to hear any faint answers...

Time went by; while slowly, nearly imperceptibly, the afternoon sun started to disappear below the horizon. Most visitors had already left the playground; and the last ones were packing their belongings and gathering their little monkeys, to leave the zoo and go home.

Both John and Davy were dead tired from their searching, and slumped down at our table, still looking around with sad faces. Now and then, one of the security guards showed up, hoping WE would have any news about our lost boy. Every time, they told us they were still looking for him; but, so far, they hadn't been able to find him.

At last, only my boys and I stayed in what now felt like a totally deserted zoo. Again, one of the security guards showed up, this time to tell us they had done everything that they could. Probably, our lost boy had already left their zoo. Therefore, he advised us to ask their local police for help, as the zoo would close within ten minutes. He would ask night security to keep an open eye, IF our lost boy would happen to show up during the night. He was very sorry and felt very much sympathy for us, but this was all the zoo could do for us...

Suddenly, I was on the verge of throwing an enormous tantrum! How in the world could this zoo's security guard send me home, just like that, without first bringing my boy back to me? I didn't WANT to leave their zoo without my little soul mate at my side! Would he still wear his rubber mask that would be very sweaty and itchy by now? Feeling more and more devastated, I forced myself to stop despairing and start thinking logical. Perhaps, the REAL police would be able to find my lost boy, where this zoo had failed...

Reluctantly, my remaining two boys and I left the playground and followed the security officer towards the zoo's entrance. Leaving their zoo like this felt like saying farewell to my little soul mate, as if we were abandoning our youngest friend. Up to the last moment, I still hoped to see him storming towards us while shouting:

"Dad and John and Davy, please wait for me..."

Alas, my boy didn't show up at the last moment, to jump into my arms and smother my face with kisses. Would he still be alive, or had some nasty child molester murdered him and dumped his dead body into a trashcan? At that thought, a hot rage welled up in my chest, and I was ready to fight all the cruel security guards who dared send us away like this! Involuntarily, I growled and balled my fists...

Fortunately, John sensed my rage and looked at me with concern; and that calmed me down. Of course, I had to stay in control of my own feelings, because I was still responsible for my two other boys who needed me! After taking a couple of deep breaths, I forced myself to shut down my feelings and to think reasonably.

Slowly, my boys and I followed the security guard towards the exit. There, the guard first waited politely until we had left the zoo. Then, he closed the iron gate, and secured it with a huge padlock. He turned around and sauntered back, probably towards his office to drink some coffee. HIS case was dismissed...

Chapter 4. A talk with John; remembering past lives.

Unwillingly, my two boys and I went to our old car, the only one that was still in the empty parking lot. Secretly, I hoped that my boy would be waiting for us in our car. I even thought I saw his small shadow, jumping up and down while impatiently waving at us...

Alas, my boy wasn't there, and I saw only a shadow from a nearby tree. Feeling sad, I worked my keys out of my pocket and unlocked our car doors. My remaining boys and I entered our car in silence and buckled up, still looking around and hoping to see our little friend.

Finally, I started the engine, stared at the zoo one last time, and slowly drove off towards a police station, to report our missing boy. Helpfully, the security guard had already told me where we could find their local station. Soon, I parked our car in its small parking lot, we crossed the road, and entered the dull looking small building.

Inside, two police officers stared at us with bored faces, and one of them told us to sit down and wait our turn. Clearly, we weren't the only ones who had lost something! They offered me a cup of coffee, and my two nervous boys got a glass of cola. Then, we waited...

After nearly half an hour of waiting, another door opened, and a woman left the police station in a hurry. Now, one of the officers pointed to the open door and told us to go in. We entered a small room, where a tired looking officer greeted us and asked:

"Please, take a seat, and how may I help you?"

Feeling very uneasy, I explained how we had lost our youngest boy in the zoo's playground, and even the zoo's security guards could find him any more. At that moment, I suddenly choked up from sheer sadness, and almost couldn't talk any more.

Fortunately, John and Davy jumped in. Filling in for me, they continued to tell the intently listening police officer their part of our sad story. Then, we had to answer several annoying questions:

Was this the first time the little boy suddenly disappeared?

Could he have a reason to run away, maybe without our knowing?

Had he ever felt frightened, or done any unexpected things?

Could he be afraid of some sort of revenge or punishment?

Could we think of any reason why he would want to leave us?

Could someone else have taken him home without our consent?

Had our boy ever talked about any unknown people, perhaps from around our neighborhood or from the Internet?

Had he ever wanted to kill himself, or wanted to live elsewhere?

The officer wrote our answers down, then asked for our address and phone number, and did we have any pictures of our lost boy? Yes, I still had a small picture in my wallet, that Peter had taken after my happy looking boy got his new mask and showed it off.

At last, I had to sign a couple of papers, and the officer promised to call me as soon as he had any news about our lost boy. From now on, their entire police corps on duty would look out for our lost boy. He strongly advised us to go home, stop worrying, and wait for the next day, before we started searching again. Normally, most lost children showed up at home within twenty-four hours after they had disappeared, usually voluntarily and unharmed! Did our lost boy know our telephone number by heart? Of course, he did!

Then, our time was up. Another officer walked us to the door, and we shook hands. Feeling numb, we left the police station and returned to our car. I unlocked its doors, we buckled up, and I drove off.

Again, we were on our way home, feeling sadder than ever...

5. John feels Harry's energy; he is still alive.

On our way home, my two boys and I were deep in thought, still thinking about our suddenly disappeared youngest friend. What could have happened to our little Shaman, in the relative safety of that secluded zoo? Was he dead, or had somebody kidnapped him? Where was he now? Would we ever see him again, or would we have to pay an enormous ransom first? Of course, I would gladly pay anything to anybody, to have my little soul mate back alive and in good health!

Now and then, I had to tell myself to stay calm and keep my eyes on the road, to avoid drifting to the wrong side and ending up in a hospital. In our backseat, John and Davy leaned into each other, staring out the windows, now and then sobbing while comforting each other. Now and then, my empty stomach rumbled, telling me I hadn't eaten anything since noon. Only, how would my boys and I be able to eat, knowing that our smallest friend could be hungry or worse?

Halfway through our way home, I saw a small restaurant along the roadside, and decided to stop. Of course, my two remaining monkeys in the backseat were still bottomless pits that needed to be fed, and I was responsible for their well-being! Therefore, I turned our car into its small parking lot and stopped. Without saying a word, I left my seat and went inside the building. At this time in the evening, they were only selling burgers, so I ordered two large ones and a medium one. On second thought, I added three cans of cola, took my wallet out of my pocket, and paid for everything. Patiently, I waited, until our burgers were ready and I could take them to our car.

John and Davy started to cheer and rub their empty stomachs, when they saw that I had brought something to eat! Then, they fell silent again, suddenly looking ashamed. How could they ever be hungry, while our little Gypsy friend could be starving or worse?

Looking at their sad faces, I tried to cheer them up:

"Boys, we absolutely have to eat something substantially, to be strong and healthy when Harry shows up again. I am sure it will do both Harry and us no good to see us wasted and meager when he returns home and shows up in good health..."

After some pondering, John hesitantly responded:

"Dad, I think you are right, and I really feel starved! Come on, Davy, let's attack those burgers before they are cold."

Both boys immediately started to stow away their burgers at lightning speed, as usual. However, halfway through wolfing down their food, they suddenly looked at each other and shook their heads. Looking deeply ashamed, they opened the car doors and threw the remainders of their burgers into a nearby waste bucket.

After returning, Davy had tears in his eyes while he told me:

"Sorry, Dad, but I just cannot enjoy my food while Harry probably doesn't have anything to eat at all."

John sadly nodded in agreement, and both boys started to stare out the windows again. Hesitantly, I took a few bites of my own burger, but my boys were right. The food tasted like cardboard, and I too went outside and threw it into a waste bucket. After drinking our colas and adding the empty cans to the bucket, I restarted the engine and slowly drove off. Again, we were on our way home.

An hour after we left the police station, I parked our car in our driveway and stopped its engine. Immediately, John snatched my keys out of my hand, bolted out of our car, and raced towards our front door, where he opened the door in a tremendous hurry and quickly disappeared inside. Davy and I followed John into our living room, where he quicky checked our answering machine. Alas, its little red light didn't blink, indicating nobody had tried to call us in our absence. John even checked our phone line; to be sure that everything was still working correctly.

Because it was past nine o'clock, Davy had to go home. He asked us to accompany him, but both John and I shook our heads. We wanted to stay next to our telephone, in case any police officers or the zoo's security guards phoned us with news about our lost boy.

Fortunately, Davy understood, and only asked me:

"May I please come back tomorrow, early in the morning, to hear any news about Harry?"

While ruffling Davy's hair, I promised:

"Of course you may come back tomorrow! Only, don't try to wake us too early, because we still need our beauty sleep..."

Chapter 5. Seeing Jack's 'spirit'; meeting 'little Harry'.

This time, nobody laughed or made any funny remarks about our 'beauty sleep'. Davy hugged John, offered me a big kiss, and slowly sauntered home, with a sad face and still teary eyes.

After Davy went home, John and I slumped down on our couch and immediately put our arms around each other. Within a second, we started to cry together, while desperately trying to release our built-up tension and cumulated sadness. One time, I thought I heard the voice of my little soul mate, whispering into our ears:

"Let it go, Dad and John, and don't bottle it up! Within a few minutes, you will feel a lot better."

Nearly hiccupping from the intense pain in my heart, I started to cry uncontrollably. Would I ever hear my boy's deep baritone voice again? Would my boy ever again crawl onto my lap, to try to wipe my tears away and let me blow my nose? I already missed him! I already missed my little soul mate terribly! Where was he now? Was he asleep, or was he awake and feeling just as sad as we were?

For a long time, John and I cried together, while trying to support each other. Now and then, we wiped each other's teary eyes, or we blew our dripping noses in the tissues John had fetched from the huge packet in my bedroom. Despite our sadness about little Harry, it felt good to be together and help each other like this. Again, we could feel our powerful mutual love radiating between us, since today growing more than ever, by huge leaps and bounds.

After we had calmed down, we tried to guess what terrible things could have happened to our youngest friend. Could some unknown person have kidnapped our little Gypsy Crown Prince, perhaps because he knew that I had some money to spend? However, how could anyone know that, today, we would be at this particular zoo?

Or, had my boy lost his way while looking for a good hiding place, perhaps by going too far away? John was convinced this would be totally impossible, because his little Gypsy brother always knew his way everywhere. According to John, he had an infallible 'sixth sense' for knowing where he had to go, and had demonstrated his Real Trapper abilities many times before!

Could our lost boy have bumped his head against something and perhaps lost consciousness? Only, why hadn't the zoo's many security guards found him and brought him back to us, although they had searched every nook and cranny in and around their zoo?

To read all our famous 'Gypsy Series' books, please visit www.gypsyseries.com

Would our lost boy still wear his rubber mask to hide his scars? It always started to itch after a couple of hours...

Slowly, John's voice started to fade away, while I drifted off into slumber. Feeling dead tired from my unaccustomed emotions, I just couldn't keep my eyes open any more. Immediately, an unearthly bright light started to surround me, while many powerful waves of Cosmic Love started to engulf my tired body. All my sorrows seemed to fade into oblivion, while I started to feel like being reborn. In my mind, I thanked our Spirit Guide, Jack, for helping me like this with his powerful Cosmic Love, while I basked in the consoling feeling of being totally loved and cared for...

Suddenly, John's voice jolted me out of Jack's induced trance, making my shocked heart almost stop beating! For several seconds, I had no idea where I was or what could have happened, while John tried to wake me up by forcefully shaking my arm.

With very much relief in his voice, my young friend told me:

"Dad? I am sure that Harry is still alive and kicking, because I can feel his energy! ...Dad? Are you listening?"

Still feeling numb and sleep-charged, I mumbled:

"Sorry, John, but I nearly fell asleep; and your unexpected voice almost caused me to have a heart attack. Are you sure that Harry is still alive and kicking? How did you feel Harry's energy? Did Jack help you from within his own realm?"

With a slightly angry voice, John explained:

"I haven't felt Jack around me for quite some time, and I am a bit angry with my 'real Dad' for not showing up now that we need him. But, I closed my eyes and tried to talk to Harry in my mind. Suddenly, I could feel his energy, but he feels like being asleep. I only sensed a dark room around him, but I cannot find out where he is. He has cried a lot and his energy feels very tired, but he IS alive!"

"How can you be so sure that you felt Harry's energy? Perhaps, your wishful mind played a trick with your perceptions..."

"I am absolutely sure, Dad, because I know how Harry feels from when he talks to me in my mind, and this IS his energy! Now and then, we had a silent conversation in our minds, but it only works when both he and I are thinking of the same things."

Chapter 5. Seeing Jack's 'spirit'; meeting 'little Harry'.

Unexpectedly, I got some more confirmation! Although I couldn't know how they did it, my two boys WERE talking to each other in their minds! I had always suspected they were doing such a strange thing, but I hadn't been sure until now. While putting this newest information away for later use, I asked John:

"John, do you have any idea where your 'real Dad' is, now that we need his help to find Harry? As our 'Spirit Guide', Jack once promised me he would always be around me and help me with everything, whenever possible; but where is he now..."

At that moment, I suddenly heard Jack's warm and soulful voice in my inside, sounding loud and clear! This time, even my analytical brain was convinced that I hadn't made up his voice in my mind. Jack's voice seemed to sound a bit tired, while he told me:

"My dear brother, please don't worry any more and just go to bed, because you will need your rest!"

With a surprised face, John stared at me while he exclaimed:

"Did you hear that, Dad? Jack tells us not to worry any more and just go to bed, because we will need our rest! Yippee, my real Dad is still around me, and he didn't forget me!"

Feeling very happy now that his real Dad had talked to him, John worked himself back into my arms and snuggled up to me. Again, my too analytical mind was going through a heavy turmoil; because I could never again deny Jack's existence. Ultimately, John had heard exactly the same words that Jack had spoken to me in my own inside! Therefore, this was the ultimate evidence that our 'Spirit Guide' really was around us, and I really could hear Jack's messages from 'the beyond', because he had contacted both John and me and had given us the same unexpected message at the same time!

Only, why didn't Jack help us find our lost little Gypsy friend? Couldn't we really rely on our so-called 'Spirit Helper'? Or, had Jack lost little Harry too, and didn't he know where my boy was? Would that be possible, for our powerful 'Spirit Guide' from 'the beyond', to lose somebody and be unable to find him or her? Although I wanted to know a lot more about this strange phenomenon, I decided to do what Jack had advised and go to bed early. Both John and I were dead tired from living through our turbulent emotions, and we absolutely needed our beauty sleep! Therefore, while turning towards my young friend in my arms, I told John:

To read all our famous 'Gypsy Series' books, please visit www.gypsyseries.com

"John, let's do want Jack advises, and go to bed immediately."

While showing me his best puppy doe eyes, John wheedled:

"Dad, may I please sleep next to you in your double bed, now that Harry is still missing? I am a bit afraid to sleep alone, because I might get bad dreams about my disappeared little brother..."

For a moment, my too analytical mind pondered about what our 'Big Brother' society might think of me. Then, my Own Heart told me, loud and clear, to stop worrying and, from now on, just be there for my young friends, always and everywhere. From this moment on, I would never again deny any of my boys the safety and togetherness they so obviously craved! Besides, I too missed my little soul mate terribly, and I too was afraid of feeling lost and lonely without having my little 'octopus' attached to my chest! Therefore, I would need John's close togetherness at least as much as he needed mine.

I nodded my consent, and we went upstairs. John just followed me into my bedroom, dived under the blankets, and I crawled next to him. John glued himself against my left side, we wished each other goodnight and happy dreams, and we closed our eyes. Fortunately, both John and I fell asleep almost immediately.

Halfway through the night, John's worried sounding voice woke me up and desperately urged me:

"Dad, WAKE UP! Our phone rings and you have to answer it!"

While I woke up in sudden shock, I first couldn't understand what all the tumult was about. Next to me, John shook my shoulders to wake me up. When that didn't help, he started to push me out of bed! Still feeling sleep charged and dizzy, I glared at John's worried face. Why should I leave my cozy bed this early? I wanted to get lots and lots more beauty sleep first! Slowly, I wrestled upright and squinted at my still worried looking young friend, while I groaned:

"Wassup? What are you doing here, and what time is it?"

"It's nearly four o'clock, but our telephone rings! Come on, Dad, you have to answer it. It could be news about Harry!"

At that moment, our telephone downstairs started to ring again. Immediately, I was in a tremendous hurry and jumped out of bed. For a couple of seconds, I had to hold onto a chair, until my dizziness faded away and I could stay upright without swaying too much.

Chapter 5. Seeing Jack's 'spirit'; meeting 'little Harry'.

In the meantime, my telephone stopped; but it soon started to ring again. As fast as I could, I staggered downstairs and trotted towards my phone in our living room, inwardly hoping it wouldn't be some stranger dialing the wrong number. Still trying to dispel my sleepy cobwebs, I took the receiver from its cradle and grumbled into it:

"Yes? What do you want from me, at this time of the night? Do you know how late it is?"

The receiver nearly slipped out of my trembling hands when I heard a well-known deep baritone voice exclaiming:

"DADDY! Finally, you are answering our phone! All the time, I've dialed your number, but every time your answering machine took over and I was afraid I had to wait until tomorrow before you woke up. I am sorry, Daddy, but this isn't my fault and I cannot help it. Suddenly, that barn door locked and I couldn't leave it any more. Are you very mad at me? Please, don't yell at me... Everything was so creepy in that darkness, and I thought nobody would ever find me in that locked barn and that I would die from hunger and thirst..."

Clearly, my little soul mate had started to hyperventilate, because he sounded like stumbling over his own words. Then, I heard lots of scraping noises, as if my boy let the receiver slip out of his hands and it fell onto the floor. Only, I still needed to know where he was, and where I could find him! Therefore, I started to yell into my phone, to get my boy back on the receiver. Was he okay? Where was he? Was he alone? Could anybody please help him?

Fortunately, after some more scraping noises, a chuckling man took over. He told me he was the night guard at the zoo and walked his rounds every two hours. While crossing the empty playground, he suddenly heard an unexpected sound, as if somebody pounded on a closed door. Quickly, he walked towards the sound, and saw a small barn behind a closed fence. A young child seemed to have locked itself in, shouting and pounding the closed door, wanting to be freed. Only, he had to return to the zoo's office first, to find the correct keys and unlock both the padlocked gate and the closed barn.

Five minutes later, the night guard freed a very grateful young child that nearly cried from happiness. He used his flashlight to look at the kid, but almost fainted at seeing a small boy with a terribly burnt face! At first, he thought something horrible had happened and that he had to call for an ambulance immediately...

Only, the little imp started to chuckle at seeing his worried face, and assured him that everything was okay and his burns were over two years old. Now, my son was drinking hot chocolate in the zoo's office; and could I please come over and take my little deserter home?

"I am on my way! Please wait for me and don't go anywhere..."

First, I needed a moment to let the happy message sink in. Then, I put the receiver back onto its cradle and started to cheer loudly, immediately joined by a relieved looking John. We threw our arms around each other and started to dance around the room from sudden relief. Instantly, all our worries were gone. We had our lost little Gypsy Prince back, alive and kicking, just as John had predicted!

Quickly, we went upstairs and donned our clothes in record time. Within two minutes, we were ready, left our house, and raced to our car. Then, I had to go back to get the hidden spare key and open our backdoor. Of course, I needed my keys to be able to drive our car to the zoo! After I got my keys and my wallet, I put the spare key back onto its nail, raced back to our car, and quickly unlocked its doors. In no time, we left our village and entered the highway, where John started to yawn, sagged down in his seat, closed his eyes, and fell asleep. Of course, I too could barely keep my eyes open.

Around four o'clock in the morning, the long and boring highway was almost deserted. The surrounding darkness looked spooky, only now and then illuminated by the blinding headlights of a quickly approaching car that soon passed by and again disappeared. Desperately trying to stay awake, I reached for our car stereo and switched it on, hoping that some merry melody would help me stay awake until we reached the zoo's parking lot. Immediately, our joyful song reverberated through our old car, making John stir in his sleep:

"You are soooo beauuuutifuuuullll..."

Chuckling inwardly, I thought this HAD to be a positive omen! Again, everything had turned out for the best.

6. We have little Harry back, lost and found.

Humming with the happy music from our car stereo, I tried to stay awake while keeping my eyes on the boring road. In the meantime, I started to think. Fortunately, everything had turned out for the best, and I would soon have my little soul mate back alive and kicking! Only, why hadn't Jack, our 'Spirit Guide', helped us find our lost boy a bit earlier? Couldn't we really reckon on him?

Suddenly, I heard Jack's warm and soulful voice in my inside:

"My dear brother, because you are driving your car and it is in the middle of the night, my friends and I will do our best to keep you awake while I am talking to you. Of course, we have been around you and our three young friends all the time, but we couldn't intervene or tell you anything important until you had learnt your valuable lessons first. By living your lessons through to the end, you are even more aware of your responsibilities, so that you can guide not only your three sons safely through their spiritual development, but soon even more young friends. Our Crown Prince had to overcome the last bits of his remaining fears, so that he will have enough faith in himself to be an excellent Gypsy Leader in his future. My own son had to become more aware of his growing capabilities as a competent leader, so that he will be a good friend and trustworthy assistant to all of you, always helping you with everything that comes up. Your 'third son' had to feel more welcome in your company, so that he starts trusting his own feelings. Soon, a fourth young boy will enter your life, and this little sunshine will bring all of you a lot of joy! Now, go get your 'little soul mate'; and, soon, his surgeons will put new skin on him. We, your Beloved Ancestors and Spirit Friends, will always be with you, to help and guide you whenever we are allowed. Thank you, my brother and dear friend, for being who you are. May our Supreme Being be with you and your steadily growing family, and bless you!"

Jack's warm voice slowly faded away, while I tried to stay awake and keep my eyes on the road. Soon, Jack's spiritual influence had disappeared completely, and my own consciousness took over and kept me awake. For a long time, I still remained deep in thought, while driving on autopilot. Now and then, my too analytical mind started to doubt, but I silenced it immediately!

To read all our famous 'Gypsy Series' books, please visit www.gypsyseries.com

Jack HAD been around us; therefore, we really could rely on our Spirit Guide! We only had to learn our important lessons first... Soon, my sleepiness disappeared, making driving my car a lot safer.

Just before five o'clock, I parked our car in the darkness of the desolate zoo parking lot. At this time of the morning, its surroundings looked spooky and surrealistically silent. John woke up from the sudden absence of engine sounds, and first stretched his limbs out at full length to loosen his stiffening muscles. Then, he yawned a couple of times and smiled at me apologetically.

Looking a bit guilty, my young friend told me:

"Sorry Dad, for being such a sleepyhead. I wanted to stay awake, but the sleep overwhelmed me and I just couldn't help it."

"Well, there is no need to feel sorry. You are a still growing boy, and that means your body need lots of beauty sleep, although the beauty may be wasted on you. Come on, let's go to the zoo's office and collect our little deserter before you fall asleep again."

"Dad, again, you are no fun! Just wait until I am more awake and able to think straight again."

Chuckling, while bumping into each other on purpose, we left our car and walked through the darkness towards the desolate zoo. Its iron gateway was still locked, and all the lights were off. What should we do now? Where could we enter this closed zoo and go to its office? Could the zoo have a backdoor with a bell, perhaps at its backside?

Tentatively, I pulled at the closed gate; but, of course, it didn't give way. Fortunately, John found a small push button in a pillar next to the gate, and pressed it. In a far distance, a buzzer sounded; and, after a few seconds, lots of lights were switched on and suddenly flooded the gateway. Then, a security guard appeared, followed by a timid-looking little Harry. The broadly smiling guard unlocked the gate, let us in, and beckoned us to follow him to the zoo's office.

Much to my surprise, my little soul mate reacted extremely timid. He didn't look at us, seemed to avoid our eyes, and mainly stared at his feet... I tried to read his protective aura; but he kept his mind tightly shut, so that I couldn't read him like the 'open book' he usually was. Why didn't my boy trust me any more? Had something nasty happened to him, and didn't he want me to know about it? What the heck could have happened to my little soul mate?

John asked him a question, but his little brother only shrugged it off without saying a word. Now, John felt a bit rejected, because he looked at me with a questioning face. Although I didn't know what to think of it, I decided to give our little deserter some more personal space. In time, he would open up and tell us what bothered him...

My boy walked up front to the zoo's office and just went inside without looking back. We followed our little leader, and entered a small room where the invigorating smell of fresh coffee already welcomed me. The friendly guard offered me a huge mug of it, and I thanked him for his hospitality. Little Harry got another mug of hot chocolate, and John politely asked for only hot milk.

In silence, we sipped our drinks, while waiting for our deserter to come out of his shell. What could have happened to our boy that made him this clammed up? Now and then, he peeked at John and me from under his eyelashes. Only, the same moment we looked back at him, he immediately resumed staring at his feet. Why did he do that; and how could I reach him without forcing him to do anything he didn't want to do? I knew how proud and stubborn he could be! Tentatively, I asked him in my mind to please open up...

Immediately, my little Shaman picked up my thoughts. This time, he opened up to me a tiny bit, to let me sense he was afraid of what I could do to him. Only, what could have made him afraid of me? Never before had my little soul mate reacted like this! All the time, I continued to send him my love, while I again asked him in my mind to please trust me and let me know what was bothering him...

Suddenly, a frightened looking little cannonball jumped up and threw himself into my arms, now sobbing loudly:

"Please, Daddy, don't yell at me! I didn't do it on purpose, and it wasn't my fault. Are you very mad at me for being such a nuisance?"

Feeling happy again, I folded my arms around my boy's trembling little frame and held him very close to my chest, while trying not to squash him too much. Only, why was my boy afraid I would YELL at him for 'being a nuisance'? For as far as I remembered, I had never yelled or even shouted at any of my boys, or at any other young child. Therefore, I just continued to pour as much tender loving care as I could muster into my still frightened looking little soul mate, to make him feel safer and loved again.

For a split second, I was a bit afraid I would drown him in too much love. Then, I realized that was impossible, because real love can never do any harm to anybody! While kissing the top of his still trembling little head, I asked my boy:

"Why are you afraid I would yell at you? For as far as I know, I've never even shouted at you, or at any other young child..."

Two teary bright blue eyes looked up at me, while my boy sobbed:

"No, Daddy, you never yelled at me because I never did any too foolish things. But, Eric always yelled at John for being a nuisance or for doing things he thought were foolish. Afterwards, John always felt horrible and only wanted to die. Therefore, I was afraid you too would yell at me and make me feel horrible and wanting to die too, because you are now my official father..."

Great goodness, this was the very last answer I ever expected! During the time my boy had lived in John's house, he had seen how John's 'official father', Eric, always treated his 'official son', and how devastated John had felt afterwards. Although my boy was extremely mature for his age, he also was only eight years old, and his primary emotions still reacted accordingly... How would I ever be able to explain this to my boy? Becoming more and more angry at Eric who really didn't seem to have a heart, I gasped:

"My dear son, John's 'official father' doesn't love John; while I love you dearly, both as your 'official father' and as your adopted Dad, with all my heart, my mind and my soul! Therefore, I promise I will never ever yell or shout at you; unless it is for an extremely good reason, for example to prevent you from being run over by a too fast car. Cross my heart and hope to die! Do you believe me now?"

"Yes, Daddy, I do believe you now. But, I really did something foolish, by sneaking into that open barn that suddenly closed..."

Still sobbing, my boy started to tell us what had happened:

While playing their games of hide and seek, my boy had tried to find a better hiding place at the backside of the small labyrinth, where he entered an oblong square. Feeling curious, he peeked through an overgrown fence, and saw a small barn with an open door. After some searching, he found a small hole in the rusty iron netting, and worked his lithe little body through it. Silently, he sneaked towards the barn, and saw a huge pile of food bags in it. Still feeling curious, he stepped inside and tried to read the attached labels...

Chapter 6. Meeting -and losing - my little Soul Mate.

Suddenly, the barn door closed with a click, and he was trapped in the darkness! At first, he only laughed, and fumbled around in the dark until he found the closed door. He tried to open it by pulling its handle, but the door had locked itself and didn't give in. Still laughing, he started to pound on the door, expecting to be freed in no time. When nothing happened, he again fumbled around, found an old shovel, and tried to force the door, but his muscles weren't strong enough to break through the lock. He pounded the door with the shovel, but nobody showed up to free him. From a distance, he heard the muffled sounds of playing children, but nobody heard HIM...

After a long time of alternately yelling and pounding on the door, his dry throat started to hurt and his arm muscles started to cramp, forcing him to stop and take some rest. Now, he started to feel a bit worried. What would happen if nobody found him? Would he die here from hunger and thirst? Panicking, he started to yell and pound the door again, but his hands started hurting and he had to give up.

Still panicking, he slumped down onto one of the food bags, and started to think. Where were Dad, John, and Davy, now that he needed them to open the locked door? Why didn't we show up to free him? Didn't we miss him? Perhaps, we were glad to be rid of him, with his creepy burnt face and his so awfully scarred body... Suddenly feeling frightened at such an awful thought, he broke down and started to cry his heart out. What should he do now?

One time, he thought he sensed my energy, but he was too emotional to be able to respond to it. Soon, my energy was gone again, and his upcoming Shaman powers weren't strong enough to break through my own Shaman defenses and contact me. Again, he sagged down on a food bag and cried his heart out, afraid that nobody would find him in this hidden barn. Now and then, he yelled and pounded on the door again, but nobody heard him or rescued him.

At last, the sounds of playing children started to disappear; until everything around the barn went dead silent. Obviously, the zoo's visitors had gone home! Panicking, he again pounded on the door and the walls with all of his might. His mask started to itch terribly, so he peeled it off and put it into one of his trouser pockets. Then, he just cried and cried, until he finally fell asleep from exhaustion...

Sometime during the night, he woke up from his restless sleep and listened to the distant and strangely spooky sounds that came from all those exotic animals that couldn't sleep either. Again, he started to feel frightened, until he decided to stop being foolish and no longer exhaust himself! He knew he had a bright brain, so he decided to put it to good use and find another way to get out of this barn. Again, he took the shovel and tried to force the lock, hoping to be able to break its pin. Until the old shovel shattered, and he threw it away with an angry yell. Then, he thought he heard faint footsteps! Immediately, he started to yell at the top of his lungs and pound the door again, hoping to be heard. Finally, a grown-up voice outside the barn told him to wait, because he had to return to the office to find some keys... Never before had he felt so happy. Finally, somebody would free him!

Five minutes later, the door unlocked, and he was FREE. A security guard aimed a flashlight at him, but the man almost fainted at seeing his burnt face. The paling guard even wanted to call for an ambulance, until my boy started to laugh and told the trembling man he was okay and that his burns were over two years old. He only was very thirsty and hungry. The nice security guard took him to his office, where he got one of the man's own sandwiches and a huge mug of hot chocolate. After he took a bite of his sandwich and a sip of his drink, he wanted to call me. Of course, I would miss him and probably wait next to my receiver... Only, every time he dialed our number, my answering machine took over and asked for his name and number!

The guard thought I could have fallen asleep from tiredness, and that my boy should give me more time to wake up. While giving me some 'time to wake up', he again started to feel nervous, because he didn't know what could have happened to me. Perhaps, I wasn't home yet, or I really felt too disappointed in my 'little soul mate' and didn't want to be his Dad any more, or I had moved away to another village, to get rid of him and his foolish behavior. Or, I had suddenly died and left him alone, as Jack had done two months ago... Panicking at the frightening thought, he didn't know what to do, and again started to cry his heart out.

Fortunately, the guard knew how to handle frightened little boys. The man assured him that his Dad missed him terribly, but also needed his sleep after looking for his son all day. Probably, my boy would have to wait for the next morning, until his Dad woke up and listened to the messages on his answering machine! That calmed my boy down, and he switched into his powerful Shaman abilities to force himself out of his panic. Suddenly, he wondered why he hadn't thought before of using his powerful Shaman skills...

Chapter 6. Meeting -and losing - my little Soul Mate.

Immediately, he tried to talk to John in his mind, but John was deep asleep and didn't hear his little brother's voice. Next, he tried to talk to me; but, even in my sleep, my protective aura was too powerful for him to penetrate. After some thinking, he thought he could try to wake John by entering his dream and projecting a ringing phone into it. Quickly, he worked himself into John's dream, projected a ringing phone, waited until he was sure that both John and I were awake, returned to the guard's phone, and again dialed our number.

Finally, he heard my sleepy voice while I muttered: 'Yes? What do you want, in the middle of the night? Do you know how late it is?' Now, he only was afraid I would yell at him for being a nuisance and acting foolish; because Eric always yelled at John when he thought John had acted too foolish and should be punished. Afterwards, John always went upstairs to his bedroom, where he slumped down on his bed and cried in his pillow to muffle his sounds, while feeling awful and thinking about committing suicide...

With a tiny baritone voice, my little soul mate asked me again:

"Please, Daddy, don't yell at me; because I don't want to feel like John always did, and I also don't want to die any more, now that I am freed from that locked barn and can go back home with you and with John... Hey, where is Davy? Did Davy get lost too?"

While John explained that Davy went home and would join us again the next morning; I finally understood why my little soul mate had been afraid of me. He had seen what Eric's hateful yelling had done to John, and he didn't want to feel like another 'bastard child'...

With sudden tears in my eyes, I pulled my vulnerable little son even closer to my chest. How could I ever yell at my precious boy, my son and little soul mate, the light of my life... While putting my hand under his chin, so that he looked up at me, I explained:

"Young kids are curious by nature. They always try to discover their world by exploring everything interesting that catches their attention. Therefore, it is up to us grownups to create a safe enough environment for our children, so that they can be curious without any risk of getting harmed. Unfortunately, this zoo did not create a safe enough environment, by allowing a hidden barn to be open. That was not your fault, and nobody will be mad at you or yell at you for feeling curious and peeking into that barn! Of course, I am not mad at you, but I WAS afraid after you suddenly disappeared and nobody could find you any more. I also felt guilty for not looking properly after you... John, Davy and I have been searching for you until the zoo closed and we had to leave. I even feared that somebody could have kidnapped you and that I would never see you again..."

This time, I started to cry my heart out, probably because I was dead tired and totally mellow from all my fears and spent emotions. Indeed, I really had been terribly afraid that something bad could have happened to my precious little soul mate... Immediately, my little therapist threw his arms around my neck, and whispered:

"Let it go, Dad, and don't bottle it up! In a few minutes, you will feel a lot better."

In sudden surprise, I stared into my boy's bright blue eyes full of love and care. At that same moment, as in a flash, I knew that Jack had taught him and his friends to use such a statement, every time somebody cried their heart out! Already feeling a lot better, I started to laugh and couldn't stop any more.

Soon, I felt my little Shaman reading my mind, to understand why I laughed. When he found out what was so funny, he started to laugh too, while John shared our hilarity and laughed with us. Although the security guard looked surprised, he too soon started to laugh. It felt wonderful to be able to get rid of our built-up tension like this!

Then, we wanted to go home. First, we thanked the security guard for looking after our little deserter, while my boy threw his small arms around the man's waist and hugged him fiercely. The surprised looking man hugged my boy back, but also warned him to keep his curiosity in check from now on. Did my boy know the well-known proverb that stated 'curiosity kills the cat'? Of course, he did!

The nice night guard walked us to the still open gate and towards our car, and waved us out until we disappeared around a corner. Finally, I was happy again. I had my boy back. My precious little soul mate, lost and found...

7. Anti-anthropoid; and teasing each other.

On our way home, John and little Harry stretched out at full length and entangled into each other in our backseat, yawning and shivering from the nightly cold. Soon, they fell asleep and started to snore in unison, while our car heater started to heat up and nicely warmed my cold feet. Of course, I felt tired and sleepy too. Therefore, I turned the sound of our car stereo a bit up to help me stay awake, hopefully without hindering my two peacefully sleeping boys too much. Of course, they still needed their beauty sleep, after living through their own emotional turmoil! Trying not to yawn too much, I just kept my eyes on the still pitch dark and boring road that only now and then showed an approaching car on its other side.

An hour later, I parked our car in our driveway, killed its engine, and woke my still snoring boys. John woke up immediately, but little Harry just went on sleeping and only mumbled some. Therefore, I opened his door and gently carried his tiny frame out of our car, while John helped me by keeping the door open. Still looking sleep charged, John got my keys and opened our front door, while I carried my little soul mate inside and went upstairs, followed by a yawning John.

In my bedroom, I undressed my sleeping boy, while John shucked his clothes and dived under our blankets without asking for approval. Well, I didn't mind any more, while I put my boy under our blankets and joined my two sons. Suddenly, my boy turned around, adeptly crawled onto my stomach and 'octopussed' himself onto my chest, while putting his little nose in my left armpit as usual. Heaving a deep sigh of content, he started to snore again, while John snuggled up against my left side and wished me a good night and happy dreams. Soon, all three of us were deep asleep, fortunately without getting any nasty dreams or frightening nightmares.

Way too soon, the bright morning sun peeked through a crack in my curtains and woke me up. Still feeling sleepy, I tried to get away from the irritating sunbeam, while my boys started to stir and yawn and unwillingly opened their eyes. This morning, waking up a bit early was a good thing, because we had to shower and dress into our neatest clothes, to drive to what my boy called his 'face clinic'.

John left my side and wrestled upright, while he grumbled:

"I am very happy that Harry has returned home in good health, but I also hope we will never have to go through such a terrible nightmare again! I still feel very tired and sleep charged after yesterday's turmoil and collecting Harry from that zoo in the middle of the night. All of this started happening after we played another game of hide and seek around the zoo's labyrinth, and Harry tried to hide too well..."

Looking mischievous, my boy on my stomach teased John:

"The last time, you couldn't tag me, so I've WON our last game!"

For a few seconds, John fell silent. Then, he turned around and glared at his little brother with a face full of disbelief and brooding eyes that seemed to radiate fire and brimstone. For a moment, I was afraid that John would attack his little brother, and that I had to protect my too cheeky little monkey against attempted fratricide...

Then, John started to chuckle while he told my boy:

"You cheeky pipsqueak monkey, how DARE you! They should have kept you in that zoo, not in a barn but in a real ape cage, for the remainder of your life, playing hide and seek with the public!"

Chuckling, John kicked our blankets out of the way, dived onto his little brother, and started to tickle his tiny ribs wherever he could find any sensitive spots. Of course, my little monkey immediately tried to tickle John back, while desperately wrestling to get away from his merciless torturer. Only, at the same time, he also didn't want to leave his cozy place on my stomach... While trying to retrieve his blankets, my boy's deep baritone voice teased John:

"You are only jealous, because I really won our last game. Please, Dad, protect me from that mean 'antipoid'..."

At hearing his little brother's semantic error, John chuckled:

"Jeez, this little anthropoid cannot even pronounce his parentage correctly. You really think you've won our last game? Then, I will let you feel who is winning our last game of tickle-torturing!"

Again, John started to tickle his little brother; who still didn't want to leave my cozy stomach, but only squirmed a little bit while trying to escape John's ferocious attacks. Of course, lying prone on my stomach was an emormous disadvantage.

Chapter 7. Misinterpretations and misunderstandings.

Suddenly, our doorbell rang, sounding nice and civilized now that Davy had repaired it with a tiny wad of tissue. Only, who could be at our front door, this early in the morning? Could our 'disturbed lady' have informed the police again, after seeing the same young boys frequenting my house? My trembling little soul mate on my stomach planted his fingernails into my bare skin, while he moaned:

"Nooooo... Please, not again those stupid police officers with their condemning 'improper' sex things..."

At my side, John growled what sounded like a curse, while he left our bed and stomped towards a window. Again, my young friend was ready to defy all the meddlesome police officers in the world, to protect his little brother and me from them! Involuntarily balling his fists, he tried to look outside, with a grim face and fire-shooting eyes. For a few seconds, he scanned our front yard and driveway, and he even craned his neck to look at our front door.

Then, he started to laugh, while he told us:

"Nah, Davy is here a bit too early, probably because he wants to talk to our lost and found pipsqueak monkey..."

Quickly, John left the window and hurried downstairs, to open our front door and let our mutual friend in; while I tried to calm down my still trembling son. Fortunately, he had withdrawn his nails from my skin, although my chest now showed a couple of bloody scratches.

While using his powerful Shaman abilities to pull himself together, my boy muttered under his breath:

"I was a bit afraid that those oversexed police officers were here again, to arrest and interrogate us..."

At that moment, Davy stormed up the stairs and bolted into our bedroom, probably because he didn't know if the zoo or the police already found our little deserter. When Davy saw my little soul mate lying on my chest and smiling at seeing his 'younger brother from a past life' showing up with a worried face and concerned eyes; he stopped dead in his tracks. For a second, Davy only stared at my boy as if he saw a ghost. Then, he nearly started to cry with the sudden relief. While wiping his teary eyes, Davy exclaimed:

"Thank heaven you are home again! All night long, I was so afraid that something bad had happened to you... Where the heck have you been, and why couldn't we find you any more?"

Davy shucked his shoes and kicked them into a corner. Then, he threw himself onto our bed and dived next to little Harry on my stomach, so that I could give him his own cuddle. A few seconds later, John threw himself onto the pile, to join his friends and have his own share. Only, my body wasn't wide enough to carry three squirming boys; and all three boys tumbled off my overloaded stomach and landed onto the wobbling bed next to me, in a disordered pile.

My little soul mate protested, and Davy admonished John:

"Couldn't you wait until it is your turn to get a morning cuddle?"

Chuckling at seeing two indignant faces, John stuck out his tongue and laughed at their protests. Only, that made both boys even angrier! Working together, they attacked John and started to tickle his belly and ribs mercilessly, until John almost peed our waterbed, wrestled free from their combined attacks, and hastily left the battlefield.

My boy stuck out his tongue towards John, while he told Davy:

"This will teach that 'antithropoid' to leave us monkeys alone!"

With a suddenly questioning face, Davy responded:

"Huh? What the heck is an 'anti-thropoid'? Is that somebody who hates apes? The word sounds funny..."

Laughingly, John teased his little brother some more:

"Our pipsqueak anthropoid just discovered a brand new species of apes that is called 'anti-anthropoids'."

With a sly grin, our pipsqueak anthropoid immediately rebutted:

"Then, I suppose you are an inferior species of apes that has to be called 'anti-funny-thropoids'!"

John tried to tickle his little brother again, but Davy jumped in and started to defend his 'brother from a past life'. Together, they rolled off our wobbling waterbed and onto the carpeted floor, squealing while trying to tickle each other wherever they could.

Then, three hungry stomachs started to rumble loudly, because they hadn't eaten anything since yesterday and wanted to be fed! Immediately, our three inseparable friends stopped their romping. Davy quickly shucked his clothes, and my three musketeers threw their arms around each other and marched off towards our shower, where they started to use our shampoo to tease each other even more.

Chapter 7. Misinterpretations and misunderstandings.

Soon, three freshly cleaned boys returned into my bedroom and quickly dressed. While I took my own shower, my happy threesome already frolicked downstairs. Ten minutes later, I was ready and joined them in our kitchen; where my three boys had already prepared a healthy breakfast, set the table, and even brewed my first cup of coffee. Proudly sitting on their folding chairs, they waited impatiently for their 'ancient grandpa' to show up. They cheered loudly when I finally entered our kitchen, and John rose from his chair and politely offered me my own folding chair to sit on.

Now, it was time to feed my three young monkeys and one old 'beard-anthropoid'. In no time, all the food had disappeared into three bottomless pits, and three naughty looking boys burped loudly to thank our food spirits. Fortunately, and just in time, I had rescued enough food for myself, to fill my own stomach properly.

After my threesome cleared the table, Davy turned towards my little soul mate and asked him:

"I still want to know why you suddenly disappeared during our last game of hide and seek..."

Happily, my boy started to tell how he saw a small barn with an open door, and decided to have a closer look at it. He found a hole in the rusty iron netting that was big enough for him to worm his lithe frame through the overgrown fence. Next, he went to the open barn, stepped inside, and curiously peeked at a huge pile of food bags, trying to read the labels. Suddenly, the door closed with a loud click, and he was trapped in the dark and unable to free himself.

At first, he only laughed, because he was sure his friends would show up and free him in no time. Therefore, he pounded on the door, listened, yelled, and pounded again. Only, nobody seemed to hear him, and nobody showed up to rescue him. After some time, he tried to force the door with an old shovel, but his muscles weren't strong enough to break through the lock. Now, he started to panic, because nobody showed up to free him, and he was afraid that he would die here from hunger and thirst. Feeling terribly, he slumped down onto a couple of food bags and cried himself asleep.

Sometime during the night, he woke up and again started to pound the lock with the wooden shovel, hoping its pin would break and set him free, but the old shovel broke into pieces. Fortunately, the zoo's night guard heard him and freed him. They went to the guard's office, where the man gave him his own sandwich and a mug of hot chocolate. From time to time, he tried to call home; but, every time, Dad's answering machine took over. At last, he started to concentrate on John's dreams, and projected a ringing phone into them... Finally, sleepyheads John and Dad woke up, answered the phone, drove to the zoo, and took him back home, where they resumed their beauty sleep. And, of course, because nobody could tag him, he had WON their last game of hide and seek!

My boy's declaration made John grumble in protest:

"Our little pipsqueak 'anti-fun-poid' really thinks he has won our last game, by just disappearing into thin air..."

John's grumbling protest made Davy chuckle:

"Then, let's change our playing rules, before our little pipsqueak 'anti-fun-thropoid' decides to be curious again! Harry, a next time, please remember the proverb 'curiosity kills the cat' before you want to play cat again, because I was terribly afraid and couldn't sleep all night from worrying about you! Dad should buy us some cell phones, to carry with us all the time, so that we can call each other in case anything unexpected like this ever happens again..."

Well, I had already thought about buying a couple of cell phones, one for myself and one for each of my boys, but they had to be a surprise, perhaps next time we went shopping downtown. For now, we had to start preparing for our two hours' ride to my boy's skin transplant clinic, where my boy's skin transplant surgeon wanted to take a first look at his terribly burnt face and body.

Therefore, I told my still bantering three musketeers:

"Boys, we have to drive to Harry's 'face clinic' within half an hour from now; so let's start preparing for our two hours' trip. Harry, where is your rubber mask, and do you want to wear it during our voyage? Then, please, glue it on now."

Hesitatingly, my boy put his hand into a back pocket of his trousers, where he had put his mask after it had started to itch too much. With a suddenly worried face, he tried to get it out, but it seemed to be stuck to the fabric and didn't want to show up.

With a very unhappy face, my boy asked me:

"Dad, could you please help me get my mask out of my pocket?"

Chapter 7. Misinterpretations and misunderstandings.

Hesitantly, my boy stepped towards me and turned around, to let me see where his mask was stuck. Indeed, he had folded the floppy thing and put it into his back pocket while it was still sticky! First, I tried to pull the fragile rubber mask out of his back pocket, without doing too much damage. Only, the sticky thing had glued itself to the fabric, and my clumsy efforts were in vain.

Soon, I gave up my futile efforts, and asked my boy:

"Please, step out of your trousers, so that I can have a closer look at your mask and at how it is stuck."

Without protest, my boy shucked his jeans and offered them to me. After a few more vainly attempts, I finally immersed his trousers in warm water, to dissolve the glue. Fortunately, that helped, and the mask reappeared, looking a bit crumpled but still undamaged.

Little Harry first raced upstairs, to get another pair of trousers and put them on. Then, he took his bottle of sticky substance, and glued his crumpled mask onto his face with a little help from John. Working together, they carefully rubbed it into all directions, until its crumples were gone and it fitted like new.

Still looking a bit sheepish, my youngest son asked me:

"Dad? What time are we going to my face doctors?"

"Huh? What are 'face doctors'? Ah, I think you mean your 'transplant surgeons'. Well, we have to be on our way within ten minutes. Davy, could you please tell your Mom where we are going?"

Unfortunately, Davy couldn't join us, because he had promised his Mom to do some much needed chores, but he left us with a happy face and quite a story to tell. He promised to be back after our visit to Harry's 'face clinic', to find out what his 'face doctors' had told us.

John and little Harry walked Davy to our front door, while I went to my desk to gather my boy's identity papers and the address of our transplant clinic. In our hallway, little Harry and John had already donned their shoes. Boys will be boys, and they suddenly were in a tremendous hurry, wanting to leave immediately!

Chuckling inwardly, I stepped through our front door, ready to leave our house and drive to my boy's face clinic. Only, John looked at my hand with only a few papers in it, and shook his head...

While John took the papers out of my hand, he admonished me:

To read all our famous 'Gypsy Series' books, please visit www.gypsyseries.com

"Old grandpa, you forgot to take your keys and your wallet!"

My two boys started to laugh at seeing my offended face; while I returned to our living room to get my keys and my wallet from my desk, where I had left them without thinking. My smallest imp snatched the keys out of my hand and raced to our car. He opened its doors, and both boys entered its rear seat and quickly buckled up.

I got my keys back, gunned the engine, and we left our driveway and drove off. Finally, we were on our way to my boy's 'face clinic', to meet his 'face doctors' and have his thorough physical...

8. My boy's face clinic and our 'face doctor'.

Soon, we left our small village and turned into the long and boring highway. Happily, I scanned our car stereo for some nice background music... and almost immediately found our own fun song!

Turning the volume high, I let it resonate through our car:

"You are soooo beauuuutifuuuullll..."

Happily, we started to sing along with the catchy melody, clapping our hands and stamping our feet, while our deafening sound tried to raise the roof of our old car that almost started to swing at the cadence. Until a dull advertisement took over, and I lowered the volume.

After some time, my boys stopped their bantering and fell silent. I looked over my shoulder to see what they were doing, and smiled at the heart-warming sight. Both boys had stretched out over the full width of our car, with their arms around each other and happily snoring together. Of course, they were still sleepy, after going through our nightly adventures, and we had two hours of driving ahead!

Helpfully, I lowered the volume of our car stereo even more, while keeping my eyes on the long and boring road...

Two hours later, I entered the big city where we had to find my boy's transplant clinic. Both boys woke up to the noise of the heavy traffic, and all the starting and stopping at the many traffic lights. Still yawning, they rubbed their eyes to get rid of their sleepy cobwebs. Then, they started to look around at all the concrete multi-story buildings, several green parks, and lots of enormous warehouses.

A moment later, I stopped along a sidewalk and asked a sauntering police officer to direct us to the 'transplant clinic'. The nice officer (yes, they do exist) knew where the clinic was, and gave me its directions. I thanked him politely for his help, and drove on. After some searching, we suddenly saw our clinic that turned out to be a modern brick building, situated at the edge of a spacious park. I parked our car in its parking lot, my boys and I exited, and I locked our car doors and put my keys in my pocket. Together, we walked to the clinic's glass entrance and stepped through its automatically opening sliding doors, with a strange feeling of anticipation.

To read all our famous 'Gypsy Series' books, please visit www.gypsyseries.com

Inside the building, we were welcomed by soft background music and a noticeable antiseptic smell. Little Harry shivered, looked at me, and silently worked his small hand into mine. Obviously, he remembered his past operations and didn't like the smell. At the reception area, I told the waiting nurse our names and the name of our surgeon. She smiled at little Harry, looked up his name on her list, and took her phone to announce us. Next, she pointed to a small but cozy looking waiting room, and told us to wait there for our surgeon to show up.

Feeling impressed with the obvious efficiency, we sat down on a nice leather bench along the wall and started to wait. My boy crawled onto my lap, to be held and feel a bit safer, and John started to study a couple of medical magazines from a table.

After only a few minutes of waiting, a tall man in his fifties, with a friendly and open face, entered the waiting room. He smiled at me, winked at John, and then turned towards my little soul mate who suddenly looked a bit unsure. With a warm and pleasant voice, the friendly surgeon asked my boy:

"I suppose you are Harry Romani? And you brought your father and your brother to support you during your physical? That is good. Please, follow me to my private office, where we can get acquainted."

My boy seemed to like his 'face doctor' at first sight, because he immediately started to smile broadly. Quickly, he hopped off my lap, and we followed the friendly man through a passageway towards his cozy-looking consulting room, where he asked us to sit down.

We started with some small talk about our voyage, and my boy's surgeon told us he was a bit curious how we knew about his private transplant clinic. He also told us he had already contacted my son's previous surgeons, and they had sent him their medical information about his past operations, plus a couple of pictures. Smilingly, he took a couple of colored photos from a thick folder, and handed them to my intently listening little soul mate.

Again smiling at his little client, the surgeon asked him:

"Harry, may I please ask you a few questions about these pictures that were taken before and after your last skin operations?"

The surgeon started to ask my boy his medical questions; and both John and I listened in sudden surprise to my boy's astonishing mature and intelligent answers. All the time, he answered with precise and detailed information, and he even added a couple of relevant things

Chapter 8. John's parents; and taking 'my boy' home.

all on his own. He really was an amazingly special boy, and I started to feel even more proud of my brave little soldier!

After our surgeon had scrabbled down all the new information, he put his papers away and told my boy:

"Thank you very much, my young friend, because you've helped me quite a lot with your detailed answers and extra information. Now, may I please have a closer look at your burns? And, do you want your father and your brother to stay with us in the room, as you have to remove all your clothes and will be clad only in your 'birthday suit' for quite some time, until all our tests are ready?"

Still smiling, my mature boy simply answered:

"Nah, we always see each other naked in our shower stall, at least every morning and every evening, so that's no big deal. Dad, could you please help me peel my rubber mask off, because I am now a little bit too nervous to do it myself?"

After I helped my son remove his sticky rubber mask, my boy's surgeon looked at it in marvel and exclaimed:

"Wow, this flexible rubber mask is a truly beautiful specimen of craftsmanship! Harry, do you happen to know who made it? I am sure that such a rubber mask will be a wonderful solution for at least a couple of our inoperable or too badly burnt patients..."

With a proud face, my boy answered:

"Yes, I know who made it! Peter first made a negative mold of my face, and then fit this rubber mask onto the positive mold. I always glue it to my face with some sticky substance from a bottle. Dad, do you have Peter's business card in your wallet?"

Of course, I had Peter's business card in my wallet, because it also held the address of this transplant clinic. Happily, I dictated Peter's address and phone number to our 'face doctor', who wrote it down. Again, he told us that some of his too badly burnt patients would feel delighted and very grateful. Immediately after we were ready and went home, he would call Peter and greet him from us.

In the meantime, my boy undressed and put his folded clothes onto an empty chair. Now, he turned around and performed a playful bow towards our surgeon. Our 'face doctor' chuckled at seeing the antics of my now naked son, and politely bowed back at him.

Now, he started to examine my boy's burns, by scrutinizing every single scar and colored stain. Now and then, he scribbled a few notes onto his papers, before he went on with the next burn or scar.

All the time, my brave little soldier helped our surgeon with his examination; by turning around, flexing his body, and stretching his limbs, assisting his 'face doctor' as a real professional.

Finally, our surgeon put his papers down and told my boy:

"Thank you very much for such a professional assistance, and I wish that all my clients could be as helpful as you are! Now that I have seen your burns, I am sure we can do quite a lot to make your body more presentable; and, even more important, to restore your burnt face. Fortunately, all your important nerves are still working sufficiently to be able to reconnect your senses to your new skin within a short time. By the way, do you know what 'circumcision' means? Shall I remove the burnt skin from the top of your penis, or do you want me to give it a smooth foreskin that covers its top?"

With very much determination in his voice, my boy responded:

"Yes, I know what 'circumcision' means; but I prefer my penis to stay undamaged, just like my Dad's and John's are, with a smooth foreskin that covers the entire top of my penis. I only hope you don't forget to put a hole in it..."

With a suddenly questioning face, my boy's surgeon asked:

"What do you mean by 'don't forget to put a hole in it'? Could you please clarify your question some more?"

"Well, sometimes, I have to pee; and that would be difficult without a hole in the top of my foreskin to let my pee squirt through!"

My boy's surgeon started to bellow with laughter, nearly falling off his chair from sudden fun! After he recovered, he tousled my boy's unruly blond hair, and made his humble excuses for laughing at such a serious question. Solemnly, he promised not to forget to create a nice opening in the top of my boy's foreskin.

Together, they went to a technical looking computer and sat down in front of its enormous monitor screen. After switching everything on, our surgeon asked my boy to start creating the nice new face he wanted to see in a mirror, after having his skin transplant and looking at his own reflection...

Chapter 8. John's parents; and taking 'my boy' home.

With a happy smile on his so terribly burnt face, my boy started to control the computer mouse like a professional. Enthusiastically, he created face after face, by choosing items from the available combinations of all different noses, lips, and eyebrows. After playing around and trying out its possibilities, he became more serious and finally chose a cheerful little pug nose, small eyebrows, and not too thick lips that would nicely accentuate the oval shape of his head. With a questioning face, he turned around and looked at John and me...

John and I were pleasantly surprised; and we assured our proud looking boy he had made an excellent choice, which our impressed looking surgeon confirmed. He also instructed my boy how to save his new face into a newly created map, and let him print his new face out on an attached color printer. After handing my son an extra copy, he let him switch off the computer and the monitor.

Finally, our surgeon went back to his chair, sat down, and told us to ask him any questions we could have about our boy's pending skin transplant and his healing afterwards...

For quite some time, our 'face doctor' answered all our questions, while explaining what he wanted to do. Although my son's burns and scars looked bad at first sight, in fact, they were not that bad! Fortunately, the fire hadn't damaged any important nerves or muscles, so that only his outer skin was burnt away and all the underlying tissues were still intact. Therefore, my son would very soon have an almost normal feeling in his transplanted new skin.

After only three healing weeks, my boy would be able to feel again all the important things like touch, warmth, cold, and pain, without any restrictions. Compared to other severely burnt victims, he could consider himself extremely lucky! Soon after my son had his skin transplant, his renewed body would feel almost 'normal', without any remaining restrictions or impediments.

Of course, John and I felt elated at hearing such extremely good news, while my boy raced towards his 'face doctor' and offered him an enormous hug and a big kiss on his cheek! Our surgeon started to blush from sudden emotion and even got tears in his eyes. Furtively, he wiped his tears away with a tissue; while my boy left him and happily climbed onto my lap.

Smilingly, my boy asked his still blushing face doctor:

"When can we start? Now that I know that I will look normal again, I want to have my new face as soon as possible!"

Smiling back at our over-enthusiastic boy, the surgeon took his phone and called for a nurse. Soon, a friendly looking nurse entered our room, greeted us, and offered little Harry a bright blue gown to put it around his unclad body. With a proud face, my boy dressed up into his beautiful gown that made him suddenly look like a Foreign Prince! Striding majestically, he followed the nurse towards the laboratory, followed suit by John and me.

For quite some time, several doctors and nurses were busy around our little Prince, making X-rays, CT-scans, and photographs of his burnt face and body, while patiently answering my boy's questions and explaining what they were doing. A nurse drew some blood from a vein in his arm, and he had to pee in a cup and transfer part of it into a bottle. Another doctor listened to his heart and lungs, and tested his reflexes with a small rubber hammer. All the time, my boy underwent everything like a real professional. Obviously, he had lots of experience with the preparations from his past operations.

Finally, 'our' nurse took us back to the consulting room and our 'face doctor'. Little Harry nestled onto my lap, still clad in his bright blue Princely gown, and John sat down next to us. Our surgeon told us that, so far, all the tests had turned out to be absolutely positive. Therefore, he now wanted to discuss what he intended to do with his young friend before he got his major surgery, around three weeks from now. Today, he would like to peel a couple of thin layers of living skin from my son's body. He thought the best place would be the insides of his thighs, where the fire hadn't damaged his skin.

After the peeling, the insides of my boy's thighs would look slightly reddish, like scratched surfaces, but they would be painless; and Mother Nature would heal the scratches within a few days, without any visible scarring whatsoever. During the next three weeks, the laboratory would stretch and cultivate my boy's peeled skin under special conditions, to let it grow and increase its quantity.

After three weeks, my son had to return to the clinic, to have his major skin transplant. Under narcosis, the surgeon would first remove all of his old scars and wild flesh, and then apply the newly cultivated skin to all of the cleaned places. He would also rebuild my boy's nose, and reconstruct his burnt lips and wrinkled little pecker.

Chapter 8. John's parents; and taking 'my boy' home.

After the surgery, their anesthetist would keep my boy asleep for at least a week, to keep him immobilized and allow his body to heal sufficiently. Once awake, my boy had to stay in the clinic for around another two weeks, to allow his doctors to observe him and monitor his healing process. Although any major operation always implied some risk, our surgeon was convinced that everything would work out for the best, as my son was both very young and in perfect health.

Looking more and more enthusiastic, my boy exclaimed:

"Yes, I really can have my new face even before I go to school! When can we start the peeling?"

"We could start right now! Our nurse will put you to sleep for a few minutes, so that I can peel a few thin layers of living skin from the insides of your thighs. After the peeling, I will put some analgesic spray onto your scratches, and you will have to keep the insides of your thighs dry for at least two days. What do you think, shall we now go to our operating room for your peeling?"

"Yes, please, let's do it immediately; and thank you very much for everything that you are doing for me!"

In rank, we followed our surgeon to an operating room. First, my boy had to enter a shower, where a nurse scrubbed him thoroughly before she applied some brown disinfectant to the insides of his thighs. Then, my brave boy climbed onto a stretcher and laid down, with an expectant smile on his proudly beaming face.

A smiling nurse handed him a mask that was attached to a nitrous oxide container, and asked him:

"I suppose you already know what you have to do now?"

My boy nodded, took the mask, and firmly pressed it around his mouth and nose. Without any fear, he started to inhale the sleeping gas, while looking up at John and me with beaming eyes. A few seconds later, his eyes slowly closed, his body relaxed, and he just fell asleep. He really was a remarkable brave little soldier!

John and I left the operating room and went to the reception area, to wait for our little friend to wake up after his peeling. Only, before we sat down, the receptionist pointed us to a small cafeteria and suggested to wait there while having a drink. We thanked her and went to the small but cozy place, where I ordered a cup of coffee and John took a glass of cola.

In silence, we waited for our surgeon to be finished, while sipping our drinks. Now and then, we looked into each other's eyes and smiled at each other. Again, we could feel our mutual love radiating towards each other, and also towards our sleeping little friend.

Fifteen minutes later, our nurse showed up and asked us to follow her to our consulting room, that now held a gurney with a yawning and groggy looking little Harry on it... Slowly, our little soldier woke up some more, until he sat upright and lifted his bright blue gown. Proudly, he showed us a couple of reddish stripes along the insides of his thighs that were now covered with some silky film.

After we had admired my boy's scratches, he put his gown back down. With a still sleepy sounding voice, he told us:

"Jack was in my dream and we cuddled all the time, until I had to return into my body and woke up. Jack had already seen the print of my new face, and he told me I have made a perfect choice! He also asked me to greet his own son and my new Dad from him. Now, the insides of my thighs start itching, but my face doctor already told me not to scratch them for at least two days."

Our nurse offered him a glass of water and a colored pill, and he swallowed the pill and gulped the water eagerly. Still looking drowsy, he slid off his gurney and wavered towards me. I lifted him onto my lap, where he settled down against my chest with a happy sigh.

Because his stomach suddenly started to rumble, he joked:

"My stomach tells me it is hungry! Where can we eat?"

Our surgeon tousled my boy's unruly hair, while he told me:

"Feeling hungry is a good sign; and, within a few minutes, your boy will be his joyful self again. You have a wonderful son, and I am sure that this extremely special child will achieve extraordinary things during his long and busy life! Now, I have to leave you to our nurse, because my next appointment is already waiting, but we will see each other again within three weeks from now."

After our surgeon left us and went to his new appointment, our nurse took a schedule to plan my boy's skin transplant; and we set a new appointment for his major surgery, three weeks from now. Then, John and I helped our still drowsy little friend with his dressing. I took his rubber mask from the table and helped him put it onto his face. Fortunately, its inside was still a little bit sticky.

Chapter 8. John's parents; and taking 'my boy' home.

Finally, I lifted my boy onto my shoulders, and he clamped his small hands around my forehead to keep his balance, with his little legs dangling free. Together, we went to the clinic's small cafeteria, to eat and drink something substantial before we drove home.

Soon, our brave little soldier started to laugh and joke again, as if nothing extraordinary had happened. John and he ordered copious amounts of delicious junk food, and wolfed it down at lightning speed as usual, while I nibbled at some meat sandwich and sipped my coffee. Chuckling inwardly, I thought that, although my sandwich tasted reasonable, it absolutely lacked my little cookie's tasty herbs!

In the meantime, my boy had started to pluck at the insides of his thighs, as if trying to remove his trousers from his itching wounds. Clearly, he didn't feel too happy with his fresh 'scratches'.

After a moment of struggling, he complained:

"Dad? My scratches feel like they are sticking to the fabric..."

Without feeling worried, I took my boy to a bathroom, where I took a quick look at his fresh wounds in case something would be wrong. Fortunately, his silky scratches didn't show any visible blood, and nothing in that region looked extraordinarily sticky.

While I pulled up my boy's trousers, I reassured him:

"I am sure the stickiness is only sort of an unusual feeling. After we get home, I will take another look at your scratches."

Before we went home, we said our goodbyes to the again smiling receptionist, and my boy told her with a proud face he would be back within three weeks from now; to get a brand new face and cultivated skin on his burns! Smiling back at him, she reassured him he would be welcome any time, and she would look out for him.

Looking happy again, my boy asked for my keys and proudly led the way towards our car. John and I followed him, chuckling inwardly at seeing him walk like a little rodeo rider, with his legs wide apart. My boy opened our car doors and carefully got in, while still plucking at the insides of his trousers. He almost forgot to give me my keys back, and I had to ask him for them to be able to drive off.

On our way home, I again switched our car stereo on; but, this time, our fun song didn't pop up. After a few minutes, both yawning boys stretched out along the backseat and threw their arms around each other. Soon, they were sound asleep while softly snoring.

Feeling full of love for my two sleeping imps, I helpfully lowered the stereo volume some more, while keeping my eyes on the road...

9. Harry goes outside and gets a new friend.

Two hours later, we entered our small village, and it felt good to be home again. Happily, I drove into our own street, backed our car into our own driveway, and turned its engine off. For a few seconds, I just sat still and enjoyed the sudden silence, while my two boys slowly woke up from their sleep, yawned, sat upright, and started to look around with surprised faces.

Still yawning, my little soul mate asked me:

"Dad, are we home already? What time is it? I am very thirsty from my narcosis, but I have to pee first."

"It's four o'clock in the afternoon; and yes, we are home already."

Quickly, my boy snatched my keys out of my hand, left our car, and galloped to our house; while John and I followed him at a slower pace, chuckling at again seeing him walking like a little rodeo rider with his legs wide apart. Inside our house, my boy first raced to our kitchen and eagerly gulped a lot of water, while John entered our toilet, and I lined up to wait my turn. A few seconds later, my boy appeared from our kitchen, now clamping his little boyhood with both hands. Only, he had to wait his turn to bless our ceramic god, because John heard him coming and quickly locked himself in!

My boy started to pound on the closed door, while begging:

"John, please let me in! I'm nearly peeing my pants..."

Chuckling at his little brother's sudden hurry, John responded:

"That's your own fault, after drinking so much water. Ask Dad to buy diapers and put them on you."

My fidgeting boy started to look more and more frustrated, now kicking John's closed door while shouting:

"John, you are mean! Please let me in before it's too late!"

Finally, John flushed the toilet, waited some more, and teasingly slowly opened the door. His desperate little brother nearly ran him down in his hurry, with his pants already halfway down to his knees. He left the door wide open, and we heard him sigh with relief.

Within a minute, my boy reappeared in our hallway and sent a murderous look at his chuckling older brother, before he disappeared into our living room. Now that it finally was my turn, I went inside, closed the door, and happily took all my time.

After I showed up in our living room, John politely asked me if he could phone his mother. He wanted to tell her everything about the zoo where Harry suddenly disappeared, the transplant clinic where Harry got his physical, and that Harry's 'face doctor' would give him a brand new face within three weeks from now. He also promised to greet his Mom and Mark and Marrie from Harry and me.

To give John some more personal space, I took my little soul mate with me and went to our kitchen, to brew my first heavenly tasting cup of real coffee. In the meantime, my boy cozily leaned against my stomach, from where he wheedled:

"Dad? Now that I still have my rubber mask on, I want to take a closer look at our neighborhood. Can I please go outside?"

Feeling a little bit surprised, I responded:

"Of course you may go outside whenever you wish; but don't you want to wait for John, to join you when he is ready?"

"Do I really have to wait for John, because he always hangs on the phone for at least an hour? I promise I will not again play 'curious cat' and disappear into some silly barn that suddenly locks me in..."

"In that case, have fun! Will you be home before dinner?"

"Yes, I will be home in time to cook; and I love you very much!"

My boy offered me a big kiss, shouted 'bye' to John in our living room, and quickly disappeared outside, to take a closer look at our neighborhood. Again, I felt very proud of my brave little soldier. My shy little boy certainly had changed quite a lot, since I first met him! Inwardly, I admired his newly found courage, and I hoped he would enjoy himself outside, although this was the first time in two years that he went outside in plain daylight and all alone...

Feeling full of love and very happy with my three boys, I drank my coffee, rinsed the empty cup in the sink, and decided to act as a good parent and start tidying our kitchen. Then, I looked in our nearly empty refrigerator, and made a long list of the many things we needed to restock within the upcoming few days.

Half an hour later, John returned from our living room and started to help me. Working together, we went upstairs, where I cleaned our bathroom and changed our bed sheets, while John vacuumed our rugs in the bedrooms, the hallways, and the stairs. Feeling very proud of ourselves, we returned into our kitchen to fetch some drinks.

Suddenly, our nicely sounding doorbell rang; and I went to our front door and opened it, expecting to see Davy. However, much to my surprise, a firmly built young boy with snow-white hair and bright emerald green eyes looked up at me from a curious and open face full of sunshine and happiness. I estimated the boy to be around the same age as my little soul mate, and immediately liked him at first sight, although I had never seen him before. Behind him, my little soul mate showed up, smiling at me with a proudly beaming face. While my boy tried to push the new boy past me, he explained:

"Dad, this is my new friend! His name is Nicky, he lives only a few blocks away, and we want to play Davy's games on our computer because Nicky's Dad doesn't have enough money to buy their own computer. Is that okay with you?"

Smiling at seeing my son's enthusiastic face, I responded:

"Of course that is okay with me! Nicky, you are always welcome in our home, and any new friend of my son is a new friend of mine! Would you too care for a coke or perhaps another cool drink?"

Nicky nodded enthusiastically, while looking up at me with a trustful face and sparkling emerald green eyes. Without thinking, I reached out and ruffled his snow-white hair. Immediately, he leaned into me and threw his arms around my waist, with his firm body pressing against my stomach... Wow! This young boy certainly wasn't shy or distrustful, although he had never seen me before.

Within a second, my little soul mate joined our cuddle and leaned against me to get his own hug. Then, he grabbed Nicky's hand and impatiently dragged his new friend into our house. Reluctantly, Nicky left my stomach and obediently followed his new friend into our kitchen, where he started to look around with curious eyes.

My boy went to our refrigerator, and asked his new friend:

"What kind of cool drink do you prefer? Coke, juice, milk, hot chocolate, or perhaps cool water from the tap?"

"You can make hot chocolate? That's my favorite drink!"

Chuckling, my son took a fresh bottle of milk and put it onto our kitchen table. Then, he took a folding chair and clambered onto it, to get a pan and two mugs. While he got our chocolate powder from one of the cupboards, Nicky took the milk and helpfully poured some into the pan. My son pushed his chair towards our electric cook top, Nicky gave his friend the pan, and my son put it onto our cook top, switched it on, and waited until the milk was hot. In the meantime, Nicky put two helpings of chocolate powder into each of the empty cups...

In surprise, I stared at both silent boys, while trying to understand what could be happening. All the time, they were doing everything without saying a word or even looking at each other! Could they have done this before, or were they reading each other's thoughts? I knew that my little Shaman could talk to John in his mind, but that worked only when both he and John were thinking of the same things...

Soon, both friends took their steaming drinks to our living room, already slurping them while walking shoulder to shoulder. Feeling more and more curious, I followed them from a short distance. Nicky entered our living room, stopped, and quickly slurped another sip of hot chocolate while looking around with curious eyes. After a short silence, he nodded approvingly and told little Harry:

"It feels really nice here! Your house is much cozier than ours, and your Dad seems to be totally neat."

Involuntarily, I started to blush, while the two new friends finished their drinks and brought their empty mugs back to our kitchen, before they went to our computer. Smiling at each other, they wriggled their bodies into the same armchair. Little Harry switched our computer on, and explained to his new friend why they had to wait until the screen showed up. Next, they paged through Davy's games, deliberated for a moment, and decided to play one of Davy's racing games. Little Harry started the game, while explaining all the different driving movements to Nicky. Nicky seemed to pick up his explanations very fast, and soon started to play enthusiastically.

A moment later, both friends were totally immersed in their racing game, while frantically wriggling and jumping up and down in their shared chair. Suddenly, Nicky roared with laughter when his car broke down and collapsed into a huge fire! Immediately, they started to push each other's racing cars off the tracks and into the banks, trying to wreck them while having lots of fun.

Chapter 9. The Kingdom of Heaven belongs to these.

Smiling at their happy antics, I went to our couch and sat down next to John. Much to my surprise, my young friend muttered under his breath, while he stared at little Harry's new friend with an angry face. Clearly, he didn't like what he saw, but I had no idea why that was. Could John be jealous because his little brother had been outside without waiting for him? Or, could John be jealous of Nicky, who suddenly became little Harry's best friend? While both new friends again roared with laughter, John turned towards me and whispered:

"What is Nicky doing here? He is the little brother of Jason, the sixteen-year-old big boy who kicked Harry off his skateboard and called him a 'freaky alien'! I don't like that family, because his always drunken father is just as big a bastard as his oldest son."

Feeling shocked by John's venomous outburst, I whispered back:

"John, what are you doing now? Please, try to think first, before you start judging from the outside! For example, are you a 'bastard' only because Eric might be one? Or, is Davy a 'bastard' only because his father has been such a... let's say such a bad person?"

For a few seconds, John stared at me as if he wanted to argue but couldn't find the right words. Then, he got a thoughtful expression on his face. After some more pondering, he shook his head and started to blush. Again, he stared at both new friends who sat squeezed together in their shared armchair. Obviously, they already liked each other very much, and they certainly had lots of fun together!

Slowly, John's facial expression changed towards shame, until he suddenly looked at his feet and mumbled:

"Sorry Dad! Of course, you are right again, and I will have to learn to think first before I open my too big mouth and start talking nonsense. Davy is a good boy, and he cannot help it if his father has been such a beast. Nicky seems to be very nice to Harry, and he too cannot help it if his older brother behaves as a dork and his always-drunken father is such a bast... err... such a grumpy alcoholic."

Obviously, my young friend already regretted his too harsh words; and I hoped he had again learnt a valuable lesson. Gently, I folded my arms around my young friend's firm frame and pulled him even closer to my chest, to support him, and also to let him know we were still friends. Trying to distract him from his shame, I asked him:

"How is your mother doing, and Mark and Marrie?"

"Mom was very pleased to hear from me, and she told me she misses me. Of course, I miss her too; but not too much, because I like it here even more, with you and with Harry and Davy. I told her what had happened in the zoo and in Harry's face clinic; and she answered she is glad she didn't know that Harry was missing! She is also very happy to hear that Harry will get his new face so soon. Eric tried again to take Mark and Marrie to a juvenile home; but Mom told him to stop his efforts, or she will sue him for leaving her without any money and for abandoning his children. Hopefully, he will leave us alone from now on. By the way, Mom invites all of us, including Davy, to visit her next week and have dinner at my grandma's house."

Exactly at that moment, Nicky jumped up and overturned their shared chair in his exuberant over-enthusiasm! Both boys fell onto the carpeted floor, while Nicky again threw his arms high into the air in exaggerated triumph. Shouting at the top of his lungs, Nicky yelled:

"GOTCHA! This time I WON, so I really am the greatest!"

Chuckling, Nicky dived on top of his new friend, while John and I started to laugh at the funny sight and my little soul mate playfully poked Nicky in the ribs. Of course, Nicky immediately turned around and poked his new friend back. Now, they started wrestling on the carpet, trying to pin each other down. Then, little Harry started to tickle Nicky's ribs; making Nicky squirm while desperately trying to escape from his torturer. My clever boy seemed to have found Nicky's weakest spots, and easily won their wrestling match. In triumph, my boy straddled Nicky's chest and told him:

"Now, I am the greatest! Therefore, say 'uncle'."

"Aunt..."

"Not 'aunt', but 'UNCLE'!"

"Nephew..."

"I warn you! Say 'uncle'; or I will ask Dad and John for help."

"Grandpa..."

"Dad and John, please help me. I won our wrestling match, but Nicky refuses to say 'uncle'..."

Chuckling at my boy's funny antics, I teasingly responded:

"Why should Nicky say 'uncle', while YOU already did that for him, at least four times..."

Chapter 9. The Kingdom of Heaven belongs to these.

For a split second, my boy looked perplexed. While counting the 'uncles' in his mind, he totally forgot to hold onto Nicky. Immediately, Nicky threw his hips high into the air and easily wrestled free from under his torturer. Cleverly, my boy started to tickle Nicky's sensitive ribs again, making Nicky squirm around and around on the carpeted floor while trying to escape from his relentless torturer.

Suddenly, Nicky stopped wrestling, sat upright, and blushed:

"Sorry Harry, but I think I've peed my pants..."

Looking ashamed, Nicky rose from the floor, now showing a still growing wet spot in the front of his blue jeans. Then, he cringed when he saw me looking at him, and started to tremble all over...

In the meantime, my little soul mate teased his new friend:

"Ah, poor baby, did your Mom forget to put diapers on you?"

However, Nicky couldn't respond any more to his teasing friend. Still trembling all over, he stared at me with fearful eyes...

As a trained psychotherapist, used to working with young children, I knew that some young kids have weak bladders, especially when they are ticklish and start laughing. Could Nicky's parents have punished their son too fiercely for wetting his pants? Some fathers tend to see such behavior as an unwanted weakness in their son that has to be rooted out before it is too late... Therefore, I only smiled at my frightened and still trembling new friend, to reassure him and let him know I understood it had not been his fault, and that I still liked him very much. While pointing upstairs, I asked my little soul mate:

"Harry? Could you please take Nicky upstairs to let him shuck his wet clothes and wash up; and could you also lend him a pair of your own trousers, until his are cleaned and he can wear them again?"

Helpfully, my boy took Nicky's hand and dragged him out of our room and up the stairs. On their way towards our shower, we heard them teasing each other again, as if nothing had happened.

Chuckling at hearing their renewed antics, John mused aloud:

"Nicky didn't look very happy after he suddenly wet his pants! I think his drunken father has been a bit too harsh with punishing his sons. Dad, are you in for a racing game on our computer, now that our toddlers are upstairs to change their diapers?"

Of course, I was in for a racing game against my young friend! First, John and I wrestled for the best place in front of our computer. Unfortunately, we didn't fit together in the same chair, although we really tried it out... Then, John started to slaughter me. Every time I thought I could win, he pushed my car to the sideline and passed me, leaving me with a wrecked car on fire. I even thought he let me pass on purpose, to tease me even more.

A sixty-five-year-old man was racing against a thirteen-year-old young boy; and having my driver's license was NOT an advantage. Never underestimate youth!

10. What is a 'homo'; and Jason is in trouble.

After John had saddled me with another wrecked car on fire, for the umpteenth time, I decided to give up and sighed:

"Sorry John, but I am too old for those lightning fast games."

"Ah, poor senile ancient grandpa... Shall I get you a soft pillow for your old back, to sit more comfortably?"

Pretending to be offended, I turned towards my young friend and poked his ribs. Immediately, John rose from his seat and pushed me off my chair, so that I tumbled down and landed on the carpeted floor. Quickly, John dived on top of me and tried to pin my arms down onto the floor. However, because I still was the strongest one, I WON! Proudly straddling John's chest, I teased my squirming young friend:

"This time, I am the greatest! Therefore, say 'uncle'."

"Aunt..."

"Not 'aunt', but 'uncle'!"

"Nephew..."

"I warn you! Say 'uncle', or I will ask Harry and Nicky for help."

"Then, I will pee my pants, on purpose!"

"Ah, poor baby, did you forget to put on fresh diapers?"

Now, John and I nearly wet our pants from laughing too much! Hurriedly, I left John's chest and raced to our bathroom, followed suit by John who groaned loudly because he had to wait for me. While I happily blessed our ceramic god, John continually pounded on the door, until I flushed the toilet and he nearly ran me over in his hurry. Fortunately, for him, he was just in time...

On our way back to our living room, John suddenly halted, with a surprised face. Silently, he tiptoed to our stairway, looked upstairs, listened, and slowly shook his head, as if he didn't trust the unexpected absence of any boyish sounds. With a suspicious face, he turned towards me and whispered:

"What are our toddlers doing up there? They are too silent..."

Indeed, we only heard the splashing sounds of a shower stream, but nothing more. Feeling curious, I tiptoed up the stairs, followed by John. Even in our open hallway, everything was silent, except for the continuously streaming water. What were our youngsters doing, after their loud bantering and frolicking? Silently, I opened the door to our shower room and tiptoed inside, followed by John...

Then, I started to chuckle, when I saw that both my little soul mate and his new friend were relaxing under the splashing warm water stream, lying brotherly together with their eyes closed. They were a lovable sight to behold, and I motioned John to stay silent.

Only, within a split second, my little soul mate started to stir, opened his eyes, and looked up at John and me, making me think my little Shaman could have felt our approaching auras and immediately reacted to what he suddenly sensed.

Showing us two sparkling bright blue eyes, my boy exclaimed:

"Hi, Dad and John, are you spying on us?"

At hearing his new friend's deep baritone voice, Nicky too opened his eyes and looked up. When he saw me, he suddenly cringed and stared at me with a shocked face and lots of fear in his emerald green eyes! Quickly, he jumped upright and tried to dive for the still open door, as if wanting to escape; but he stumbled over little Harry's outstretched legs and fell onto his knees. Keeping his hands in front of his face as if trying to protect himself, Nicky begged:

"Please, don't kick me off the stairs! Harry and I did nothing bad and were only lying still..."

For a couple of seconds, I felt too confused, and didn't know what to think of Nicky's sudden panic. Why, for heaven's sake, was Nicky afraid I would kick him off the stairs? That didn't make any sense! What could be Nicky's problem?

After I pulled myself together, I 'tuned in' into Nicky's protective aura, to try to understand what could be bothering him. Immediately, I sensed an enormous wave of panic and fear that almost choked me! This boy was terribly afraid that I would punish him, but for what?

I looked at John, but my young friend seemed to be as bewildered as I was, while my little soul mate only stared at his new friend with a questioning face. Obviously, my little Shaman too didn't know what to think of Nicky's strange reaction. What should I do now?

Chapter 10. Getting used to seeing little Harry's burns.

Again, Nicky jumped up from the wet floor and tried to dive past me, as Davy had done when he felt too frightened and ran away... Fortunately, I could catch his dripping wet body in my arms before he could run outside and alarm our too nosy 'disturbed lady'. Quickly, I wrapped my arms tightly around his naked little frame, to keep him immobilized and prevent him from running away.

Still struggling to free himself from my arms, Nicky cried:

"Please, don't kick me off the stairs. We didn't do anything bad, honestly! Please, let me go..."

While I tried to keep Nicky from running away, my too analytical mind already started to doubt. Here I was, an old 'grandpa', holding onto a naked little boy who seemed to be afraid of me. What would our meddlesome society think of me, if they ever heard of this? What would Nicky's father think of me, if he ever heard of my assaulting his frightened son? Would he immediately inform the police, or would he first come here to kick ME off my own stairs?

Fortunately, Nicky already calmed down some, now that I didn't do anything to confirm his fears. Slowly, he stopped struggling and sagged down into my enveloping arms, although still trembling all over. What the heck could be this new boy's problem?

Tentatively, I loosened my tight grip on Nicky's surprisingly firm frame; and I felt happy to see that he didn't try to run away any more. Therefore, I just opened my heart to my frightened little friend, and started to send him as much Universal Love as I was able to muster. While kissing the wet top of his small head, I asked him:

"Nicky, why are you so scared? You haven't done anything bad, and you are NOT in trouble..."

At hearing my consoling voice, Nicky's bright emerald green eyes looked up at me and pierced straight into mine, as if looking directly into my soul! For a few seconds, he seemed to feel surprised, as if he didn't know what to think of such unexpected kindness. Then, with a still quivering small voice, he stuttered:

"I... I was afraid you would be angry at me..."

"And what made you think I would be angry at you?"

Hesitatingly, Nicky's quivering voice answered:

"For... for being a homo..."

At hearing this totally unexpected 'confession' coming from such a small child, I was completely out of words! Did Nicky really think he could be a 'homo', supposed he understood the meaning of this nasty word? Stealthily, I looked at John for help, but my young friend only looked back and me. Although I sensed that John knew a lot more about Nicky and his surprising statement, he clearly didn't want to talk about his knowledge in Nicky's presence.

Still not knowing what I should do, I decided to take some more risk and withdrew my arms from Nicky's firm frame. Fortunately, my new friend didn't try to run away from me any more, but he looked up at me with some more trust. Therefore, I just turned around and took two towels out of my chest of drawers. After offering one towel to John, I wrapped Nicky's firm frame into the second towel and started to dry his still slightly trembling body. Again, Nicky let me do as I liked, and just leaned into me without any more protest.

At the same time, John had started to dry his wet little brother. Only, my little soul mate started to protest fiercely:

"No John, you cannot do that! You have to look out for the scars inside my thighs, because I forgot to keep them dry."

Still trying to dry his now loudly protesting little brother, John just wrapped him in the towel and only curtly responded:

"Then, stand still for a second, and stop squirming around like some slithery eel in a bucket of snot!"

For a second, silence fell over our shower room. Then, everybody started to bellow with laughter, including Nicky! Our heartfelt laughter also made our built-up tension vanish, and the tense atmosphere around us changed noticeably, feeling as a welcome refreshment.

Still laughing, John and I finished drying our youngsters. My little soul mate went to his bedroom, and soon returned with yellow snoopy briefs and blue jeans for Nicky. After both boys dressed and were ready, little Harry dived back into our shower stall and quickly fished his crumpled rubber mask from behind the soap.

With a slightly guilty face, he looked at me and explained:

"Sorry, Dad... but I'll take it downstairs and clean it immediately."

Of course, Nicky followed his new friend towards our stairway, where they raced downstairs together, again shoulder-to-shoulder and teasingly bumping into each other on purpose.

John and I followed our youngsters down the stairs at a slower pace, chuckling at seeing their renewed antics and returned happiness. Downstairs, we went straight to our kitchen, where little Harry got a pan of warm water and our liquid soap. First, he immersed his rubber mask into the water and painstakingly cleaned it, of course helped by his new friend who had started to ask him thousand-and-one questions about his mask and about his so badly burnt face.

Meanwhile, I brewed a fresh cup of coffee, while John filled a tray with glasses of cola and the cookie jar. Together, we went to our living room, where my little soul mate placed his cleaned mask onto his green model. He also switched our still running computer off, and followed us to our couch where we sat down.

John plopped down at my left side and leaned against me as usual. My little soul mate claimed his usual place on my lap, where he tried to melt away into my chest. Nicky stepped towards me and seemed to hesitate, while staring at me with a longing in his emerald green eyes. Then, he just plopped down against me and trustfully leaned into me!

Tentatively, I put my arm around Nicky's firm frame, not knowing how my new little friend would react... Well, he just melted into me even more! Clearly, my 'fourth boy' had found his own place in my 'steadily growing family'. Chuckling inwardly, I remembered Jack's warm and soulful voice while he promised:

"Soon, a fourth young boy will enter your life, and this sunshine will bring a lot of joy to all of you..."

Could really Nicky be my 'fourth young boy' and 'sunshine' our Spirit Guide had predicted? His name sounded like my oldest son's Gypsy name from my past life, 'Nikki', when I was our 'Gypsy Monarch Harold the Great'. Was that why I immediately liked my new friend at first sight? Nah, that was too much of a coincidence...

However, I still wanted to have a serious talk with Nicky, about why he thought he could be a 'homo', whatever that nasty word might mean in his boyish vocabulary; and why he had been afraid I would be angry at him and kick him off the stairs...

While I tickled Nicky's belly to make him laugh, I asked him:

"Nicky, could you please explain why you were afraid I would be angry at you and kick you off the stairs?"

Immediately, Nicky tensed up and stared at me with his emerald green bottomless orbs. Then, he again sagged down against my right side, and heaved a deep sigh of frustration. Obviously, he didn't know how he should answer my unexpected question...

With a slightly saddening voice, he tried to explain:

"A year ago, my older brother, Jason, wanted to take a shower with his friend, Carl; and they asked me to warn them in time in case Dad came home early. Suddenly, Dad showed up and went upstairs to take a shower, before I could warn them. When Dad found Jason and Carl in our shower stall, cuddling and kissing, he started to swear, called Carl a 'filthy homo', kicked him off the stairs, and threw him his clothes. Then, he called Jason a 'filthy fag' and nearly beat him to death. Our family doctor brought Jason to a nearby hospital with bruises and two broken ribs; but Jason only told them he fell down the stairs, because he felt too ashamed to tell the truth. After Jason returned home, Dad told him he would never tolerate a 'filthy homo' in his house; and, next time, he would castrate him, by cutting his balls off! Since that time, Jason is mean to everybody, including me, he swears and shouts at almost nothing, and he has turned into a real bully. I think Jason still misses Carl, and I also think he hates me for not keeping my promise to warn them in time..."

Nicky started to cry from regret and frustration, while he trustfully buried his little head into my side to muffle his heavy sobs... At my other side, John suddenly stirred and tensed up when he realized what Nicky had told us about Jason. Again, my young friend had to learn a valuable lesson, this time of never judging a person from the outside!

For a few seconds, my little soul mate on my lap stared at his sobbing new friend, with lots of understanding in his bright blue eyes. Then, he hopped off my lap, turned around, and stared intently into my eyes... Suddenly, I knew how my little Shaman always 'talked' to his friends in their minds! Although I didn't hear his voice, I felt his energy entering my brain and just knew what his intentions were! Without saying a word, my little soul mate asked me to take his sobbing new friend into my arms, to help him overcome his sadness...

Feeling very proud of my boy, I sent him my pride and love; while I lifted a still sobbing Nicky off our couch, pulled him onto my lap, and folded my arms around his firm frame. Immediately, Nicky buried his face into my chest and started to sob even more; while I started to send him as much Universal Love as I was able to muster.

Chapter 10. Getting used to seeing little Harry's burns.

Patiently, I waited, until my new little friend had emptied his huge bucket full of sadness and sorrows. In the meantime, my little soul mate had plopped down onto Nicky's vacant place, from where he first sent me his own love and gratitude. Then, he cuddled up to me and happily worked his small head under my free arm.

This time, my heart almost burst with Pure Love for my warm and soulful little Gypsy Prince with his enormous heart full of love and compassion! To me, he had absolutely proven to be a real Prince, and I was sure he would be an excellent future Gypsy Leader.

A moment later, my boy peeked from under my arm and told his still silently sobbing new friend:

"Just let it go, Nick, and don't bottle it up! In a few minutes, you will feel a lot better..."

Nicky seemed to listen to his new friend, because he curtly nodded his head and immediately started to cry his heart out, with loud wails that seemed to come from the very bottom of his soul!

John rose from our couch, went to our kitchen, and returned with a fresh packet of tissues and a glass of water. He put everything onto our table, sat down, and started to wait until our sobbing little friend would recover from his tormenting pain and agony.

My little soul mate showed me an enormous smile from ear to ear, as if he already knew that everything would turn out for the best with his new friend. I just continued to hold Nicky close, still sending him as much Universal Love as I was able to muster.

Two minutes later, Nicky suddenly stopped crying and bashfully looked around, although he didn't seem to feel overly ashamed. Could Nicky have used the same Shaman technique my little soul mate and I always used to stop our emotions and pull ourselves together?

John took a couple of tissues from his packet, helpfully dried Nicky's eyes, and then let him blow his nose. Little Harry left his cozy place under my arm, and offered his friend the glass of water. Looking a bit timid but also grateful, Nicky gulped the water, while his teeth chattered against the rim of the glass.

I continued to cradle my 'fourth boy', until he had calmed down and again looked around, with still puffy eyes. Then, with a still sad sounding voice, Nicky continued his explanation:

"My Dad always tells us that 'real boys don't cry'; but I cannot help it because I just am too sad and I want to get it out of my system. Although Jason now acts as a bully, I still love him, and I miss my big brother terribly. We always did everything together, even after Jason met Carl and they started to love each other. Carl too was always very nice to me, until my Dad kicked him off our stairs and told him he would never tolerate a 'filthy homo' in his house. Then, Jason stopped being my big brother and became a real bully. Now, he always tells me to 'piss off' when I want to talk to him. I think that Jason hates me for not warning him in time; and I also think that Jason still loves Carl. When I saw that Jason kicked a young boy with a burnt face off his skateboard and called him a 'freaky alien', I fought with him and told him not to hassle that boy ever again! Of course, I didn't know that Harry would become my best friend, but I just couldn't let Jason pester that poor boy. Now, Harry is my best friend, and I wish that you could be my second Dad and John my second big brother..."

Spontaneously, Nicky crawled upright on my lap and put a wet kiss onto my bearded cheek! Feeling a bit surprised, I returned the kiss onto his wrinkling little nose, making his emerald green eyes sparkle with joy and happiness. After offering me another wet kiss, he hopped off my lap and went to our kitchen to wash his tear-streaked face, of course immediately followed by my little soul mate. This joyful 'sunshine' was already working his way deeply into my heart!

Within a minute, Nicky returned into our living room. He looked at our wall clock, and told us with a disappointed face he had to go home on time; because, else, his father would forbid him to visit us ever again, and he didn't want to take any risk in that department!

My little soul mate took Nicky upstairs to collect his wet clothes, and helped him put them into a plastic bag from our kitchen. Then, Nicky threw his arms around my neck and again offered me a wet kiss, before he told me:

"Thank you very much for everything! Tomorrow, first thing in the morning, I will bring Harry's borrowed clothes back."

My little soul mate wanted to walk his new friend home, and just followed him outside without his mask. Of course, both inseparable friends immediately threw their arms around each other's shoulders and started to giggle again. Frolicking and bumping into each other on purpose, they wrestled through our front door and disappeared outside. Clearly, my boy had found himself a friend for life!

Chapter 10. Getting used to seeing little Harry's burns.

In the meantime, John continued to lean into my left side, still staring into empty space with a sad face and teary eyes. Now and then, he looked at me, with deep brown orbs full of anguish... Suddenly, John left my side and climbed onto my lap, obviously to be held and feel safe and comforted. Although my rusty old body started to groan under John's heavy weight, I folded my arms around my young friend and pulled him even closer against my chest.

After a moment of sobbing in silence, John mumbled:

"Dad, I never knew that Jason could be in so much trouble... Now, I feel terribly ashamed for calling him a 'bastard', and I wish I could help him get a better life! Could you please try to find out where Carl lives now, so that Jason can meet him and be his friend again? I also wish I knew how I could help Nicky, who still loves his big brother, but it looks like Jason doesn't want to see it any more. Again, you have been right about everything, Dad, and I hope I have learned this important lesson of never judging anyone from the outside. Thank you very much for being my Dad and helping me again!"

Our nice sounding doorbell rang again; and John hopped of my lap, quickly dried his still teary eyes with a tissue, and went to our front door to open it. He returned with a happy looking little Harry who still carried the same plastic bag. My little soul mate dropped the bag onto the floor, crawled onto my lap, and explained:

"Nicky took me upstairs to his bedroom and first changed into his own clothes, so that I could take mine home. Then, we went to their living room, where Jason recognized me but he only looked sad and didn't say a word. I am now sure he feels unhappy because he still misses Carl, and I wish I could help him with his sadness... Their father wasn't home yet, and they don't have a mother in the house. Nicky asked me to ask you if he may come back tomorrow morning. He says he likes it here very much, and he also says he wishes you could be his second Dad, or perhaps his Grandpa..."

What? Did I hear this correct? Nicky really wanted me to be his GRANDPA? I never knew I could be looking THAT old... Suddenly chuckling inwardly, I started to realize how 'old' I actually looked with my grayish beard, at least in the eyes of this eight-year-old little boy who saw me for the first time. Obviously, John had been right all the time, and I really was becoming an 'ancient grandpa'.

At my side, John too started to chuckle; but, this time, the chicken didn't dare to say a word about me being 'old'... Together, we went to our kitchen, where my little soul mate prepared one of his famous meals, with the help of a couple of tasty herbs from his own garden.

Within twenty minutes, our little cookie's tasty meal was ready; and, again, our food tasted more than delicious. After finishing our meal, we did the dishes, cleaned our kitchen table, and returned to our couch in our living room, with coffee for me and colas for my boys...

11. I am Davy's new Dad; and meeting BJ.

While we leaned into each other and sipped our drinks, we started to talk about Jason who missed his former friend, Carl, and became a real bully after his father kicked Carl out of the house and nearly beat his own son to death for being a 'filthy homo'. How would we ever be able to help Jason, and perhaps his friend Carl as well?

John thought I should try to talk to Jason's father first, to explain what the man was doing to his own sons in his righteous ignorance. My little soul mate thought our efforts would probably do no good, as long as Nicky's Dad continued to hate what he called 'filthy homos'. Just look at what those police officers did to us when they arrested and interrogated us, without listening to our answers! Ignorant people always tend to think they are right, and therefore refuse to listen to anyone else who disagrees or who thinks different. Couldn't we try to concentrate on Jason and his ignorant Dad and send them our Love, to let them experience how Real Love feels? Hopefully, it would change their attitudes and make them feel less hateful, so that they could start to feel some more love and compassion for each other...

For quite some time, John and I only stared at our little Gypsy Prince who suddenly brought forth such an astonishing deep insight in how 'normal' people tend to react when confronted with things they cannot or do not want to understand. Was this so extremely mature little deep thinker really only eight years old? Wow!

Before we could respond to my boy's clever reasoning, our little Shaman sat upright and tilted his head; as if he sensed something he didn't expect and now used his outstretching aura to contact it.

Looking a bit surprised, my boy announced:

"Here comes Davy, but he is not alone..."

Ten seconds later, our melodious sounding doorbell rang, and John went to our front door to welcome our unexpected guests. Soon, he returned into our living room, followed by only Davy. Could my little Shaman be wrong, for the first time since I knew him? Then, Mary, Davy's mother, followed her son and entered our living room! Again, my boy's amazing Shaman skills had worked flawlessly.

Davy immediately raced up to me, threw his heavy frame onto my lap, and offered me a big kiss on my cheek. Chuckling inwardly, I thought that my poor lap had to endure a lot of heavy weight today. Smilingly, I folded my arms around my third son and returned the kiss onto the top of his head, while John and little Harry disappeared into our kitchen to fetch more drinks for our unexpected guests.

Mary smiled broadly at seeing her proudly beaming son sitting on my lap, and told me with sudden tears in her eyes:

"Every day, I am more and more thankful that Davy found YOU! For the first time in his life, my son is a happy boy, thanks to you, Big Harry! Thank you very much again, for being there for my son and helping him whenever necessary. When I saw you for the first time, I didn't know what to think of you being so close with my abused son. But now, I am sure you will never ever harm him and only help him with everything that he needs. If you wish, you can take him to those Gypsies in Rumania; and I will pay you for his lodging and sign any official papers that you need for the customs and other officials. Next week, we will go downtown, to get Davy his own passport and buy him a traveling outfit. Just tell me whatever else he needs. From now on, I totally accept you as Davy's new father, without any restrictions, and I am very grateful that you allow my son to call you 'Dad'."

Davy's beaming face lit up the entire room, while he responded:

"Mom, can I really go to Rumania and visit Harry's own Gypsy people and also become their honorary Gypsy and live in a caravan? Mom, I love you very, very much, and you really are the best Mom in the whole world! Dad, when are we going?"

Chuckling at my third son's obvious eagerness, I answered:

"Well, Harry's Gypsy people invited us to visit them in Rumania, but they forgot to give us their address and to tell us when we are expected. I think we first have to wait until Harry gets his new face and his own people send us a fax or an email."

In the meantime, John and little Harry had returned into our living room, carrying a tray of fresh coffee and colas. They put everything onto our table, and settled down on both sides of Davy and me. After thanking them, we all took a drink and started to sip it.

Then, Davy turned towards little Harry, and teased him:

"This time, you will have to wait your turn to sit on Dad's lap!"

Smilingly, my little soul mate responded:

"That's no problem! After you go home, I can sit on Dad's lap for as long as I want, and John will have to wait his turn."

Again, our melodious doorbell sounded. Feeling surprised, John and I looked at our little Shaman, wondering why he didn't announce our new visitor in advance. Didn't his amazing clairvoyant abilities work every time, perhaps because he had been too busy?

Only, our boy had already picked up our thoughts. Smilingly, he left his place under my arm and followed John towards our front door. I thought he could have sensed our visitor in advance, but didn't want to leave our conversation and his cozy place against my side... Now, he hopped off our couch and quickly followed John.

Soon, both boys returned into our living room, followed by Nicky. My 'fourth boy' first went to Mary and politely shook her hand. Then, he pushed Davy towards one knee, happily clambered onto my other knee, and offered me another wet kiss on my cheek. Looking up at me with sparkling emerald green eyes, he explained:

"My Dad told me I can stay here until eight o'clock, but only if you allow me and I am not too much of a burden to you. And, my Dad wants to have a private talk with you, perhaps later this evening, because he has another appointment first."

Smiling at my little sunshine's obvious happiness, I responded:

"Nicky, you will never ever be a 'burden' to me; and your Dad too is always welcome in our humble home."

"Okay, and thank you very much! Harry, shall we set up another racing game? I want to crash you and set your car on fire again..."

My little soul mate followed his friend to our computer, where they again joyfully wriggled into the same chair. Sitting closely together, they waited impatiently until the computer started up and they could play their favorite game. Then, they immediately began to cheer and shout enthusiastically, while trying to steer each other's racing cars into the banks so that they collapsed into a huge fire.

Trying to act as a good parent, I admonished them:

"Harry and Nicky, please, try to muffle your voices! And, from now on, tickling or wetting pants is strictly forbidden..."

For a split second, both boys turned around in their shared seat and stared me down in obvious disdain! Then, they just went back to their racing game and ignored me completely. However, they really tried to muffle their voices, by whispering instead of cheering.

John chuckled at seeing their indignant faces, and asked Davy:

"Davy? Do you want to lose a game of checkers?"

Chuckling, Davy stuck out his tongue towards John, offered me a quick kiss, and hopped off my lap. My two young friends fetched my old checkerboard from our hallway closet, settled down at our living room table, and soon totally immersed in their game.

A couple seconds later, Mary suddenly left her easy chair, cozily joined me on my couch, and whispered:

"Yesterday, Davy told me you had helped him with his itchy scar. Only, this was the first time ever Davy let a MAN look at it! Even in the hospital, only a female nurse was allowed to wash him and help him. Therefore, I am now sure that you have earned a very special place in Davy's heart, and he trusts you absolutely. He told me you also massaged a few drops of oil into his scar and stitches?"

Involuntarily, I blushed, at remembering Davy who showed up in my bedroom and asked me to help him because his 'scar' started to itch. Of course, I supposed he would show me some itchy wound; but he suddenly shucked his briefs, pulled his legs towards his shoulders, and trustfully showed me where he had his itching scar and stitches. Then, he explained how his own 'father' had torn him open, because the man's big penis didn't fit into his son's too tight poop hole...

While I again shuddered at the thought, Mary continued:

"Being here, with you and your boys, has turned out to be the best thing that ever happened to my abused son! Now, Davy has a chance to grow up in a caring and loving environment around your boys and you. Yesterday, he even asked me to marry you, so that he could be with you and with his new family all the time..."

Feeling a little bit shocked, I fell silent, because I had to digest this new information first. Could there be a hidden message in what Mary told me? She absolutely was attractive, although, up to now, I never considered courting such a young woman. How old could she be? Being no expert in that department, I estimated her to be around

Chapter 11. Remembrances and an intellagent octopus.

thirty-five or perhaps forty years old maximum... After listening to my own heart, I decided to trust her intentions and asked:

"Perhaps, you could join us downtown, next time we have to go there to stock up? Davy would feel delighted..."

However, Mary responded with a surprised smile:

"Thank you very much for such a nice compliment, but I don't want to invade your life! I like you as a friend, but I also want to cling to my own social circle of people and family. To be honest, after the disaster of my marriage, I'm feeling quite happy without having to fend off another courting man. I am only very thankful that you want to look after my son, and you will always be Davy's special Dad!"

Fortunately, Mary wasn't concocting any sinister plans to help me out of my lonely existence. After being married and divorced, I felt quite happy without another woman interfering with my life as it was! At least, up to now... but who knows what our future brings?

After drinking our coffee, we had some more small talk, while our wall clock slowly crept towards eight. Looking at the clock, I decided to warn our car-wrecking youngsters in time, and told them:

"Nicky and Harry? Could you please stop in time, because it's nearly eight o'clock and Nicky has to go home soon..."

"But, can I come back here tomorrow, please? I like it here, and your atmosphere is much better than ours at home!"

"Thank you for such a nice compliment; and you MAY come back here any time you wish, but only when your parents agree."

"At home, it's only my Dad, Jason, and me. My Mom died when I was still little; and my Dad already agrees now that he knows where I am. Harry, will you please walk me home again? I think my Dad will be home by now, so you can meet him if you wish."

Of course, my little soul mate wanted to walk his friend home again! First, Nicky said goodbye to Mary, John, and Davy, before he offered me another wet kiss. Then, my little soul mate followed his friend outside, again without his rubber mask to hide his burnt face. Together, they frolicked out of our front door, again walking shoulder-to-shoulder and happily bumping into each other on purpose. My little soul mate had definitely found himself a friend for life!

Twenty minutes later, our friendly doorbell sounded. Thinking it would be little Harry, John left his game of checkers and went to our front door, to let his little brother in. Only, surprisingly, John returned into our living room followed by a beaming little Harry and a proudly grinning Nicky who again offered me a wet kiss.

Behind them, a HUGE man slowly entered our living room and looked around approvingly. The enormous giant had to duck his head to pass through the doorway, but he seemed to be in pain because he walked slowly and deliberately, and now and then even grimaced.

After looking around, he greeted everybody with a booming voice:

"Hello Mary and Davy, it's nice to see you again! Hi John, is everything okay? And hello Big Harry, I am very happy to finally meet you, after all the wonderful things my youngest son told me about you. Please, may I first have a short private talk with you? By the way, my real name is Jason; but everybody always calls me 'BJ', that is short for 'Big Jason'. I've always wondered why that is..."

After greeting BJ back, Mary rose from her chair and beckoned Davy to follow her, while she explained:

"Hello BJ! It's nice to see you again, but we have to go home now. Thank you, Big Harry, for your hospitality and for listening to me."

Unexpectedly, Davy asked his mother, with a pleading voice:

"Mom? May I please sleep over here again tonight?"

Mary smiled at her son's pleading face, but also looked at me:

"Of course, you may sleep over here whenever you wish, but only if Big Harry agrees..."

"Well, I certainly agree! Davy is a well-mannered boy; and, so far, he has been relatively easy to manage."

Davy beamed at hearing my compliment, but he also joked:

"Dad, you haven't seen everything of me. Just wait until I really get loose! In the meantime, thank you very much for again letting me sleep here. And, Mom, you are the best Mom in the whole world."

Before Mary said her goodbyes, she reminded us:

"Please don't forget that all of you are invited to have dinner at my house, tomorrow evening!"

After I again promised to be there, Mary went home. Immediately after she left, Nicky and little Harry raced back to our computer and again joyfully wriggled into the same chair, while John and Davy went back to our table and resumed their game of checkers. Now that everybody had settled down again, I beckoned Nicky's father to follow me to our kitchen, where I asked him:

"BJ, before we start talking, would you first care for coffee, tea, or perhaps hot chocolate?"

"I am addicted to black coffee; so, if you don't mind?"

While I quickly brewed fresh coffee, I chuckled:

"BJ, you are a man after my own heart!"

Slowly and carefully, BJ lowered his huge frame onto a folding chair, as if he was in severe pain. Still wincing, he waited until I joined him at the kitchen table. Then, he took a sip of his coffee, nodded approvingly, and started to tell me why he was here. Trying to lower the sound of his booming voice, BJ told me:

"Big Harry, I first want to apologize for my behavior! A few days ago, my sixteen-year-old son, Jason, complained that four big children had attacked him without any reason. They ran him over with their skateboards, a huge boy beat him up, another big boy kicked his balls, and a girl like a panther punched him a bloody nose! Of course, I believed my son and was mad as hell, because his nose was bleeding, his balls were bruised, and his new trousers were ruined. Therefore, I took Jason to our police station to ask for recompense. The officers heard Jason's story, and promised to start an investigation. Two days later, street gossip told me that the police had arrested a newcomer in our village, together with two small boys who had spent the night in his house. That made me think... They arrested a man and two small boys, and not three big boys and a girl like a panther? Feeling curious, I asked around about your household; and the 'huge boy' turned out to be Eric's thirteen-year-old son, John; while the other 'big boy' was twelve-year-old Thomas, and the 'girl like a panther' was his little sister, Chrissy. Apparently, Jason was 'run over' by John's eight-year-old little Gypsy brother with his burnt face who now lives in your house. Then, Nicky told me what he had seen from behind our windows, and that he had a fight with Jason over the assaulted Gypsy boy. Nicky even told Jason to leave the poor kid alone from now on, or else... Well, I assure you that I had a good talk with Jason!"

BJ first took another sip of his coffee, before he went on:

"Of course, I took Jason back to our police station to tell the truth, but the officers told me that everything had already turned out for the best. Both boys were in your custody, and your conduct had already been proven to be beyond any reproach! After some more asking, I discovered that our habitual blabber-mouth had a hand in it; and I assure you she will never again spread any gossip about you. From now on, our entire neighborhood will stand up for you, and we will always help and assist you whenever we can. While asking around, I also had a short talk with Mary about her abused son, Davy; and I can assure you that Mary already thinks the world of you, and Davy even asked his Mom to marry you so that you could be his Dad for real! For the first time in his young life, Davy starts feeling loved and happy, and he also starts losing his remaining mistrust. Unlike my own flesh and blood, my sixteen-year-old oldest son, Jason..."

BJ worked a handkerchief out of his pocket and wiped his welling tears away, while I rose from my chair to brew fresh coffee. Although my own heart told me to put my arms around BJ's slumped shoulders and comfort him, I just didn't dare to touch the huge giant. What if he turned out to be a real homo hater, didn't want to be touched by another man, and decided to kick me off my own stairs?

After BJ blew his nose and took a sip of his coffee, he went on:

"When I returned home this evening, Nicky waited for me with sparkling eyes and totally in awe. He told me he had made a new friend, and this boy's father was the nicest person he had ever seen! His new friend had tickled his ribs, and Nicky had wet his pants. That happens now and then, because he has a weak bladder. Much to Nicky's surprise, you didn't shout at them and throw a tantrum, as I undoubtedly would have done. You only sent them upstairs, to take a shower and put on dry clothes. In the shower, your boy suddenly peeled his skin off his own face, making Nicky nearly faint, until he recognized the burnt Gypsy boy who had been assaulted by Jason! Now, your boy and my son are sworn friends, and they already vowed to stay good friends for all eternity! While they lazily lounged under the warm water stream, you suddenly showed up; but, again, you didn't shout at them or throw a tantrum for being lazy, as I certainly would have done. You just took a towel and started to dry Nicky, while John dried Nicky's new friend. Now, you are Nicky's hero, and he is sure you can walk on water! He even told me he fantasizes you could be his second Dad, or perhaps his Grandpa..."

Chapter 11. Remembrances and an intellagent octopus.

Again, BJ took a sip of his coffee, before he went on:

"Unfortunately, I am NOT such a good father. Seven years ago, my spouse suddenly died; and I started to drink to forget my pain, although Jason was only eight years old and Nicky was still a toddler. Soon, I started to drink too much and I became a real bully, always bad-tempered and shouting at my boys for nothing. Last year, I came home, wanted to take a shower, and suddenly found Jason and his friend under the warm water stream, kissing and playing homo. At that moment, my entire hetero world shattered into pieces, and I went completely berserk! Feeling betrayed, I threw Jason's friend out of my house, and kicked Jason two broken ribs. Jason went to a hospital, but he told his doctors he fell off the stairs. After that incident, Jason changed a lot and became a total jerk. Now, he even bullies his little brother he once was so fond of, and I am afraid that everything is MY fault. Many times, I've tried to talk to Jason, but he never listens to me and only shrugs it off. I think I am too impatient, because I always start yelling again. Perhaps, Jason is afraid of me, with my big mouth, but I also think he still misses his former friend, Carl, even after such a long separation... Of course, I want my oldest son back and I still love him; but I don't know how to reach him, because he never listens to me and always shuts down immediately..."

This time, BJ nearly started to cry, while he again blew his nose before he went on, now sounding a bit shivery:

"During the last few months, I started to feel extremely tired and got pain everywhere in my body, so I went to a hospital, where they told me I have cancer in the last stage and will probably die within a few months. Unfortunately, I don't have any trustworthy family or real friends, because everybody seems to be afraid of me. Of course, that is my own fault, for drinking too much and being such a bully... Now, I've stopped drinking, and I am seriously trying to better my life, by helping my kids and also trying to be nicer to them. I've even tried to contact Jason's former friend, Carl, to ask him to forgive me. Only, nobody seems to know where Carl's family lives after they suddenly moved out of town... I also want to ask you for a favor. Although I probably am way too forward, could you please take my youngest son, Nicky, into your house after I am gone? I know he already adores you, and I am sure you will be a much better father to him than I have ever been. Just look at how much John, Harry, and even Davy love you..."

Again, BJ blew his nose before he went on, with a sad voice:

"Although I sincerely regret everything that I did to my boys, and I wish I had done better, it is too late now, and I have to live with the consequences. I want to go home now because my pain is getting worse, but I hope you will consider my request about helping Nicky, because I don't want to send him to some unknown orphanage..."

12. Nicky sleeps over; two little whisperers.

For a few seconds, I felt totally flabbergasted, and just didn't know what to answer. All of a sudden, and totally out of the blue, BJ asked me to take his youngest son, Nicky, under my wings after he passed away, just like that... BJ would probably die within a few months, exactly now that he had started to better his life and he wanted to ask Jason and Carl to forgive him for his misdeeds... Why was life so cruel to this now honest man who had decided to change his attitude and really wanted to become a better human?

Hesitatingly, I responded to BJ's unusual question:

"Yes BJ, I promise I will seriously consider your unusual request. Only, what are you going to do with Jason?"

Still looking sad, BJ answered:

"Well, Jason is already sixteen years old, and I am afraid that nobody wants to take such a moody teenager into their house. Therefore, I suppose I will help him rent a room, so that he can try to fend for himself after I am dead and buried... Now, I have another question for you. Could Nicky please stay here tonight, so that he can get used to being around you, and you also could get used to have him around in advance? Now, I really want to go home, to take some medication before my pain gets worse and I cannot walk any more."

Again wincing from the pain, BJ carefully rose from his chair and slowly stumbled outside, without waiting for an answer.

After BJ went home, I first slumped down on a folding chair and closed my eyes, suddenly feeling horrible. BJ had told me he would die within a few months, but my inside refused to accept such a fate. Couldn't BJ first go to another hospital, where the doctors knew how to cure his lethal cancer and they could help him?

My next thought was unrelated to BJ: Where will everybody sleep tonight? This night, I suddenly had four young boys sleeping in my house, and I had only two folding beds to accommodate them! Of course, little Harry and John could sleep next to me in my double waterbed, as they already used to do.

Only, wouldn't Davy and Nicky be jealous of their younger friends and want to join them? My waterbed certainly wasn't big enough to accommodate me plus four growing boys!

Still pondering, I brewed another cup of coffee and returned to our living room. Little Harry and Nicky were still racing and wrecking all types of roaring cars, while John and Davy watched some film on TV. They seemed to be too engrossed in their own businesses to see me enter the room, until Nicky looked up and noticed me, standing in the doorway and watching them. His face lit up as a torch when he saw me, but he also started to look around for his father...

When Nicky didn't see BJ, he asked me:

"Where is my Dad? Sorry, Harry, I think I have to go home now."

Quickly, he left their game to his friend, wrestled out of their shared chair, trotted towards me, and asked me:

"Can I please come back tomorrow? I like it here, and I like Harry as my new friend, and I also love you very much!"

"Well, thanks a lot for such a nice compliment, and I love you too, very much! Your Dad already went home to take his pain medicine, but he also thought you would like to stay here tonight and return home tomorrow morning..."

"Can I really sleep here tonight? YEEEAAAHHH! Then, I want to sleep next to Harry in Harry's room!"

Okay, the first part of our sleeping arrangements was now settled. Nicky and little Harry were certainly small enough to fit into a shared folding bed. I only hoped that John and Davy would want to share the other folding bed, because it would be for only one night. Tomorrow, first thing in the morning, I would drive downtown to buy two bunk beds, so that my two adopted sons could have their own double beds in their own rooms, to have their sleepovers in style!

Soon, Nicky wrestled back into their shared chair, and little Harry and he resumed their racing game. Smiling at Nicky's enthusiastic reaction, I joined John and Davy on our couch and tried to catch up with their film. However, every time, my thoughts went back to BJ and his pending death. Had BJ already tried to get a second opinion for his lethal illness? Perhaps, some advanced doctor could cure him with a newly discovered medication?

Of course, in case Nicky's father really died, I would happily take Nicky into my house! Yet, I still hoped that Nicky could keep his own Dad, next to having me as his 'grandpa'.

Only, what would happen to sixteen-year-old Jason? What if nobody wanted to take such a cranky teenager into their house? Perhaps, I could take Jason into my house and give him his own room? Only, even with two bunk beds, my house still had only two bedrooms, next to mine. Jack, our Spirit Guide, once asked me to guide and mentor even more young kids. Could Jason be one of those young kids? If so, I had to hire a contractor to lift the roof of our attic and create a few more bedrooms; and I also needed to buy a bigger car...

After the film ended and all four boys started to yawn, I told them:

"Boys, it's time to go upstairs, take a shower, and go to bed."

Without protest, my boys left our living room and raced upstairs. Soon, I heard them chase after each other across our hallway, and tease each other under the water stream in our shower stall. When they had calmed down some and sounded as if being ready, I went upstairs to wish them good night and to tell them where they should sleep. Much to my surprise, they had already decided for themselves!

I entered my little soul mate's bedroom first, where I found two youngsters, jumping up and down on their shared folding bed. Both boys were of about the same height; but my naked little soul mate's body looked badly scarred and a bit skinny; while Nicky's firm body looked more robust and a bit stockier, clad in only dark blue boxers. When they saw me, both happy looking boys jumped up at me at the same time, to have a shared cuddle in my already opening arms.

While he very much enjoyed our shared cuddle, Nicky told me with sparkling emerald green eyes:

"I wish I could live here forever, with you as my new Dad and Harry and John and Davy as my new brothers!"

Feeling a bit bashful at getting such an unexpected compliment, I ruffled Nicky's snow-white hair and responded:

"That would be nice, but wouldn't your own Dad miss you?"

"To be honest, I am not sure... Now that Dad stopped drinking, he really tries to be nicer to us, especially to me. But, now and then, he still shouts at Jason and calls him a 'fag' or a 'homo'. I really wish he would be nicer to Jason too, but I think he feels too ill and has too much pain to care any more, and I suppose that Jason is still mad at him for throwing Carl out of our house..."

For a few seconds, I didn't know what to answer. How did Nicky know that his Dad was ill? Could this extremely intelligent boy have picked it up somewhere, and did he know that his Dad's illness could be lethal? Deciding not to ask him any more embarrassing questions, I tossed both boys onto their folding bed, from where they looked up at me with sparkling eyes and trustful faces.

Trying to act as a good parent, I told both boys:

"Now, crawl under your blankets and go to sleep immediately. And, please, no more talking; else I will have to separate you!"

My words didn't seem to make much of an impression. Both boys only smiled at me, while disappearing under their blankets and putting their heads brotherly next to each other on their shared pillow. Feeling all mushy, I stared at one healthy and utterly boyish face, peacefully lying next to one badly burnt face with a damaged nose and wrinkled lips. Getting tears in my eyes from my feelings of love, I thanked our Supreme Being in my mind, because I felt grateful that Nicky and my little soul mate had become such good friends!

After kissing both boys goodnight, I tiptoed out of their room and went to John's bedroom; where John and Davy had already crawled under their blankets and were now softly talking to each other. When they saw me, John pushed himself halfway up and muttered:

"Hi, Dad, I hope this narrow arrangement is only for one night! Could you please buy us double beds or perhaps bunk beds, for when our friends want to sleep over again?"

"What? You too are a mind reader? I thought only Harry was one. Yes, I have already planned to go downtown, tomorrow morning, to buy two new bunk beds, one for Harry's room and one for yours. Then, both folding beds can go back to the attic."

"That is a marvelous idea, Dad! But, I am afraid that Harry and Nicky will feel very unhappy with your decision. Our toddlers could be Siamese twins, attached to each other for all eternity..."

"Well, even with bunk beds, they can still sleep together in one single bed if they want to! A bunk bed only gives them more choice."

John and Davy wanted to talk some more before they went to sleep, so I asked them to lower their voices. They promised to be good boys, reckon with our Siamese toddlers, and go to sleep soon. Smilingly, I left their shared room, to have another look at my two 'Siamese twins'. Chuckling at the funny sight, I saw that both boys had their arms around each other. They were already asleep, with blissful smiles on their happy looking faces.

Helpfully, I straightened their blankets, kissed their foreheads, and tiptoed out of their room, leaving the door ajar. Now that I was alone, I first went to our shower stall and took a refreshing shower. Then, I went to my own bedroom and tried to sleep alone in my double bed, hugging my pillow and feeling abandoned. Much to my surprise, I already missed my heat-radiating little octopus on my stomach or glued to my side. I seemed to be so used to having him next to me, that it distracted me and nearly prevented me from falling asleep!

For a second, I even thought about going to my boy's bedroom and bringing him here, to have him sleeping next to me. However, how would Nicky react, if he woke up during the night and missed his inseparable friend? I didn't want to take any unnecessary risk of Nicky telling his Dad that Harry slept next to me in my bed! One can never know how other people will react, especially homo haters.

Ten minutes later, my door suddenly opened and my little soul mate wavered into my bedroom! Yawning and looking sleepy, he wavered towards me and crawled next to me in my bed. Could my little Shaman have picked up my selfish and unrealistic thoughts? Or, had I unwittingly woken my boy up, by longing for him and thinking about bringing him here to sleep next to me in my double waterbed? Suddenly, I felt a bit guilty. Luring my boy towards me to sleep next to me in my double bed had not been my intent...

Fortunately, my still yawning son started to scratch the insides of his thighs, while he complained:

"Dad? My scratches are itching terribly, where my face doctor has peeled the skin. I think my body is sort of punishing me, because I forgot to keep the insides of my thighs dry in our shower..."

Immediately feeling less guilty and much happier, because I had NOT lured my boy into my bed, I proposed:

"Okay, let me have a look at your itching scratches."

Happily, my little soul mate spread his legs, to let me have a close look at the insides of his thighs. His scratches looked slightly reddish and a little bit swollen, but they didn't bleed, and I thought they still looked alright. Therefore, I just took my bottle of massage oil, put a few drops onto my boy's itching scratches, and carefully rubbed the oil in. Soon, he heaved a happy sigh, yawned again, and told me that the itching was nearly gone. With another happy sigh, he started to crawl onto my stomach, as he always did when he slept next to me...

After a very difficult moment of hesitation, I decided not to act on my unrealistic desires, but to play it safe. Therefore, I left my bed, took my yawning son into my arms, and carried him back to his own bed. Carefully, I lowered him onto his part of their shared folding bed, next to his still sleeping friend. Nicky seemed to feel our presence, because he opened his eyes and smiled when he saw us. My little soul mate snuggled up to him; and they threw their arms around each other and closed their eyes again. Soon, they fell asleep and started to snore in unison, while I tiptoed out of their room and ambled back to my own bed. Again, I hugged my pillow and felt abandoned...

Suddenly, Davy wavered into my bedroom, and yawned:

"Dad? I cannot sleep because my scar starts itching again. Could you please rub some massage oil onto it?"

Again, I took my small bottle of massage oil; while Davy shucked his briefs, lifted his hips onto a pillow, and pulled his legs towards his head. Much to my delight, his reddish scar and stitches seemed to look quite a lot better than they had done before! Again, I put a few drops of oil onto them and carefully rubbed the oil in, until Davy told me that the itching had subsided. Happily, he crawled into my arms and closed his eyes, obviously planning to sleep next to me in my double waterbed for the rest of the night...

Again, I decided not to listen to my loneliness but to play it safe. Therefore, I told Davy to put on his briefs and that I would bring him back to his own bed to sleep next to John. While trying to spare my rusty old back, I lifted Davy's rather heavy frame into my arms and carried him back to his shared folding bed. He snuggled up to John, closed his eyes, and soon started to snore.

At long last, I finally fell asleep too, still feeling abandoned and hugging my pillow...

Chapter 12. My skilled cookie and amazing little chef.

Sometime during the night, I woke up again to the sounds of an opening door and whispering voices. Who were those whisperers, and what were they up to? Pretending to be asleep, I peeked through my eyelashes at the faintly lit doorway. Then, I started to chuckle. Two small figures cautiously tiptoed towards my bed, but one of them seemed to feel unsure and hesitated.

The other figure persuaded him to enter my bed, by whispering:

"Come on, just do it! I am sleeping in Dad's bed every night."

"Yes, but he is your Dad, and I only pretend to be his son..."

"Shush, don't wake him! Just do it. I'm sure he doesn't mind."

Impatiently, the first small figure pushed the second small figure into my bed, and waited until he disappeared under my blankets. Then, he went to the other side, where he crawled into my bed and happily clambered onto my chest. Heaving a deep sigh of utmost content, my little octopus had recaptured his own place on my stomach!

In the meantime, the other figure had crawled towards me until he felt my side. Cautiously, he snuggled up to me and put an arm around my waist; where he reacted a bit surprised when he felt little Harry's body. Then, his stocky little body glued itself against my side, where he melted into my safe and cozy aura with a deep sigh of content.

Feeling full of love and happiness, I could no longer pretend to be asleep. While very much enjoying my unexpected company, I threw my arms around my two young friends and pulled them even closer into my enveloping aura. Now that Nicky had crawled into my bed voluntarily and on his own account, I wasn't afraid any more of what BJ would think of me. Obviously, both boys were craving a cuddle and my feelings of safety, and I was more than willing to give it to them! From now on, our meddlesome Big-Brother society could... no, I didn't want to use any bad words, but you know what I mean.

Nicky suddenly stirred a bit when he felt my arm around his waist; and he whispered to his friend on my stomach:

"Shit, your Dad is awake!"

Trying to tease my little sunshine next to me, I whispered back:

"Please, no shitting in bed! Our bathroom is downstairs."

For a split second, both boys remained silent. Then, they jumped upright and started to shriek and bellow with laughter! Nicky started to tickle my old ribs, of course immediately helped by his inseparable friend. Although I tried to tickle them back, their combined attacks soon were too much for this 'ancient grandpa'. Wanting to give up, I begged my little torturers to have some mercy with their 'old man'...

Still chuckling, they stopped their combined efforts and tried to melt away in my enveloping aura and our safe togetherness. A second later, Nicky asked me, with a slightly worried voice:

"Pop, are you now mad at us, for wanting to sleep next to you?"

"Well, to be honest, I felt abandoned when I had to sleep alone in my double bed. Therefore, let's try to get our beauty sleep first, and tomorrow we will talk about it some more. Okay?"

"Okay, Dad, and I love you very, very much!" sounded into my left ear, followed by a big kiss onto my left cheek.

"Night, Pop, and I love you even more!" sounded into my right ear, followed by a wet kiss onto my right cheek.

Again, I started to laugh, because Nicky seemed to have promoted me to be his 'Pop'. And, to me, 'Pop' was synonym to 'old grandpa'... Again, rascal Thomas turned out to be right! Happily, I accepted my new status; feeling infinitely rich with and marveling in the unconditional love and total acceptance of my boys.

Again, I drifted off into dreamland, now holding my two softly snoring young friends in my arms and feeling on cloud nine.

13. Eat, the Magic Word for Growing Kids.

Early in the morning, I woke up from a strange nightmare. Two 'lipstick monkeys' with brightly colored behinds had started crawling all over me, while I tried to get away from their combined attacks. Shuddering with fear, I looked around for something appropriate to defend myself against both crawling animals. How would I be able to send these two little anthropoids back to their ape house, before they locked me up into their own ape cage and escaped into the crowd? I didn't want to be an ancient beard-ape and play hide and seek with the already chuckling public for the rest of my life...

Slowly, I woke up some more, until I suddenly realized that I was only having a very strange dream. Therefore, I quickly switched into my 'therapist mode', to find out what could be the hidden message in my strange nightmare. Never before had my unconscious mind sent me such a weird puzzle to interpret.

Slowly, I woke up even more, opened my eyes... and stared into two bright blue eyes on my left and two sparkling emerald green eyes on my right! Both little Harry and Nicky were already awake and had started crawling around on my stomach, wrestling and pushing each other while competing for the best place in my already enveloping arms. Obviously, their ferocious wrestling had caused me to feel attacked by two little 'lipstick monkeys' in my strange dream.

Both little monkeys started to laugh when they saw that I opened my still sleepy eyes and stared at them. One monkey offered me a wet kiss, while his happy sounding boyish voice told me:

"Good morning, Pop! I thought you would never wake up."

Immediately, an indignant sounding baritone voice protested:

"Hey, that is MY text! That is what I always say to Dad when he wakes up in the morning and looks sleepy!"

Trying to look mock-angry, my little soul mate started to tickle his chuckling friend, making Nicky squirm around on my stomach while squealing and trying to get away from his torturer. Because I didn't want to wait until Nicky wetted our waterbed, I told my boy:

"Please, Harry, have some mercy with your little monkey friend, because he didn't realize he is a plagiarist."

Looking surprised, my boy stopped torturing Nicky and asked me:

"What is a 'playgitarist'? Is that a game, and can I play it too?"

Chuckling at hearing my boy's linguistic confusion, I explained:

"A 'plagiarist' is someone who uses a text from somebody else, as if it were his own creation."

"Aha! I KNEW it... Nicky, you are a playgiaristic antithropoid. Go back to your ape cage and play hide and seek with the public!"

For a couple of seconds, Nicky only stared at his friend, with a bewildered look on his questioning face. Then he started to chuckle, pushed his friend off my stomach, dived on top of him, and tried to tickle his ribs. For another second, little Harry only groaned while squirming around to get away from his torturer. Then, he quickly turned around and deliberately tickled Nicky's most sensitive spot!

Within a second, Nicky looked stressed while he mumbled:

"Sorry, but I have to pee first!"

Quickly, Nicky pushed his friend out of the way, dived towards the floor, and raced down the stairs to empty his bladder. Of course, my still chuckling boy followed his friend in need, probably to tease him some more. At a much slower pace, I left my bed, put on my slippers, and followed them downstairs, to bring my own morning offer to our ceramic god. Only, I had to wait my turn until both little monkeys finished crossing their streams and playing sword fighting.

Two minutes later, my two little anthropoids finally turned up, still teasing each other and playfully bumping into each other. They smiled broadly when they saw me waiting, and Nicky bumped into me on purpose. Of course, I now had to prove to him that I still was the alpha ape in our house! Therefore, I pushed Nicky aside, hasted into our bathroom, and quickly locked the door, before both little monkeys could recover and possibly take revenge.

Outside the closed door, I heard them whisper to each other, clearly hatching sinister plots to get me back. Whistling, so that both boys wouldn't think I could be afraid of them, I emptied my bladder, flushed the toilet, opened the door, and returned into our hallway...

Immediately, two little towboats dived towards me and attached themselves onto my ankles! Groaning with their combined effort, they pulled my legs into two different directions, thereby effectively tackling me down! While I slumped onto the fortunately carpeted hallway floor, my little torturers jumped onto my chest, straddled my arms and my legs, and triumphantly started to tickle my old ribs wherever they could find a sensitive spot.

Groaning from helpless frustration, I first tried to grant them their innocent fun, until I started to wheeze and pant and nearly had to pee again. With my last effort, I rose from the floor and grabbed both little devils into my arms. Trying to spare my old back, I swung my precious load across my shoulders, dragged them upstairs, and dropped the wriggling bundle onto the carpeted hallway floor.

For a second, both boys sat up and only glared at me. Then, they quickly jumped up and tried to attack me again! However, this time, I only sat down and pulled both boys onto my lap and into my arms. Chuckling at seeing their surprised faces, I immobilized them, until they had calmed down and stopped their futile efforts.

With brightly sparkling eyes, Nicky looked up at me and told me:

"Pop, being here is FUN! My own Dad never plays with me, and Jason only romped with me until he lost Carl and became depressed. I wish I could live here forever, with you as my new Dad and Harry as my new brother, to have fun every day..."

While my little soul mate enthusiastically nodded his head, he assured me he would LOVE to have Nicky as his twin brother, next to having John as his older brother and me as his adopted Dad! Oops, sorry, next to having Davy as his other brother, of course.

Soon, both little stomachs started to rumble, telling us they were hungry and wanted to be fed! Chuckling, I wrestled up from the floor, with both boys still clamping onto my arms as if they didn't want to let me go ever again. Still clinging to each other like this, I carried my precious load to my bedroom and opened its door.

Inside my bedroom, we stopped dead in our tracks, and stared in surprise at two moving and giggling lumps below our blankets! For a split second, my two little monkeys fell silent, and then:

"Attack of the Dangerous Gypsy!" little Harry shouted, while he left my arms and recklessly jumped onto the first moving lump.

"Here comes the Nickering Dragon!" Nicky's enthusiastic voice shouted, while he threw himself onto the second moving lump.

Within another split second, four loudly shouting and wrestling boys were in a heavy confrontation; while their arms, legs, blankets, pillows, and our bed sheets seemed to whirl around in a vast tornado. Now and then, a broadly smiling face showed up from the whirling twister and soon disappeared again into the moving pile.

Shouting at the tops of their lungs, my four wrestling boys tried to raise the roof of our house, until they started to feel too exhausted to continue and finally stopped their war. Slowly, the whirling pile collapsed, and four panting and wheezing young boys showed up, grinning at me apologetically. Looking floored, they slumped down onto the disarranged bed and tried to catch their breaths.

After they had taken some rest and regained some strength, John suddenly decided to demonstrate his responsibilities as our competent upcoming Leader. Slyly, he used the 'Magic Word for Growing Kids' on his still tired looking friends, by telling them:

"Let's hit the shower, and then get something to EAT..."

At hearing John's magic word 'EAT', all four boys immediately jumped out of bed and raced to our shower room, already shouting and playfully pushing each other to be first. Obviously, Nicky won, because I heard him yell the loudest sheer!

While my boys were showering in our over-crowded shower stall, I tried to act as a responsible parent and quickly made my trashed bed a little bit more presentable, by straightening the crumpled sheets and blankets. Then, I went to my frolicking boys, to take a quick look at what they were doing. Smiling at the funny sight, I looked at four enthusiastic boys who were helping each other. John was already shampooing little Harry's blond hair, while Nicky politely asked Davy to kneel down so that he could rinse his brown hair.

Because I started to feel hungry too, I decided to try out John's 'Magic Word for Growing Kids' on my showering boys. Chuckling inwardly, I told them that, downstairs, in our kitchen, I had something to EAT... Instantly, they were in even more hurry! Quickly, they finished washing and rinsing each other, grabbed a couple of towels, and hurriedly dried each other. Then, they raced to their bedrooms, quickly dressed, and tumbled down the stairs at full speed.

Chapter 13. The too difficult thermostatic shower tap.

Chuckling at seeing such an unexpectedly powerful effect, I first took my own shower and dressed into something casual. When I appeared in our kitchen, my little cookie had already performed his tasteful herbs magic with a pan of greenish scrambled eggs. John had already set our kitchen table with five plates and some cutlery, and had even brewed nicely smelling coffee for me. Davy and Nicky were nearly ready buttering huge piles of toast, working closely together while chattering and playfully teasing each other as usual.

All four boys started to cheer when I finally arrived in our kitchen, and my little soul mate chuckled:

"Dad, you are the slowest ancient grandpa in the world..."

Quickly, he ducked away under our kitchen table, to escape my wrath. Showing up at the other side, he teasingly stuck out his tongue. Well, I will try to get him later on, perhaps after eating breakfast.

All of us sat down at the table and attacked the huge pile of nicely smelling food. In no time, four plates were empty, and four enthusiastic boys were licking their fingers clean and scrutinizing the pan for the last crumbs. Fortunately, I had rescued in advance another toast and a second helping of scrambled egg for myself.

While my impatient looking boys were waiting for the old man, John poured me my first cup of coffee. Did I hear John mumble something about a certain 'slow and senile old man'? Fortunately, for John, my 'senile' ears were too old and too deaf to be sure...

After Davy and Nicky had cleared our kitchen table, I took my shopping list from our refrigerator and looked it over. To play it safe, I also asked John and little Harry to take another look at my list; to be sure I hadn't forgotten anything important.

My little cookie looked at my list, and then dived into our refrigerator and rummaged around in it. Soon, he reemerged, and asked me to add some garlic, a couple of onions, and a few carrots. And could I please add a fresh fillet of salmon or some other tasty fish?

In the meantime, John had looked into our cupboards. He told me I had forgotten to add four important things: sugar, salt, salad oil, and macaroni. Davy had a bright moment and asked me if we had enough tissues left, after all our crying. Finally, Nicky looked at my list and anxiously asked if I hadn't forgotten to add more cookies...

All of us started to laugh, but we had to admit that Nicky was right! Quickly, my little sunshine took our pen and boldly added '!!!COOKIES!!!' to our steadily growing shopping list.

Now, my little soul mate trotted to our living room, and returned with his green model and a brown bottle. He put everything onto our kitchen table, sat down, carefully lifted his rubber mask from his model, and first started to make its inside sticky. Of course, Nicky immediately sat glued to his friend's side and started to help him. Working closely together, they attached the sticky mask to my boy's burnt face, and rubbed it into all directions until it fit perfectly.

For quite some time, Nicky only stared at his friend's masked face in obvious awe, until he suddenly mused aloud:

"Harry could be from that funny fairy tale, where the ugly frog turns into a handsome Prince..."

Chuckling at the thought, my Gypsy Crown Prince answered:

"Then, I hope I don't have to kiss the Princess, because I am still way too young to marry her."

Still laughing, we went to our hallway to put on our shoes. Next, I returned to our kitchen to get my shopping list, and I went to our living room to get my keys. Thinking I hadn't forgotten anything, I went to our already opened front door and stepped outside...

Much to my dismay, John started to laugh and teased me:

"Ancient grandpa, didn't you forget something important?"

For a few seconds, I only stared at my laughing young friend, not comprehending what John could be talking of. Was I again forgetting something important, despite my tries to be good this time?

My little soul mate started to laugh too, at seeing my frustrated face, while he stared at me with little fun lights in his bright blue eyes, indicating that his 'ancient grandpa' really forgot something. Of course, he had already read my frustrated thoughts; but he only laughed at me, and that didn't help me any further...

Again, I started to think. To go shopping in our supermarket in another town, I needed my keys, my shopping list, and... what else could I need? Then, finally, something started to dawn upon my too old and too forgetful mind. Again, I had forgotten to take my wallet from my desk, and I absolutely needed it to pay for our purchases!

Chapter 13. The too difficult thermostatic shower tap.

Hastily, I turned around to go back to our living room, but John already beat me to it. Quickly, he raced inside, and returned with my wallet in his hands. Triumphantly, he showed it to me, before he teasingly slowly put it into his own back pocket. Again, my teasing young friend turned out to be right, sigh...

After ruffling John's curly brown hair, I complimented him:

"Fortunately, I didn't forget YOU, as my personal assistant."

I threw my keys towards little Harry, who caught them adeptly and quickly opened our car doors. Everybody got in and buckled up. This time, John sat shotgun and searched our car stereo for some nice background music, while I started our old but still reliable car and backed out of our driveway. John helpfully told me where I had to go, and I drove off and headed for the highway.

Again, we were on our way to our usual supermarket in a nearby town. Would again my little soul mate start looking out for Kees, his friend from The Netherlands who always helped us with our groceries because he knew exactly where he could find everything? Stealthily, I looked over my shoulder at what my three boys in our backseat were doing, and silently chuckled at the funny sight...

Nicky, Davy, and little Harry were sitting squeezed together in the backseat of our too small car. When they saw that I looked at them, they started to pant and wheeze demonstratively. Of course, they were exaggerating, but our car really was too small to accommodate me plus four growing boys! My little soul mate at the side was only a tiny boy, but Davy in the middle was a lot older and firmly built, and Nicky at the other side was broader and stockier. Obviously, I would soon have to buy a bigger car...

Sitting sandwiched in the middle, Davy protested:

"On our way back home, I want to switch places with John!"

John looked over his shoulder at Davy and chuckled, but he wisely kept his mouth shut. Obviously, my upcoming leader did not want to switch places with his panting friend in the backseat!

Soon, little Harry opened a car window, and Nicky followed suit with the car window at his side, so that at least my two smallest boys had some fresh air. Only, hadn't my clever little Shaman read my thoughts? Then, buying a bigger car would be a surprise for him...

Well, to keep my surprise a secret, I only had to keep my thoughts hidden from my little Shaman's always-curious mind.

Quickly thinking of something else, I kept my eyes on the road, while John again told me where I had to turn left to reach the highway.

14. Supermarket; and I am angry with John.

Within half an hour, we arrived at 'our' supermarket, and I parked our car in its enormous parking lot. Vividly, I remembered the first time we arrived at this market, and my little soul mate decided to join us inside, despite his terribly burnt face. Today, his rubber mask effectively hid his visible burns and scars and stains, so that he had nothing to fear from any too curious customers.

Patiently, I waited until everybody had left our car, and then first carefully locked its doors. Although our old car didn't contain anything of value, one could never know.

My little soul mate held up his hand, and asked me:

"Dad, could I please have a coin? I want to drive our shopping cart, and Nicky can help me if he wants to."

Quickly, Nicky stepped next to his waiting friend, and two pairs of expectant eyes looked up at me. Chuckling at the funny sight, I put my hand into my pocket, to get my wallet and give my boys a coin. Only, where could I have left that wallet? I felt in my other pocket, but the only things in there were my keys. Could I have left it home, because I really was becoming an old and forgetful grandpa? Feeling ashamed of my obvious forgetfulness, I already started to tell my boys we had to go back home to get my wallet...

Then, I saw John, looking at me with a way too smug face. At that same moment, I remembered what John had done before we went outside. Darnit! Again, my young friend had me; and he started to chuckle openly when he saw that I remembered his teasing.

Still trying to look as innocent as possible, so that I didn't offer my chuckling young friend any more reasons to tease me, I asked him:

"John? Could you please give Harry a coin?"

Still chuckling, John responded:

"Sorry, Dad, but I haven't taken any money with me."

Trying to look stern, I admonished John:

"Don't befool me, boy, and take my wallet out of your pocket!"

Still chuckling, John fished my wallet out of his back pocket and handed a coin to his little brother. With a sly grin, he put it back into his own pocket. Now, I only had to remember where it was...

My little soul mate and his inseparable friend already raced towards the automatic sliding doors and disappeared inside; while John, Davy, and I followed them at a bit slower pace.

Inside the shop, my boy asked Nicky to take over and to steer our shopping cart, before he left us and started to race through the aisles, obviously looking for Kees. I took our shopping list out of my pocket and handed it to Nicky, who took it with a proud face and started to point out the various items we had to buy. Only, within a few minutes, my little soul mate raced back to us, looking disappointed.

Huffing and panting, he managed to bring out:

"I've asked the shop manager about Kees, but he seems to have taken a day off! Tomorrow, he will be here again."

Quickly, my boy stepped next to Nicky and helped him reading our shopping list and pushing our shopping cart through the aisles, now and then adding a few more things he thought could be useful. From now on, our shopping experience went by relatively uneventful, while Nicky and Harry steered our steadily filling cart around the corners and worked closely together to push it forward.

Soon, our cart was filled to the brim. After Nicky had checked our shopping list for the last time, we went to one of the many cash registers to check out. Of course, although we tried to choose the shortest waiting line, what seemed to be the shortest line also turned out to be the slowest one! Muttering under our breaths, we waited our turn, slowly shuffling forward while pushing our heavy cart along.

Finally, we arrived at the front of our line, where my boys started to put our purchases onto the steadily moving caterpillar band. Out of habit, I put my hand in my pocket, to get my wallet and pay for our purchases with my credit card. Fortunately, and just in time, I remembered who carried it now. Therefore, I quickly turned towards John and held up my hand, without saying a word.

Trying to look innocent, John opened my wallet and took my credit card out. After he offered the card to me, he stuffed my wallet back into his own pocket with another sly grin. Looking at my young friend's sparkling deep brown eyes, I suddenly realized that John was enjoying our innocent teasing at least as much as I did!

Chapter 14. Having lots of fun; and John's catharsis.

In the meantime, Nicky and Davy had been too busy frolicking and teasing each other to see what happened between John and me. Only my little Shaman sensed that something special was happening, because he stared intensely at us with curious eyes. Suddenly, I sensed that my little devil was again reading our minds! Inwardly, I chuckled, while I tried to send him a picture of a nasty looking devil with a green face and fire-shooting eyes...

For a split second, my little Shaman looked shocked, while he hastily retreated from my mind. Then, he started to laugh, while he sent me a picture back of an old and crippled grandpa, leaning heavily on an old and crippled walking stick!

Wow! I never thought I would be able to receive and transmit any pictures from and to my little friend! Could my own incarnation as a powerful Shaman and Cosmic Mage be waking up? Concentrating on my little soul mate, I tried to read his mind...

"Sir? Could you please check off? The others are waiting!"

Quickly forcing myself to wake up from my 'psychic experiments', I grinned sheepishly at the impatiently waiting young girl at the cash register. Still trying to dispel my disturbing cobwebs, I entered my pin code and confirmed our purchase.

The young girl had already turned around, while she mumbled:

"Thank you, sir, and have a good day."

"Thank you too, for being patient with this old man."

Suddenly, the girl looked at me, smiled, and responded:

"You are not old! Maybe a bit distracted, but certainly not old."

Well, her sudden compliment absolutely made my day! Happily, I strode forward and returned my credit card to John, who put it back into my wallet and put my wallet back into his own pocket. Feeling high and mighty, I followed my happy foursome outside.

Nicky and little Harry were already wrestling our too heavy cart through the automatically opening sliding doors; while John and Davy had snatched two empty cardboard boxes from a huge pile of litter and quickly passed our still wrestling youngsters on their way towards our car. Suddenly, Nicky uttered a shrill cry, because our too heavy cart slowly drifted off the sloping sidewalk, and overturned onto the road with a loud rattle!

All our purchases rolled across the street, forcing an approaching car to brake with screeching tires to avoid crashing into them. The angry looking driver tooted his horn, while my little soul mate held his hand over his mouth and stared at the turmoil with shocked eyes. At hearing the sudden tumult, John and Davy stopped dead in their tracks, looked at the unexpected mishap, and came racing back to us.

Glaring at our shocked looking youngsters, John snarled:

"What the heck are you two doing? Is it so difficult for you little toddlers to properly steer a shopping cart?"

At hearing John's angry reprimand, Nicky started to cry, probably because he expected to be punished for being too careless, as his own quick-tempered father undoubtedly would have done. Immediately, my little soul mate went to his crying friend and took him into his arms. While glaring back at John with fire-shooting eyes, my boy told his still heavily sobbing friend:

"Of course, this accident is not our fault! Instead of shouting at us afterwards, John could have helped us with our heavy cart. He should have seen that it drifted off of that slope, because we are only eight years old and not strong enough to keep a falling cart upright."

Meanwhile, another car showed up behind the still waiting first car, and its impatient driver hit his horn a couple of times, while two more cars appeared around the corner and drove towards us. What should I do now? Of course, this unexpected accident had been my fault as well, because I had saddled Nicky and little Harry with a too heavy cart, without considering they were only small boys.

Feeling more and more nervous, I told a still quarreling John:

"Please, stop blaming each other and help me clear the street! We are obstructing the traffic..."

Hastily, I pulled our fallen cart upright and started to collect our purchases. They had spread out everywhere, and I tried to sweep them towards our cart using two hands and a foot. Fortunately, Davy had already started to help me, by putting some fallen groceries into a cardboard box. John still muttered at our youngsters, and little Harry still tried to comfort his heavily sobbing friend.

An impatient driver steered his car past us, on his way crushing a bag of oranges while giving us the finger. Another car drove past us, tried to dodge the unexpected ravage, and almost hit John...

Chapter 14. Having lots of fun; and John's catharsis.

Feeling more and more frustrated with such a dangerous situation, I suddenly shouted at a still muttering John:

"JOHN! Come here and help me gather our purchases, dammit! This is NOT a good time for moping!"

Reluctantly, John left our youngsters and started to put some fallen purchases into a cardboard box; while Nicky dried his tears with a sleeve of his shirt and started to help me, as a brave little soldier; and my little soul mate dived towards the other cardboard box and started to fill it. Fortunately, we could collect most purchases and put them into our cart and both boxes. At last, we swept our crushed oranges and too soiled vegetables into the gutter. In silence, I wheeled the cart to our car, and put our rescued purchases into its trunk.

Nicky and little Harry volunteered to bring the empty cart back, while John entered our car and slumped down onto its backseat, still looking angry and staring out the windows. Davy slumped down onto the front seat next to me and slowly buckled up. In awkward silence, we waited until our youngsters returned and we could go home.

Of course, I didn't feel happy with this unexpected situation! For the first time since I met John, I had shouted at him, and that didn't feel right. As a psychotherapist, I already surmised what could have happened. Up to now, John's denouncing 'stepfather', Eric, had always shouted at his 'son' and belittled him for everything that went wrong. Now, not knowing any better, John started behaving exactly the same way! That is why John snarled at little Harry and Nicky. Only, next to being a psychotherapist, I also was a human being with my own feelings of pride, and I didn't like the fact that John tried to take over my task, by reprimanding my boys. From frustration, I had shouted at John, and therefore acted exactly as Eric would have done! Of course, John now projected all his built-up anger and frustration about Eric towards me. This time, I was John's scapegoat, and I deserved it.

Meanwhile, our sad-looking youngsters came ambling back to our car. Nicky handed me my coin, and he and my little soul mate stared at John as if not knowing what they should do. Slowly, they clambered into the rear seat, propped up against the car door, and tried to avoid touching a still angry looking John... This didn't feel good! Hesitantly, I turned around and told my still moping young friend:

"John? I am very sorry for shouting at you. The angry words just slipped out of my mouth, because I felt shocked and frustrated..."

With a dark gloom in his brooding eyes, John answered:

"Well, I don't like people who shout and curse at me! Please bring me back to my Mom. I want to go home!"

What should I do now? Of course, I didn't want to lose my young friend over such a silly thing. On the other hand, as a grownup and knowing I ultimately had been right, I also didn't want to prostrate for such a young child. Feeling more and more uneasy, I looked at my intently listening little soul mate, as if asking for his advice... Immediately, my little Shaman turned towards John and forcefully punched his arm! With fire-shooting eyes, my boy stared John down until John started to feel uneasy and his face turned a deep red. Still staring intensely, my boy admonished his bigger brother:

"Ungrateful pig that you are, how dare you defy Dad! Dad helps you and is only nice to you, and what do you do in return? Shame on you! Of course, this accident is your fault too, because you didn't help Nicky and me. Now, start apologizing for your stupid frustrations, or I don't want to be your little brother anymore."

Determinedly, my little soul mate turned around and started to stare out the windows, while John's face became redder and redder. For a moment, I was afraid that John would try to attack my boy; and I already readied myself to intervene if necessary. Then, John burst out towards his little brother, almost screeching:

"You little pipsqueak, what do YOU know about frustrations? Dad CURSED at me, for crying out loud, and I don't want to be cursed at by anybody! Now, leave me alone, and I only want to go home."

With a sudden smile on his face, my little therapist retorted:

"What do I know about frustrations? Well, I have lost my Mom, and my Dad, and Jack, and my family, and half of my nose... Isn't that enough frustrations for a little pipsqueak? Yet, I know that Dad's cursing made you think of Eric who would have done the same thing, and that is why you are angry with Dad. Only, Dad is NOT Eric; and especially you, as Eric's former 'bastard child', should know better than letting your anger get the best of you! Do you still want me to be your little brother? Then, you know what you have to do..."

Again, my little soul mate turned away from John and started to stare out the windows, as if demonstrating he left the choice to John. At the same time, I could clearly sense my little Shaman sending John as much Cosmic Love as he could bring forth.

122 Aad Aandacht is a Dutch psychotherapist who loves writing 'books with a message'

Chapter 14. Having lots of fun; and John's catharsis.

For ten, twenty seconds, nothing happened. Then, John slowly lifted his head and looked at his little brother. After heaving a couple of frustrated sighs, John nearly started to cry, while he mumbled:

"Of course, you are right again, and I am always doing the wrong things, with my too big mouth. Now, Dad is angry at me, you hate me, I've lost my real father, Eric doesn't want to know his 'bastard child' any more, and I'm nearly losing both you and Dad over my stupid feelings of anger and righteousness... Only, I don't want to live like this any more! Thank you for helping me again, and I hope you still want to be my little brother. Dad, I apologize for talking back to you. I am very sorry for having been such an ass, and I will try to better myself. You are the only living person in the world who still loves the 'bastard child' and accepts me as I am, in spite of my too big mouth and my stupid behavior. Will you please forgive me and continue to be my Dad? I don't want to lose you too..."

John dived towards me, threw his arms around my neck from behind, and started to cry his heart out. While trying to loosen John's death grip on my neck that nearly suffocated me, I started to send my young friend as much Universal Love as I could muster. Fortunately, again, everything had turned out for the best, and I felt very happy to have my young friend back!

In the meantime, my little Shaman and I had started working together, pulling John's frustrations out of his aura and sending them towards Mother Earth. When we were ready, my clever little therapist whispered into John's ear:

"Let it go, John, and don't bottle it up. In a few minutes, you will feel a lot better..."

Looking surprised, John first unfolded his suffocating arms from around my neck, sat upright, and stared at his broadly smiling little brother. Then, he forcefully stopped his crying and started to chuckle, despite his still streaming tears. Now sniffling and laughing at the same time, John managed to bring out:

"I know you've stolen your text from my real Dad, but thank you very much anyway. Can we now be brothers again?"

Smiling even broader, my little soul mate assured John:

"Of course, silly! I've never stopped being your brother, although I WAS mad at you for being stubborn and talking back to Dad. Besides, this morning, Dad already told Nicky and me that we are play... err... 'playgitarists'? I mean those people that steal their text from someone else, to pretend it were their own creation..."

Still wiping his eyes with the backs of his hands, John chuckled:

"I think you mean you are a 'plagiarist', for thieving Jack's text? Yes, you absolutely are one; but I love you anyway."

Exactly at that moment, Nicky's head showed up from the trunk of our car, while his concerned sounding boyish voice piped up:

"Our new packet of tissues slipped to the bottom of this cardboard box, and I cannot get it out any more..."

Of course, all of us started to bellow with laughter, even Nicky himself, while he clambered back onto the rear seat and sat down next to his friend. Our heartfelt laughter also diminished our remaining tension, while John helpfully dived into the trunk and reappeared with Nicky's packet of tissues. Quickly, John opened the package, got a couple of tissues, and dried his teary eyes and blew his nose. With a naughty smile, he offered his used tissues to Nicky, who indignantly refused to accept them. Seeing no other way, John left our car and deposited the crumpled tissues into a nearby trashcan.

After John returned, we started to talk about what had happened; and we promised each other to stay close friends for all eternity, even if we didn't like something or became angry at each other for some reason. As we were human beings, becoming a little bit angry would be allowed, but staying angry would NOT be accepted from now on!

I drove our car out of its parking spot, and we went home. This time, Davy sat shotgun, while John was sandwiched between Nicky and little Harry. Surprisingly, John didn't seem to mind at all!

Davy switched our car stereo on and searched for nice background music, but our own funny song didn't show up. Soon, we were humming along with some happy sounding song, feeling quite a lot better and certainly much closer to each other...

15. We are buying a beautiful Golden Van.

Half an hour later, I drove our car into our own driveway, and we were home. As usual, little Harry snatched the keys out of my hands and raced to our front door to open it. Of course, his inseparable friend, Nicky, immediately followed him inside; while John and Davy lifted one of our cardboard boxes out of the trunk and dragged it into our kitchen. I followed them at a slower pace, carrying the second box that fortunately was less heavy.

In our kitchen, little Harry and Nicky helped me restock our refrigerator, while John and Davy put the remaining purchases into the appropriate cupboards. I brewed a cup of coffee, while John helpfully poured four glasses of cola. After filling our cookie jar with Nicky's cookies, we sat down at our kitchen table and sipped our drinks. Now and then, we looked at each other, feeling happy with our mutual love and close togetherness. No more words needed to be spoken...

After some time, John looked at me and wheedled:

"Dad? Today's weather forecast has predicted that the forthcoming couple of days will be extremely hot. Could you please buy us such a small inflatable swimming pool, to put it in our backyard, so that we can cool off in the water when the weather gets really hot?"

At that same moment, four puppy-dog-eyed boys surrounded me, pushing each other towards me while trying to look extremely hot! Chuckling at their funny antics, I first folded my arms around my exaggerating herd and pulled them into a group-cuddle. Then, to tease my boys a little bit, I told them with my best convincing face:

"Unfortunately, our old car is too small to transport all of us plus an inflatable swimming pool..."

As I already expected, all four boys started to look disappointed, and their shoulders slumped down considerably. That is, until one little devil stealthily invaded my thoughts and quickly read my real intentions! Before I could send my little Shaman a misleading picture, he already saw through my joke.

Smiling from ear to ear, my little soul mate lectured me:

"Dad, you are only teasing us! Of course, we can deflate our swimming pool and tie it onto the roof of your car as a package, as we did before with our computer desks... John, do you happen to know a nearby store where they sell inflatable swimming pools?"

Chuckling at my little Shaman's cunning antics, I first tried to tease him some more, by admonishing him:

"You little devil, did you read my thoughts again? Only, this time, I am a little bit disappointed in your Shaman abilities, because you didn't find out my other decision..."

For a split second, my little Shaman looked surprised, as if he hadn't expected me to detect his stealthy mind reading. Then, he again probed my mind, this time openly entering my brain and quickly paging through my thoughts. Although I tried to hide them behind a brick wall; he only chuckled, dived under my wall, and found out what I had planned to do! Wow, what a powerful Shaman was he, at such a young age. I would have to train myself quite a lot more, to be able to stop this sneaky devil from reading my thoughts at all...

Immediately, my sneaky little devil started to jump up and down with sheer enthusiasm, while he shouted:

"You really want to buy a BIGGER CAR too? Yippeeeee... Come on, Nick; let's find a bigger car on the Internet!"

Enthusiastically, my boy already stormed towards our living room, followed by his inseparable friend; while John and Davy first looked at me for clarification. Then, they too followed our over-enthusiastic 'toddlers', to see what they were up to.

When I entered our living room, all four boys already crowded around our computer, impatiently waiting for a well-known search engine to show up. Then, my little soul mate typed in: 'big car'... Would he really be able to find a decent car on the Internet? I decided to let him have his innocent fun, turned around, and returned to our kitchen to brew another cup of coffee.

Three minutes later, Nicky shouted from our living room:

"Pop, we've found a beautiful car that is big enough for all of us!"

Feeling curious, I took my coffee to our living room; where, much to my surprise, my boys turned out to be clever merchants! They really found a nice site on the Internet that advertised used cars.

Chapter 15. Looking for a toyshop and Peter's studio.

Enthusiastically, Nicky pointed to an enormous yellow van that sparkled in the bright sunlight with a golden glow. This huge vehicle would absolutely be big enough to transport all of us, plus lots of extra gear! Smiling broadly, my boy clicked on its picture, and an extensive list of details showed up. This golden van appeared to have two turnable seats in its front, next to five removable sleeping seats in its interior. If necessary, four removable seats could be placed into a square, while the fifth one could be folded down, to use it as a small conference table in the middle...

Feeling very impressed by my boys' clever choice, I told them:

"Wow, this looks like a nice vehicle! How much does it cost?"

Looking a bit surprised, my little soul mate responded:

"Aw Dad, that is no big deal to you, because you can always buy everything with your credit card!"

Chuckling at my little soul mate's youthful naivety, I decided not to disappoint his trust in me. Afterwards, I would explain to him how a credit card works. Besides, I really did have some extra money to spend, even after paying for my son's expensive skin transplant.

While ruffling my boy's unruly blond hair, I told everybody:

"Okay, let's take a look at this van. Do you know the address?"

Immediately, all four boys started to cheer loudly, while dancing around me from enthusiasm. Then, all of them wanted to hug me at the same time, which effectively floored me. I tumbled backwards onto the carpeted floor, while four over-enthusiastic boys piled up on my stomach. Their combined weight nearly suffocated me, but what a lovely way of passing away...

After some more happy cuddling and basking in each other's close togetherness, John finally fought himself free from their pile, on his way cleverly pick-pocketing my keys out of my pocket. While he raced to our front door, he shouted over his shoulder:

"Come on, lazy slackers, let's GO. What are you waiting for?"

Quickly, everybody left me and followed John outside, leaving poor old me lying on our floor. Slowly, I stood up, stretched my groaning back, and rearranged my crumpled clothes. Now, I only had to get my wallet with my 'credit card that can buy everything' and follow my boys outside, to take a look at our new conveyance!

To read all our famous 'Gypsy Series' books, please visit www.gypsyseries.com

Only, where was my wallet? Normally, I always put it on my desk or on our table, next to my keys. However, this time, I just couldn't find it. Could John have pick-pocketed my wallet again?

Just in time, I remembered the supermarket, where John slyly put my credit card into my wallet and put my wallet into his own pocket. That is why my young friend already raced towards our car without teasing his 'forgetful old man'. Again, John had me, this time without doing anything! Chuckling, but also feeling rich with my teasing young friend, I left our house and ambled towards our old car.

Inside our over-crowded car, four impatiently fidgeting boys had already neatly buckled up, while waiting for their lazy 'old grandpa' to show up. They started to cheer loudly when I finally opened the door and entered our car. This time, John sat shotgun, while my other boys again sat propped up in the way too small rear seat, with our already huffing and panting Davy in their middle.

Trying to tease John, I asked him:

"John? Do you know where my wallet and my credit card are?"

While trying to look as innocent as possible, John responded:

"Ah, forgetful ancient grandpa, couldn't you find it again?"

"Don't try to fool me, mate, or we are not going anywhere!"

Immediately, three upset looking boys in the rear started to protest fiercely. They dived forward, threw their arms around John's neck, and forced him to give me my wallet back, or else... Groaning and coughing, John quickly took my wallet out of his back pocket and ceremoniously handed it to me. Case dismissed!

While my three boys retreated into their crowded rear, I started the engine and drove off, to have a look at our new 'golden' conveyance. John thought he knew where the car company was, and started to direct me towards it with a still hoarse voice. However, after twenty minutes of driving around and searching in vain, John sighed:

"Sorry, Dad, but I think the car company has moved away..."

At exactly that moment, Nicky dived forward and shouted:

"HERE IT IS! Pop, you have to turn into the next side street!"

Enthusiastically, Nicky pointed to a small signboard with 'Used Cars' on it that was attached to a lamppost.

Chapter 15. Looking for a toyshop and Peter's studio.

Feeling happy again, I turned into the side street, where we saw an enormous sales yard that was filled to the brim with all types of used cars! With a strange feeling of anticipation, I parked our old car into one of the empty spaces and switched its engine off. Four impatient boys quickly unbuckled and jumped outside in a hurry, where they immediately started to look around at all the used cars.

Soon, John pointed to an enormous van with a beautiful metallic golden color that sparkled in the bright sunlight. As if already feeling totally in awe, he sighed:

"There she is! Wow, what a beauty..."

"WOW!" Davy reiterated his friend, with beaming eyes.

Both my little soul mate and his inseparable friend were unusually quiet, as if they felt truly impressed. With their arms around each other's shoulders, as usual, they only stared at our brightly sparkling golden van, this time silently and open-mouthed.

A smiling sales vendor approached us and politely asked:

"Good day, sirs! How may I help you?"

"Could we please take a closer look at that gold-colored van over there, and perhaps also have a test drive?"

"Of course, sir, but I have to open it first. Just a moment, please."

Quickly, the man disappeared into his office. Within a minute, he returned with a small black box in his hand. He showed the small box to my curious looking boys, and told them with a mysterious voice:

"Now, I'm going to perform some magic! Just look at this..."

The man pushed a white knob on his black box; and, at that same moment, all the van's lights flashed two times.

"Now, all five doors are unlocked, and the van's alarm is switched off! Isn't that real magic?"

Politely, my boys tried to look a bit impressed. Then, they raced towards the unlocked golden van and dived inside. Immediately, they started to try out its turnable chairs, by arranging six seats around a folding table in the middle so that they had a small conference room. Little Harry accidentally pressed its horn, making the van respond with a nice and civilized hooting sound. Smilingly, he did it again.

Nicky thought we would be able to camp out in our golden van, making John and Davy put four chairs into sleeping positions. All the boys seemed to be truly impressed and over-enthusiastic, while acting as if this beautiful golden conveyance were already ours...

At first, I let them do as they liked; feeling truly impressed myself, but trying to behave as if I were not too interested. I thought that, if I were too enthusiastic, my behavior could inflate the price of this splendid vehicle. Therefore, when all four boys finally started to calm down, I told them to turn the seats into their starting positions, leave the van, and wait outside until we had decided.

A few seconds later, four fidgeting boys surrounded the broadly smiling car vendor and me. They still looked at 'our' golden van with yearning eyes, as if silently begging me to buy this beautiful vehicle... Only, I first wanted to know how much money I would get back for my old car, before making any too hasty decisions. Therefore, I asked the vendor about its price minus the value of my old car.

My question tempered the excitement of my boys considerably; while the vendor looked thoughtful, walked around my old car, opened its doors, and finally shook his head... Suddenly, I heard Jack's voice in my inside, mentioning an unbelievable low price! Nah, my too enthusiastic brain clearly fantasized Jack's voice in my inside, because I was sure this splendid van would cost quite a lot more...

Much to my surprise, the vendor told me exactly the price that Jack had mentioned! Although I felt truly surprised, I still tried to keep a straight face, while I politely asked to be allowed to test-drive the van first. Supposed its behavior on the road was not to my liking, or this beautiful vehicle turned out to be moody or unreliable...

Without any objections, our still broadly smiling sales vendor just took the ignition key out of his pocket and handed it to me. Again, my boys entered 'our' golden van and quickly rearranged four seats next to each other. They sat down, fastened their seatbelts, and looked around with expectant faces, while the vendor sat shotgun and showed me how to operate its many knobs and handles. Then, I started our golden van, and drove off for a short test drive.

Immediately, I felt like a King in my golden conveyance, and my boys reacted ecstatic! Jumping up and down in their seats, they craned their necks to look everywhere at the same time. Soon, they started to discover even more nice and useful facilities:

Chapter 15. Looking for a toyshop and Peter's studio.

"Pop, we can talk to each other without raising our voices!"

"Dad, this van has little cabinets in the backs of all its seats!"

"We can switch our ceiling lights independent from each other."

"Dad, I think that, if we shift our movable seats together, we can easily create one big bed to sleep on during a camp-out."

While driving my new van, I suddenly realized that this beautiful golden vehicle was exactly the car I had always dreamt of but never bought! Driving my new conveyance felt as if I already owned it, because I immediately felt totally at home in it, while driving around and listening to the friendly sound of its softly humming engine.

Then, my too analytical mind took over and started to doubt again. Why was this beautiful van for sale for such an extremely low price? Could it have any hidden defects that would show up only after I bought it and owned it? Again, I heard Jack's happy sounding voice in my inside, this time assuring me:

"Please, accept this conveyance as a small present from us. She is reliable, and you will soon need her more than you think."

At that same moment, my little soul mate leaned against my back and whispered into my ear:

"Dad? Jack is here, and he asks me to assure you that this cum... err... this 'cumveians' is a small present from our Spirit Friends, she is reliable, and you will soon need her more than you think."

This time, I felt totally dumbstruck! Was this for real? Had really Jack asked my little soul mate to give me exactly the same message, except for my Gypsy boy's linguistic mistake because he didn't know our unusual word 'conveyance'? Had Jack also put the idea into my little soul mate's mind to look for a bigger car on the Internet?

Whatever it had been, I now felt totally content with our golden van! Silently, I thanked Jack and our other Spirit Friends in my mind, for giving my boys and me such a splendid present. Almost humming from sheer happiness, I drove our golden van back to the sales yard.

First, I followed the broadly smiling vendor into his office, where I paid him with my 'inexhaustible' credit card. In exchange, he handed me the papers, the spare keys, and the small remote transmitter. Next, I went to my old car, and entered it for the very last time.

While my boys swiftly moved our possessions from our old car to our new golden van, I handed the vendor my old keys and papers. For the last time, I looked around in my old car that had offered me its means of transportation for many years. Then, I just turned around and went to my new golden van, without any feelings of regret.

Again, my boys and I entered what was now OUR beautiful golden van. I used my new ignition key to start her engine, and we drove off without looking back. John climbed onto its front seat and started to try out its built-in modern digital stereo. Immediately, our own cheerful fun song reverberated through its surround speakers, sounding much warmer and with a nice booming bass:

"You are soooo beauuuutifuuuullll..."

Feeling elated and very happy, we started to sing along with our warm sounding fun song, already feeling at home in our golden van.

Trying to act as a good parent, I told my enthusiastic boys to sit down, put their seat belts on, and postpone their playing for as long as we were on the road. However, they didn't really listen to me, because they were way too busy trying out all its interesting new possibilities; and who cares? They were just too excited! Therefore, I let them do as they liked, and only drove a bit slower and more careful.

16. Buying a big inflatable swimming pool.

While my four enthusiastic boys happily hummed along with our warmly booming golden car stereo song, I asked John:

"John? Do you happen to know where we can find a shop that sells inflatable swimming pools?"

Immediately, three enthusiastic boys in their backseats started to cheer loudly, while John answered:

"Of course, Dad, and I will show you the way to where it is. At the second crossing, turn right..."

Within a few minutes, John had guided me towards a parking lot. With some difficulty, I managed to park our enormous van into one of its spaces, as she was much bigger than our old car. Fortunately, or was it luckily, I managed not to hit one of the other parked cars.

We left our golden van, and I used her magical remote transmitter to lock her doors and put her alarm on. Obediently, she winked at us with her lights, twice, and Nicky loved it and asked me to do it again. Then, all the boys wanted to try out our magic transmitter a few times, until they got bored and wanted to go on. Together, we crossed the small parking lot, and entered a huge building.

Inside the building, we looked around in awe, because this huge shop seemed to sell absolutely everything that you ever needed for camping outdoors! Only, did they also have a pool department?

After some searching, I asked an approaching vendor if they sold inflatable swimming pools. The smiling vendor politely asked us to follow him, and guided us to an enormous side wing of the shop. Suddenly, we entered a semi-tropical surrounding, where they had set up several nice looking indoor and outdoor pools.

Of course, my boys immediately went to the largest outdoor pool there was, enthusiastically jostling each other to be there first. In awe, they looked at a dark blue inflatable swimming pool of around nine by eighteen feet (3x6 meters) with a huge electric air pump and an enormous water filter. Almost trembling from enthusiasm, John told me, with sparkling brown eyes and a broadly smiling face:

"This inflatable pool will be big enough for all of us, even after Thomas and Chrissie return from their vacation and want to join us."

Looking at four pairs of yearning and openly begging puppy-dog eyes, I started to chuckle inwardly, because I thought I should have known this in advance. Boys will be boys; and, of course, they would immediately go for the biggest pool there was! Well, would it be a very bad thing to spoil my enthusiastic brats a little bit more, because it would be only a one-time occurrence? Still chuckling inwardly, I asked my four expectantly looking boys:

"Would you really want to swim in such an enormous bathtub?"

Immediately, four over-enthusiastic voices answered:

"YES, Dad! Please..."

"Okay, then let's buy it."

The shop's roof almost raised and its windows rumbled, when all four boys started to cheer at the tops of their lungs! Obviously, I was making them very happy. While they started to play and splash each other with the pool's chlorinated water, I followed the broadly smiling vendor into his office, where I used my 'inexhaustible' credit card to pay for our newest purchase. Clearly, I had made the man's day, by buying the biggest inflatable swimming pool there was!

After I left the office and returned to the pool, the vendor asked my happily playing and water-throwing boys to help him fetch three packages from their stock room that was around the corner. Together, we followed our vendor outside, where my boys left me and followed the still broadly smiling man into a separate building.

Soon, they returned, driving a cart that carried one huge package, two smaller ones, and some ropes. My little soul mate pick-pocketed the remote transmitter out of my pocket and proudly unlocked our van. With sparkling bright blue eyes, he stared at how she winked back at him with all her lights, twice, while unlocking all her doors.

Working together, we first lifted the huge package onto the roof of our golden van and carefully tied it with the ropes. Then, both smaller packages disappeared into her trunk, safely tucked away behind two removable backseats. Everybody shook hands with the still broadly smiling vendor, and we waved him out until we disappeared around a corner and he had disappeared from our vision.

Chapter 16. Harry gets a mask to hide his burnt face.

Twenty minutes later, we were home. Very carefully, I backed our golden van into our driveway, and first listened to her melodiously purring sound before I stopped her engine. For another few seconds, I remained silent, still marveling in the happy feeling of being the proud owner of such a nice vehicle. Then, I left my driver's seat and joined my four boys who proudly walked around our new conveyance and again admired her sparkling golden countenance. Davy even used a sleeve of his shirt to wipe away some almost invisible stain.

John stared at her with pure adoration in his eyes, while he softly caressed her golden sides and thought aloud:

"Yes, I absolutely like her very much, because she is the most beautiful van I have ever seen!"

Nicky nodded approvingly, while also tenderly caressing her side, but then he asked us:

"Why are we calling our new van a 'she', and not a 'he' or an 'it'?"

Immediately, we were in a heated discussion about our golden van being male or female. John was sure she had to be a 'she', because she clearly looked female! Davy argued that John's explanation wasn't a valid criterion, because it was a personal taste and not a proven fact. My little soul mate smugly declared he couldn't care less, as long as our new 'comeveiance' was functional and reliable. Nicky mused that our van didn't have any visible male organs, therefore, she had to be female. I added that calling our golden van a 'she' would pay even more homage to her already beautiful aura.

At long last, we decided to vote about which word we were going to use to indicate our beautiful golden van, from now on. Of course, without any doubt, the word 'she' won with five to zero!

Feeling very happy with our decision, we first went inside, to drink coffee and colas. Then, John and Davy started to untie our huge package, while Nicky and little Harry helped them by collecting the pieces of rope and putting them into our trashcan.

Working together, we lifted the huge package off the roof of our van and put it down into our driveway. While little Harry and Nicky helped me lift the air pump and the huge water filter out of the trunk, John and Davy unpacked our enormous deflated pool and laid it out on our driveway, so that it was ready to be turned into an enormous dark blue inflatable swimming pool.

Now, we only had to find out where we could set it up in our backyard. Together, we went to the backside of our house, to decide where we would set up our pool. It had to be in some shadow, easy to reach from our house, and difficult to see from the street...

John and Davy thought they had found the ideal spot, in the shadow of a couple of big trees, next to little Harry's herbs garden; and Nicky agreed. Only my little soul mate protested fiercely, because he was afraid we would trample his precious herbs or drown them in too much chlorinated water! After some more deliberation and argumentation, my boy agreed, on the condition that we would keep our swimming pool at least six feet away from his herbs garden.

I went to our garage to get my old tape measure, while John and Davy started to outline where we could put our new swimming pool, using four wooden stakes. After measuring the distance between John's wooden stakes and his white cobblestones, even our little cookie was satisfied. Working together, we first dragged the huge blue canvas object to its place, where we unfolded it. Sweating and panting, we pushed and pulled its crumpled canvas bottom between the wooden stakes, until it was exactly where we wanted it to be.

Now, I went to our driveway, to get the air pump and the water filter, while little Harry and Nicky reentered our house to look for a long electric cord, and John and Davy went to our garage to put two water hoses together into one long one. In the meantime, I attached the air pump to its canvas inlet and connected the electricity.

Finally, all four boys gathered around me, while I switched the air pump on. Teasingly slowly, the crumpled canvas lump started to take shape and turn into an enormous dark blue swimming pool! In the meantime, John and Davy had attached the extended water hose to our outdoor water tap. Now, we only had to wait until our swimming pool was sufficiently inflated and could be filled with water.

Teasingly slowly, our crumpled canvas object started to look like an enormous dark blue swimming pool. Finally, John went to our outdoor water tap and turned it on, while Davy took the other end of their extended water hose and put it into our dry pool. Only, much to our surprise, nothing happened! Had our old and wrinkled plastic water hose a kink in it, or could it be clogged? Impatiently, Davy took the end of the hose out of the pool, stared into its opening, and shook it forcefully... Suddenly, a forceful water stream spouted out of the crumpled water hose and splashed straight into Davy's face!

Looking shocked, Davy yelped from sudden surprise, and angrily threw the now spouting hose back into the pool. Of course, everybody started to roar with laughter, while Davy coughed and spluttered... His revenge was sweet. Before we knew what happened, Davy took the spouting hose out of the pool and pointed it at us. Now, it was our time to yelp and jump out of the way, but to no avail. The spouting water stream just followed us wherever we went. This time, it was Davy's turn to roar with laughter!

After Davy had his revenge and we stopped laughing, he put the spouting water hose back into our swimming pool and followed us upstairs, where we quickly changed out of our soaking wet clothes. Then, my clever boys decided to put on their own or their quickly borrowed swimming trunks. Immediately when they were ready, they raced back to our backyard, where they plunged into our slowly filling pool and started to splash, laugh, and have lots of fun.

While chuckling at hearing my happily playing boys in our new inflatable swimming pool, I first put on some dry clothes. Then, as a good parent, I gathered my boys' wet garments and put them into my electric dryer. Now, I went to our kitchen, to prepare enough food and drinks for four hungry growing boys plus myself. Helpfully, I boiled a couple of eggs, sliced a few tomatoes, and even gathered some of my little cookie's tasteful herbs to spice our sandwiches.

Suddenly, our backdoor opened, and my dripping wet little soul mate entered our kitchen and asked me:

"Dad? Could you please keep my rubber mask for me? Its glue doesn't want to stick any more in all the water..."

"Of course, and I will also clean it for you and put it onto its green model. Do you have any fun with our pool and the water hose?"

"LOTS of fun! Thank you very, very much, for buying us such a marvelous swimming pool! We only are still waiting until it contains enough water to swim properly. When are you going to join us?"

"Well, I will think about it... For now, just go back to your pool and have fun, while I take care of your mask."

My little soul mate offered me a quick cuddle and a big kiss, but he unintentionally pressed his wet body against my stomach. Then, he turned around and disappeared into our backyard, from where I heard him plunge into our new pool with a loud Indian shout.

Chuckling about being soaking wet again, I cleaned my boy's mask with some liquid soap, dried it, and put it onto its green model. Then, I peeled the boiled eggs, took the sliced tomatoes, some lettuce, and my boy's tasty herbs, and created a huge pile of sandwiches. From my kitchen, I heard my four boys yelling and having lots of fun with the spouting water hose in our still slowly filling pool.

Chuckling, I took a tray, and filled it with my pile of sandwiches and four colas, to feed my four happily playing boys. Feeling rich and full of love, I stepped outside; and looked at my six children who seemed to have the time of their lives in our new swimming pool...

Involuntarily, my mouth fell open from the unexpected surprise. Did I really count SIX happily playing children? Quickly, I recounted their heads, while trying to recognize them in spite of their soaking wet hair. Again, I counted John, a young girl, Davy, little Harry, a somewhat older girl, and Nicky. What the heck... Today, my small household was growing extremely fast!

John was the first one who saw me and enthusiastically waved at me. A split second later, he noticed that I carried a tray full of food. Immediately starting to look famished, my young friend shouted:

"Look, Dad is bringing us something to EAT."

At hearing the 'Magic Word for Growing Kids', all six children turned their heads towards me. At lightning speed, they tumbled out of our swimming pool and raced towards my filled tray, on their way nearly slipping on the wet grass. Within a split second, six dripping wet children surrounded my food tray and me, looking at me with yearning eyes as if they really were famished.

The around twelve-year-old oldest girl politely asked me:

"Hello sir, are we allowed to play in your swimming pool? Your boys said it was no problem..."

Trying to tease my guilty looking boys, I asked the girl:

"Well, I suppose you've already paid my boys at the entrance, to enhance their scanty allowances?"

Involuntarily, the oldest girl started to blush, while she looked a bit timid and stared at her wriggling feet. However, the youngest girl, who resembled her and seemed to be her around two years younger sister, already saw right through my little joke. Conspiringly, she winked at me, while she smugly declared:

"Of course, your boys have to pay everything for us, because they invited us into their swimming pool!"

"In your dreams!" my little soul mate chuckled...

Quickly, he dived towards the filled food tray and tried to thieve one of my sandwiches. Trying to act as a good parent, I stopped him just in time and told all six children to sit down, so that I could distribute my sandwiches amongst them. While they wolfed them down, I returned to our kitchen to fetch two more colas. Fortunately, I had made enough sandwiches to at least still some hunger...

After I returned, the youngest girl leaned into me and whispered:

"At first, I didn't recognize Harry, until his mask unglued and he took it inside. Without his mask, he already looks nice and friendly, but he looks really handsome when he wears it!"

Obviously, my little soul mate had heard the girl's whispering, or he had picked up her thoughts, because he started to blush fiercely and hastily took another bite of his sandwich. Nearly choking on his too big mouthful, he started to cough and almost spit it out.

Immediately, the girl doted all over him and helpfully patted his back, while telling him to relax. Her help only made my suddenly shy boy blush even more, while he jumped up in a tremendous hurry and quickly raced towards our kitchen to drink some water...

Chuckling at seeing my boy's sudden shyness, I followed him into our kitchen with my now empty tray. I was still hungry, because my boys' girlfriends hadn't left anything edible for me. Therefore, I made myself an extra large sandwich, and filled it with double helpings of everything that I could! It felt really good, to take good care of myself like this, and to act a little bit naughty.

In the meantime, my shy little soul mate had returned to his new 'girlfriend', in his obvious hurry even forgetting to say goodbye! From our backyard, I heard everybody's happy laughter, splashing, and joyful yelling. All six children in our now filled to the brim new swimming pool seemed to have the times of their lives!

After finishing my super sandwich and drinking another cup of coffee, I ambled to my living room. After switching my computer on, I first sorted the few real e-mails from all the unsolicited spam that had started to streamed in. When would a clever computer technician finally invent a good working spam filter, sigh...

Now that I finally was alone, I went on writing my 'Gypsy Series' of several books about meeting my badly burnt little Gypsy Crown Prince and taking him into my house. Soon, the words started to flow straight from my brain into my typing fingers, while I vividly remembered how I met John and his badly burnt little Gypsy brother.

Although we had been together for only a few weeks, we had already lived through an enormous amount of quality time! I only hoped that my readers would appreciate reading my 'Gypsy Series' books at least as much as I liked writing them...

17. Dinner with Mary; my boys' sleepover.

Time flew by, until the afternoon sun started to descend the sky and my living room became too dark. After finishing the paragraph I had been working on, I saved this part of my manuscript and switched my computer off. Then, I sauntered to my backyard, to have another look at my six happily playing children, and to tell my boys' two girlfriends to leave our swimming pool and go home. This evening, we had to dress up for dinner, because Davy's mother, Mary, had cooked dinner for us and expected us around six o'clock!

While I entered our backyard, a loud cacophony of sounds from all the happily laughing and yelling young friends enveloped and greeted me. Chuckling, I went towards our new swimming pool and enjoyed the funny sight of all these frolicking kids. They were still jumping up and down in the water, spouting at each other with the water hose, or playfully dunking each other, chasing after each other, or trying to catch each other. My nine still enthusiastically playing children seemed to have the time of their lives!

Then, my mouth fell open from sudden surprise. Did I really count NINE playing kids in our new swimming pool? Trying to recognize them, I looked at them one by one. Indeed, one new girl and two small boys had joined my steadily growing family in my absence. They were frolicking and splashing water at each other just like the others, as if they already felt totally at ease in our backyard...

Finally, it started to dawn on me that having a swimming pool in my backyard was an enormous attraction to ALL the neighborhood children! At the same time, I also realized that this was a valuable experience for my little soul mate with his so terribly burnt face and body. Having so many new friends around, who could see his burns but nevertheless accepted him for what he was, would certainly boost my boy's already growing self-esteem to an even higher degree!

Feeling full of love and all mushy at seeing so much happiness, I told my five happily playing little neighbors:

"Sorry, my friends, but you have to leave our swimming pool and go home now, because my boys and I are eating out."

Reluctantly, all five new kids clambered out of our pool, looking a bit disappointed. Three young girls who were clad in only wet panties, and two naked small boys started to gather their clothes; while my 'own' boys trotted inside to dress up for Mary's upcoming dinner.

Again, little Harry's girlfriend leaned into me, while she pleaded:

"Please, sir, can we... oops, sorry, sir, MAY we come back tomorrow? This is much more fun than playing around the block!"

"Yes, you may come back tomorrow, but only when a responsible grownup or one of the older boys is around to keep a close eye on you. Please, never enter our swimming pool without supervision."

"I promise, sir, and thank you very much! Could you please tell Harry that I will be back and see him tomorrow?"

Before my little neighbors went home, all three girls politely thanked me, clad in only wet panties and carrying their clothes in their hands. Two small boys just took their tiny clothes in their hands and followed the three girls across the street, although they were still completely naked! For a second, I started to doubt, while staring at their unclad little bottoms. What would my nosy neighbors think of me now? Would they again feel suspicious and send their 'reports' to the police about my questionable conduct? Or, would they now complain about me 'collecting neighborhood children' by luring them into such an enormous swimming pool...

Just in time, I remembered my new 'friend', BJ, and the healthy influence this enormous giant seemed to have in and around our meddlesome neighborhood. Therefore, I decided not to worry any more. Feeling reassured, I waved my five little friends out, turned around, and ambled inside to dress up for dinner.

In my hallway, Nicky happily jumped up at me and offered me a wet kiss on my bearded cheek, while he told me:

"Sorry, Pop, I have to go home now, but thank you very much for this marvelous day! Can I come back tomorrow, please?"

"Nicky, you MAY come back any time you wish, because you are one of my boys now. Please, greet your father and Jason from me, and I am sure we will see you back tomorrow, probably early in the morning. What about eating breakfast with us?"

At hearing my invitation, Nicky started to beam all over and quickly offered me another wet kiss. Smiling from ear to ear, he left me and trotted home, skipping all the way, now and then turning around and waving at me until he disappeared around a corner.

In the meantime, my remaining threesome had reappeared from upstairs, with John and little Harry already clad in their neatest clothes. This time, my boy asked me to help him with his mask; because he felt a bit tired after swimming and playing outside all day long. Ultimately, he was only eight years old and still a bit small for his age... Trying to act as a caring parent, I sent both John and Davy back upstairs, to comb their still disheveled hair.

Chuckling at seeing my stern face, both young friends trotted upstairs and did as I told them. Now, we were ready to go to Mary and Davy's house, where Mary expected us around six o'clock for dinner. Just in time, I remembered to get my keys, my wallet, and a bottle of wine, without any help from an already chuckling John.

Outside, I stealthily looked around for any suspicious neighbors, but nobody stared at me with accusing eyes. Helpfully, I lifted my tired looking little soul mate onto my shoulders, where he clamped his small hands around my forehead with his little legs dangling free. Involuntarily, I smiled, when I remembered the first time I took my boy home on my shoulders, as a trophy snatched away from Eric...

In no time, we arrived at Davy's front door, where Davy fished his key out of his pocket and let us in. He brought us straight to their nicely furnished living room, where he told us to sit down and wait for his Mom to show up from her kitchen. Soon, Mary entered the room and came up to us, acting a little bit nervous. We shook hands, and Davy offered her a fierce hug and a big kiss.

While I handed Mary my bottle of wine as a present, I told her:

"Thank you very much for inviting us to have dinner here! Is there anything we can do to help you?"

"Well, you could help Davy set the table, but let's have a drink first. Would you care for coffee; or a glass of your own wine?"

I decided on a glass of wine, while my boys voted for colas. Davy followed his mother into their kitchen, from where they soon returned with our drinks and some cookies. Now, Davy started to tell his Mom about the events of our joyful day. He described our new golden van with seven movable chairs, and our inflatable swimming pool with a huge air pump and an enormous water filter.

Vividly, Davy told his Mom how he took revenge, by spraying us with the water hose until we were soaking wet. He joked about their 'girlfriends' who joined them in our swimming pool but refused to pay at the entrance. Then, another girl and two small boys showed up in our driveway, shucked their clothes, and just jumped into our pool as if they were at home! He also told her that Harry had played in the water without his mask because it didn't stick any more, and his girlfriend had thought that Harry was really handsome...

At that moment, Davy yelped: "OUCH", because my little soul mate forcefully kicked his leg from under the table! Sticking out his tongue towards his 'former brother from a past life', Davy went on:

"I've also missed you, Mom. I've had a lot of fun today, but I wish you could have joined us in our new swimming pool."

"Don't bother about it, son. I've enjoyed myself with cooking for my friends and for my son, and that was a lot of fun too!"

While Mary returned to her kitchen to look after her cooking, we helped Davy set the table and put five chairs around it. Davy took a couple of candles and a box of matches out of a drawer, and little Harry helped him light the candles. John and he selected some nice background music, and Davy put the first CD into their player.

Then, Mary returned from her kitchen, carrying a huge tureen of steaming soup. We sat down around the table, and each of us got a bowl full. My little soul mate tasted his soup, frowned, savored again, and nodded approvingly. After taking another spoonful of soup, my curious little cookie asked Mary:

"This soup tastes very good, but what did you put in it? I can taste all the usual ingredients like oregano, onions, celery and parsley, but I also taste something else I remember but just don't recognize..."

Mary started to laugh, ruffled my boy's blond hair, and told him:

"Sorry Harry, but this is just a can of soup from a supermarket."

We all started to laugh, while my little cookie tried to disappear under the table. Soon, he showed up again and just continued to savor his 'soup from a supermarket' as if nothing special had happened.

Mary served us an excellent dinner! First, we had grilled steak, baked potatoes, healthy vegetables, and a delicious sauce. After filling our hungry stomachs to the brim, we also got a big ice sorbet that was topped with a mixture of fruits, to 'fill our empty holes'.

Chapter 17. The supermarket and a psychic medium.

After enjoying our delicious meal, Mary and I took a cup of coffee, while our three boys got freshly squeezed orange juice. Of course, all three boys had to burp loudly, to 'thank our food spirits' as my little Gypsy imp had taught them to do. Mary looked a bit distracted, but soon started to laugh at seeing their naughty faces. Then, Davy threw his arms around his Mom's neck and complimented her:

"Mom, I never knew you could cook so well for so many people."

"Son, this is the first time in all those years that I really enjoyed cooking. And thank you very much for your nice compliment!"

Helpfully, our three musketeers took everything to Mary's kitchen, where they washed the dishes and cleared everything away. After they returned, they settled down in front of the television and started to watch some funny cartoons, while Mary admonished them to calm down and muffle their voices. Stealthily wiping her teary eyes with a handkerchief, Mary turned towards me and whispered:

"I still don't know how I can thank you for letting Davy join your boys and you. I can see in his eyes how happy he feels with his new Dad, and how much he enjoys the company of John and Harry!"

Involuntarily talking a bit too loud, I answered:

"Well, Davy is a really nice kid with a heart of gold, and my boys and I absolutely love to have him around!"

Clearly, Davy had heard my well-meant compliment, because he looked at me with sudden tears in his eyes and responded:

"Dad, I really love to have you as my new Dad, with your own enormous heart of gold, and I hope I will never lose you."

Quickly, he left his friends, crawled on my lap, and told me with even more tears in his eyes:

"Finally, I'm having a real Dad who really loves me; and, for the first time, I am NOT afraid to feel a man's arms around me!"

YES! Finally, there was Davy's positive response that I had hoped and prayed for. Now, I had definitively reached my goal of helping my abused young friend get rid of his remaining fears! From now on, Davy would always be my 'special son', as Mary had foretold. I kissed the top of Davy's head, and he squeezed my arms to let me know he loved me back. Finally, my 'third son' had definitively found his own place in my steadily growing family!

To read all our famous 'Gypsy Series' books, please visit www.gypsyseries.com

Still sitting on my lap, Davy suddenly asked his mother:

"Mom? Until now, I never had a sleepover, and I think it will be a lot of fun. Please, could John and Harry sleep here tonight?"

"Yes, why not, but only if they want to and your new Dad agrees. Where did you think John and Harry could sleep?"

"In my bedroom; on that inflatable air mattress that we rescued from my summer camp..."

"Oh yeah, that is a double one. Okay, but I am sure you have to ask your new Dad's permission first!"

Of course, Davy's 'new Dad' immediately agreed. Especially when I remembered my own sleepovers, and how much fun my friends and I always had. That is, until my little brother tried to light an unwilling candle and burnt himself to death... While immediately suppressing my still too painful memories, I told my boys:

"Of course, I agree! Have fun, be good boys, don't be a nuisance, and always listen to Davy's mother."

My little lecture earned me an approving smile from Mary; while my three musketeers started to tease me, by telling ME to be a good Dad and not demolish our house in their absence! Chuckling at seeing my mock-angry face, they raced upstairs, to arrange Davy's room and inflate his double air mattress in advance.

I thanked Mary again, for letting my boys spend the night here and for her tasty dinner. Then, I went home, after yelling: "Sleep well and have fun!" towards the loudly cheering second floor.

Outside, the warm and humid summer night was pitch dark. This night, I didn't see a moon, but thousands of little stars were twinkling in the black sky. For quite some time, I stared at the Milky Way, tried to recognize the Polestar, and wondered about some reddish planet I thought could be Mars. Now and then, a bright star blinked; and I even saw a few falling stars shooting along the horizon.

Suddenly, I felt small and vulnerable, and shivered involuntarily. Who was I, and what was I doing here, on this strange planet called 'Earth'? Would there be any other planets in our universe with residents on them, wondering what they were doing on their strange planet? What was the real meaning of our lives? Was there really a 'God', who had created this universe in only seven days? Feeling a little bit melancholic, I slowly sauntered home.

Five minutes later, I entered my empty house, and decided to go to bed immediately. After taking a quick shower, I dived into my huge double waterbed, hugged my pillow, and tried to get some beauty sleep. Not surprisingly, I already missed my boys; especially my heat-radiating little sleeping buddy lying glued to my side or spread out all over my stomach as some affectionate little octopus. What was my boy feeling now, sleeping in a strange house on an old inflatable air mattress? Would he miss me too?

Then, I started to laugh at myself, for being such a nostalgic 'ancient grandpa'. Of course, my boy was having lots of fun with his friends, probably lying awake and joking with each other for hours! Until a perturbed Mary showed up and threatened to separate them if they wouldn't be silent and get some beauty sleep immediately...

At long last, I finally drifted off into a restless sleep, still hugging my pillow and feeling a little bit abandoned.

Halfway through the night, I suddenly woke up to the soft sounds of shuffling and whispering children. Feeling a bit surprised, I sat upright, switched my bed lights on, and squinted at three pairs of sleepily yawning faces. What the heck were my three boys doing here? Had Mary chased them out of her house? What horrible things could they have done, to be sent away like this?

Trying to look as stern as possible, I admonished them:

"What the heck are you doing here, in the middle of the night? I thought you would sleep over in Davy's room?"

Looking apologetically, John explained:

"Sorry, Dad, but Davy's air mattress has a leak! After inflating it, all three of us started to sleep on it with Harry in our middle, because we thought that would be more fun. An hour later, I turned around and suddenly bumped onto the rigid floor. Of course, we searched the mattress for a leak, but couldn't find any. Thus, we inflated it again and tried to sleep on. An hour later, the mattress went flat again, and Harry crawled onto my stomach. Only, I couldn't sleep on the rigid floor with him as a blanket, and Davy started to complain too. Then, we tried to sleep in Davy's bed, but Davy started to complain because he hit the wall every time he moved, and Harry felt too squeezed in between Davy and me. After I fell out of bed for the third time in five minutes, Davy woke his Mom, but she only laughed at us. Then, we decided to dress and go home. Harry took our hidden key from its nail and opened our backdoor, and here we are. Can we please continue our beauty sleep in your double bed tonight?"

Without waiting for my answer, all three boys quickly shucked their clothes, crawled into my bed, and closed their eyes... What should I do now, as a good parent? Should I tell my boys to go to their own rooms and sleep in their own beds?

Before I could decide, my little soul mate had already crawled onto my stomach, closed his eyes, and started to snore; while John and Davy quickly glued themselves against my sides. Obviously, I was way too late now to send my boys to their own rooms without feeling guilty for the remainder of the night.

No longer feeling abandoned, I switched my bed lights off, draped my arms around my yawning flock, and felt on cloud nine. From now on, our too meddlesome society could... well, I am sure you already know what I mean; yawnnn...

18. Birthday suit; tree house; meeting Jason.

The next morning, I woke up to a bright morning sunbeam shining through a crack in my curtains and tickling my still sleepy eyes. At that same moment, my little soul mate on my chest sat upright and looked around, as if he could have heard or felt something. His bright blue eyes started to sparkle with joy, while he clambered off my chest and nearly tripped over the legs of an angrily groaning John.

Before he left our bed and raced down the stairs, he apologized:

"Sorry Dad and John and Davy, but here comes Nicky!"

Ten seconds later, I heard my little Shaman open our front door and happily greet his inseparable friend. How does my clairvoyant boy always know it in advance when somebody plans to visit us, at least ten seconds before they actually reach our front door?

From downstairs, we heard the happily chuckling voice of Nicky who responded to his still naked friend:

"How come you're walking around in your house naked? Didn't Pop buy you enough clothes to dress properly?"

"You ever heard of wearing a 'birthday suit'? Every day I'm living here feels like it is another birthday!"

"Really? That yields you three-hundred-and-sixty-five birthday presents a year, plus one extra during a leap year..."

Both inseparable friends started to laugh, while they quickly shut the front door and stormed up the stairs. Happily, they bolted into my bedroom, of course again teasing each other and trying to bump into each other on purpose, as usual.

My little soul mate jumped into our bed and quickly disappeared under the blankets, while shouting at Nicky:

"Come on, Nick! Get rid of your clothes and join us."

For a second, Nicky hesitated and looked at me for approval... When I invitingly lifted our blankets, his emerald green eyes started to sparkle with even more joy, and his broadly smiling face started to beam from happiness. Quickly, he shucked his clothes and shouted:

"Here comes the Nickering Dragon!"

Happily, he jumped onto our waterbed and disappeared under our blankets, next to his inseparable friend. Then, two small heads popped up again, and two sparkling emerald green eyes plus two bright blue orbs full of love and happiness stared into mine. Showing me an even broader smile from ear to ear, my little sunshine told me:

"Pop, I am allowed to stay here all day, but only if you agree."

"Well, I've already explained that you are one of MY boys now, and therefore you will always be welcome here!"

"Yes, I know you've told me this before, but I wanted to hear it again. Since yesterday, I pretend you are my Grandpa for real..."

Suddenly, Nicky's stomach rumbled loudly, telling us it was time to leave our shared bed and eat breakfast! After offering me a few more cuddles, all four boys jumped out of bed and raced to our bathroom, to take a shower and begin the day. Being clever boys, they decided to put on their swimming gear immediately, because the day promised to be very hot again. Davy borrowed trunks from John, and thoughtful Nicky had already put on his own swim gear beneath his clothes. Together, they raced downstairs to prepare breakfast, while I took my own shower and dressed into something casual.

Still feeling full of love for my happy foursome, I descended the stairs and entered our kitchen, where my little cookie was already cleaning and slicing his tasty herbs. Davy had already set the table and was buttering a pile of toast, John had already poured four glasses of milk and was slicing a few tomatoes, and Nicky was boiling some eggs while happily chattering with everybody at the same time.

Soon, we sat down at our kitchen table and savored our tasty breakfast. Again, my little cookie had outdone himself! Especially Nicky nearly swallowed his own fingers, while he mumbled:

"This food tastes absolutely and totally delicious! Wow, Harry, I am sure you are the very bestest cook in the whole world!"

Our little cookie beamed proudly, while gleefully taking the next helping. Soon, all the food was gone, and all four boys offered me a quick cuddle and a kiss before they raced outside to have some more fun in our already waiting swimming pool. Chuckling at their sudden hurry, I cleared our table and did the dishes, before I went outside to take a look at what my boys were doing.

Chapter 18. Skateboarding outside, and a nasty fight.

Outside, the bright morning sun was already shining abundantly, promising to provide us with another very hot day. Feeling happy and totally content with my life as it was, I stepped out the backdoor... and nearly stumbled over two impatiently waiting little neighborhood boys who were this time clad in brightly colored tiny swimming trunks. Both little boys first embraced me enthusiastically. Then, the tallest boy, who I estimated to be around six years old, explained:

"Mom told us to put on some swim gear first, because she didn't want us to walk around naked again. She also told us to wait for you and ask for your permi... your permissing? first, before we can use your swimming pool again. Yes, can we?"

His smaller brother, who I estimated to be around five years old, forcefully punched his older brother's arm while he whispered:

"Say 'please may we', because saying 'yes can we' is impolite; and Mom told us to ask for 'permission' and not for 'permissing'."

Chuckling at their brotherly quarrel, I pulled both little boys even closer against my stomach while I told them:

"From now on, you MAY use our swimming pool whenever you want and your Mom agrees, but only when a grownup or one of the older boys is around as supervision. Okay?"

"Okay sir, and may I thank you politely."

Well, my youngest little friend certainly acted polite! With happy faces, both little boys ran to our swimming pool and immediately plunged into the inviting water. Panting from the sudden cold, they first jumped up and down to regain their stalled breaths. Then, they started to partake in my boys' games, almost outdoing them in their happy splashing and shouting. Twenty seconds later, two young girls showed up in our backyard, already clad in brightly colored bikinis.

Chuckling inwardly, I again thought about setting up a cash register at the entrance, to get some extra allowances for my supervising boys. How many more young neighborhood children would show up today, to play in our obviously very inviting swimming pool?

Still chuckling inwardly, I went inside, ambled to my living room, and switched my computer on. First, I glared at another pile of spam emails, and then just deleted them. When would finally somebody invent a reliable spam filter that really worked, sigh...

Now, I started my word processor, opened my manuscript, and again disappeared into my famous 'Gypsy Series' stories about meeting my burnt little soul mate and taking him into my house.

Some time later, four over-enthusiastic boys suddenly stormed into our living room and surrounded me, while John wheedled:

"Dad? Could you please help us, because Nicky has an excellent idea! He thinks we can build a tree house in those three birches in the corner of our backyard, and he already sketched a preliminary design. Do you have some used boards, a hammer, a saw, and nails?"

John and Davy looked at me with heated faces and expectant eyes, while Nicky smiled broadly and little Harry waved at me with a piece of paper and even tried to put it under my nose. Never before had I seen my foursome this enthusiastic!

Chuckling at seeing their expectantly pleading faces, I told them:

"Sorry boys, but I don't have any used boards; and I suppose you will also need quite a lot more equipment to build a real tree house. Perhaps, you could first look around in our neighborhood, or ask a few nice neighbors for some old wood or used lumber?"

At that moment, Nicky thought aloud, with a pensive face:

"We still have a lot of used lumber in our backyard, from Jason's old tree house. Only, can we ask Jason to give his stuff to us, because it was Carl's idea and I think he still doesn't want to talk about it?"

Responding to Nicky's hesitating question, I answered:

"Well, I think you could give it a try, but only ask for it and don't press Jason too much. Of course, it is and stays his and his friend's lumber, and it is totally okay for your brother to say no."

Immediately, my three other boys promoted Nicky to be our day's hero! They danced around him like crazy, patted his back, and ruffled his white hair. Then, they hurried upstairs, to chuck their swimming trunks and put on their normal clothes before going to Nicky's house and ask Jason to be generous. Soon, they raced outside, while my little soul mate again forgot to put on his rubber mask.

Around ten minutes later, four over-enthusiastic boys returned into our living room, and Nicky cheered:

"Pop, we can use all of Jason's wood and all of his equipment, but only if we let him help with our tree house."

Chapter 18. Skateboarding outside, and a nasty fight.

Behind my four over-enthusiastic boys, a taller carbon copy of Nicky hesitantly entered our living room, while timidly looking at his feet. This older boy looked exactly like his younger brother, except for being taller and having slightly darker hair.

Enthusiastically, Nicky took his big brother's hand and dragged him towards me, while explaining:

"Pop, this is Jason, and he already promised we can use all of his old lumber from our backyard!"

Smilingly, I extended my hand towards a still very timid looking Jason, and told him:

"Hello Jason! I am 'Big Harry', to distinguish me from my adopted son 'little Harry' over here. Do you care for a cold drink first, to fend off the excessive summer heat? Just follow us to our kitchen..."

Shyly, Jason took my outstretched hand and shook it, although he still stared at his feet. When I tried to hold his slightly trembling hand for a little longer, Jason suddenly looked up at me; and, at that same moment, I almost choked up from compassion. This was an extremely hurt and distressed boy! His emerald green eyes showed me an almost unbearable pain, while I sensed how he desperately tried to keep his suddenly welling sadness under control.

While secretly sending Jason as much Universal Love as I could muster, I slowly released his hand, rose from my chair, and went to our kitchen. Hesitantly, Jason followed my boys and me, and slumped down at our kitchen table. I started to brew fresh coffee for myself, while my little soul mate explained to his friends:

"Did you know that a hot drink fends off the summer heat even better than a cold drink can do? Therefore, do you still want a cold drink from our fridge, or shall I brew hot chocolate or perhaps ask Dad to brew some more hot coffee?"

Clearly trusting their little leader blindly, both Nicky and Davy changed their minds and voted for hot chocolate, while John voted for hot milk instead. Helpfully, John went to our refrigerator, from where he took a bottle of milk to our kitchen table; while Davy took five drinking cups from one of our cupboards and set them out in front of their folding chairs. Nicky seemed to remember where we had put our freshly bought packets of chocolate powder, because he already took them to our kitchen table and set them ready.

My little Shaman took a pan and already started to heat the milk, but he suddenly hesitated and asked Jason:

"Jason? Do you really want to drink hot chocolate just like us, or would you prefer something else?"

Looking a bit surprised, Jason stealthily flashed a worried look at me before he mumbled:

"Could I please have a cup of coffee, just like your Dad?"

I smiled at the taller carbon copy of Nicky, and told him:

"Jason, you are a boy after my own heart! Do you want any milk or sugar in your coffee?"

"Could I have it black please, with only two lumps of sugar?"

"Just like me! I don't want to spoil the taste with milk either."

For a few seconds, Jason stared into my eyes with a surprised face, as if he hadn't expected me to be so nice to him after what he had done to little Harry on his skateboard, and to his own little brother.

Again, I opened my heart towards Jason and started to send him lots of Universal Love, while I brewed another cup of coffee for my young guest. My inside told me I had to be very patient with this severely hurt young adolescent, who seemed to be totally unlike his always-happy little sunshine brother. In silence, we enjoyed our hot drinks, inwardly wondering if they really would help fend off the already upcoming summer heat.

In the meantime, my little soul mate leaned against my side and showed me their preliminary tree house design, of course accompanied by his inseparable friend. From what I could see, their drawing certainly was workable, and I complimented Nicky for his excellent sketching abilities. Nicky beamed proudly, but also confessed he had copied the drawings from Carl's old tree house sketches...

Unexpectedly, my boy turned towards Jason and told him:

"Jason, I am glad to see that you can be nice too! Therefore, let's forget our past and try to become friends..."

For several seconds, Jason only stared back at the 'freaky alien' with his so terribly burnt face, who didn't seem to loathe him for what he had done but only wanted to be his friend. Slowly, he got tears in his emerald eyes, as if he lingered on the verge of crying...

Chapter 18. Skateboarding outside, and a nasty fight.

Then, Jason pulled himself together and hesitantly shook my boy's outstretched hand. As if feeling a bit shocked by his own bravery, he angrily wiped his tears away before again staring at his feet.

Looking at my now broadly smiling little therapist with his golden heart full of Love and Forgiveness, I felt extremely proud of my so special boy! Again, my little soul mate had shown us he was a real Royal Crown Prince; and I was absolutely sure that this tiny Gypsy boy would be an excellent Gypsy Leader in our future!

While John tactfully offered Jason a few tissues, Nicky asked me:

"Pop? Could you please help us transport Jason's old stuff towards your backyard, perhaps on the roof of our golden van?"

"Well, that depends... Jason, how much stuff do you have, and could we transport it on our van without damaging its paint?"

Still looking a bit uneasy, Jason mumbled, barely audibly:

"My friend and I collected quite a lot of old wood and lumber, because we wanted to build a big tree house, until my Dad..."

Suddenly, Jason broke off and fell silent, probably because he realized he was giving away too much information. Again, he lingered on the verge of crying and stealthily wiped his teary eyes with John's tissues, probably remembering his happy time with Carl.

Again, I opened my own heart towards Jason and sent him all the Love that I could muster, while I told him:

"Please Jason, don't feel ashamed; because your Dad already told me everything about Carl, and I fully understand why you are sad."

Immediately, Jason glared at me with suspicious eyes, as if he didn't believe a word of what I told him. Then, he exclaimed:

"My Dad really told you EVERYTHING?"

"Yes, Jason, your Dad really told me everything about you and Carl. But what do you think, can I drive our van straight into your backyard, or do we have to carry your stuff to the sidewalk first?"

"Sniff... Sorry... Cough... Sorry, sir, but thinking of Carl and our happy times still makes me feel sad... Yes, you can drive your van into our backyard and get quite nearby; but do you have any strong ropes to tie all that wood and lumber onto its roof?"

Again, Jason started to stare at his feet, probably because he was made believe that 'big boys don't cry'... Spontaneously, I rose from my chair, folded my arms around Jason's firm frame, and pulled him against my chest. Much to my surprise, Jason trustfully leaned into me, just like Nicky had done when he met me for the first time!

Only, within a second, the 'big boy' seemed to feel shocked about his too spontaneous 'childish behavior', because he hastily pulled away from me. However, I saw his initial trust as a hopeful sign. Perhaps, I would really be able to help Jason with his sadness...

After drinking our hot chocolate and coffee, we went outside. John and Davy went to our trashcan to collect our discarded ropes, while Little Harry asked me for the remote transmitter to open our golden van, because he and Nicky wanted to arrange our movable seats into two rows, so that everybody had an unrestricted view to the front.

Jason and I went to our swimming pool, to tell our still happily splashing guests we would go away but be right back. Fortunately, one of the older girls seemed to be mature enough to supervise the others for a couple of minutes. Feeling reassured, Jason and I went to our golden van, sat down in its front seats, and buckled up.

John and Davy returned with their arms full of used ropes, and put them into our trunk. After they too buckled up, we drove off to BJ's house that was two blocks from ours, while Jason told me the way. Carefully, I reversed our van into their driveway, and stopped next to an enormous pile of used boards, timbers, and all other sorts of useful wood that was neatly stacked under a couple of plastic sheets.

For the next two hours, we were way too busy to think of anything else! Working together, we sorted Jason's lumber, piled the usable boards and timbers onto the roof of our van, and fastened them with our used ropes. We drove home, unloaded everything into our backyard, and immediately went back to fetch even more wood.

19. Jason still misses his former 'boyfriend'.

Finally, after two hours of hard work, we loaded the last pile of wood onto the roof of our van and fastened it with our used ropes. Then, Jason asked me to wait, and quickly disappeared inside their garage. Soon, he returned, carrying a couple of boxes that contained all sorts of nails, screws, and clamps. Again, he went to their garage, and returned with an electric saw and quite a lot of hammers, pincers, drills, punches, and all sorts of screwdrivers!

Looking very impressed, my boys and I loaded all of Jason's extra equipment into the trunk of our van. For the last time, we drove home, unloaded Jason's wood and lumber, and brought his equipment into our own garage, where it would be safe until we needed it.

Feeling dead tired from the unaccustomed work, I slumped down onto a kitchen chair, while my four inexhaustible boys already raced upstairs to jump into their swimming trunks. Soon, they went outside and immediately dived into our already crowded swimming pool; to cool off, tease the girls, and again have lots of fun.

Only Jason stayed behind in our kitchen, looking sad and now and then stealthily wiping a few stray tears away. Obviously, he again remembered his happy times with his friend Carl...

Trying to drag Jason out of his sad shelter, I first asked him:

"What do you think, Jason; shall I brew two more cups of coffee?"

"Err... May I please drink some cold water first? I am mostly thirsty after doing all that sweaty work."

"Then, you better take a cool drink first! Cola and juice are in our refrigerator, so please help yourself..."

Again, Jason stared at me, this time with an expression of pure disbelief on his face. Then, he slowly went to my refrigerator and returned with a bottle of cola. In the meantime, I had put an empty glass in front of his chair. Jason sat down at the table, stared at his empty glass, and absent-mindedly poured some cola into it. Still staring into empty space, he took a small sip of his drink. Then, he looked up at me, and asked me with again tears in his eyes:

"Why are you so nice to me, all the time? Don't you know that I kicked your burnt son off his skateboard, called him a 'freaky alien', and lied about it to my Dad, because I was angry with the whole world and just couldn't care any more?"

"To answer your first question: I am always nice to my friends, especially when they feel sad. To answer your second question: I know what you have done, but I also understand why you did it, because your Dad already told me everything about you."

"Did my Dad really tell you everything? Did he also tell you what he did to Carl and to me, around a year ago?"

"Yes, Jason, and your Dad now severely regrets what he once did to you and to your friend! Jason, could you please tell me what happened to Carl after your Dad kicked him out of the house?"

Again, Jason only stared at me; this time with a frightened face, as if he tried to probe my eyes for any telltale signs of loathe or rejection. When he found only love and compassion in my eyes, he slowly lowered his head and suddenly started to cry his heart out. In between his heavy sobs, he mumbled, barely audible:

"...Sniff... I think Carl's father murdered his son after my Dad phoned him, because that man is even more a homo-hater than my own Dad is. Since that time, I don't care any more and only want to die, but I am too chicken to kill myself..."

Without thinking any more, I reacted purely on my instinct as a trained psychotherapist, plus on my human feelings of compassion for this desperate young child that just needed to be loved and comforted. Quickly, I pulled a folding chair towards Jason, sat down next to him, and unceremoniously pulled his rather heavy frame onto my lap!

For a second, Jason tried to get away from me, probably because he still thought he was 'too big' for such 'childish' behavior. Then, he let himself go, slumped down on my lap, and started to cry even more.

Only, what should I do now, now that I suddenly had a lap full of a sixteen-year-old heavily sobbing and sniveling Jason? Immediately, my too analytical mind started to doubt. What would BJ think of me, as a fervent homo hater, if he ever found out that I had pulled his oldest son onto my lap? Or, what would my own boys think of me, if they unexpectedly entered our kitchen and found Jason like this? Wouldn't they feel terribly jealous, or maybe discarded?

Then, I realized they would only be happy for Jason; and John would probably offer him a couple of tissues to wipe his eyes and blow his nose, while my little soul mate would whisper into his ear: "Let it go, Jason, and don't bottle it up!" Next, my little Shaman would gladly help me pull Jason's negativity out of his aura...

While I pulled Jason even closer to my chest, I automatically started to pull his negativity and self-loathing out of his surrounding aura, by letting it stream towards Mother Earth as a small river of dirt. She would gladly convert Jason's negativity into her own positive energy and send it back to him. Meanwhile, I sent Jason as much Unconditional Love as I was able to muster, until his heavy sobs started to diminish and he slowly pulled himself together.

When Jason finally looked up at me and smiled bashfully, I took a couple of tissues from our kitchen table and dried his eyes for him. Only when I tried to let him blow his nose in another tissue, he started to chuckle and took the tissues out of my hands.

Smiling at seeing my again bashful 'big boy', I told him:

"Jason, imagine how many times my own daughters cried on my lap and I helped them dry their tears and blow their noses, even when they were older. Therefore, please sit still, accept my unconditional love, and tell me what really happened to you and to Carl..."

"...Sniff... I saw Carl for the first time when he showed up at my school and they assigned him to me to show him around. Although Carl is nearly a year younger than I am, we connected immediately and soon became inseparable. You will probably hate me for it, just as my own Dad hates me, but I started to love Carl and Carl started to love me back. I honestly don't want to be a 'homo' or a 'fag', but I just cannot help being who I am... From the first day on, Carl and I had to hide our true feelings, because both his Dad and my Dad are fervent homo haters, and they were always going on about those 'filthy fags' and 'worthless homos'. Therefore, Carl and I wanted to build a tree house at the backside of our backyard, where we could be together without any fear. For many months, we've worked our asses off to collect enough wood and to save up for enough equipment."

Still looking bashful, Jason first took another tissue and dried his again teary eyes, before he went on:

"One day, after working hard, Carl and I wanted to take a shower together. Stupidly, we relied on little Nicky who promised to warn us in time if my Dad unexpectedly showed up. Unfortunately, my Dad came home early and surprised Nicky. He went straight upstairs to take a shower, but found Carl and me in our shower stall cuddling and kissing. Dad went totally berserk, threw Carl down the stairs, and kicked me two broken ribs and several bruises. Our family doctor sent me to a hospital, where I told everybody I stumbled and fell down the stairs; because I just couldn't tell them the truth, that my friend and I were cuddling and my little brother didn't warn us in time when my Dad suddenly showed up... After I returned from the hospital, my Dad again called me a 'filthy fag' and a 'worthless homo', and he promised he would castrate me, that is cut my balls off, if he ever saw me with another boy. Many times, I've tried to find out where Carl lives now, but I just cannot find him any more. After his parents sold their house, they suddenly disappeared into nowhere..."

While Jason took another tissue, dried his teary eyes, and blew his nose, he bashfully mumbled under his breath:

"My Dad is right. I am only a stupid fag and a worthless homo..."

"NO, Jason! You are NOT stupid, but you are a wonderful boy with a lot of love in your heart!"

Looking puzzled, Jason stared into my eyes while he responded:

"Huh...?"

"Jason, do you still love Carl?"

Without thinking, Jason nodded vigorously, while his teary green eyes burned deep holes into mine. This time, I saw such an amount of love and longing in them that I nearly choked from my own welling emotions. Never before had I seen so much Pure Love radiating from such a young child. This boy really loved Carl, and I could only hope that Carl loved Jason back with the same amount of pure love!

For a couple of seconds, Jason continued his stare, as if he still couldn't believe that I didn't loathe him for loving his friend...

At last, trying to break our awkward silence, I asked him:

"Jason; may I try to help you find out where Carl lives now?"

Desperately trying not to cry again, Jason managed to bring out:

"Wou... woul... would you really do that for ME?"

Smiling back at my suddenly hopeful young friend, I answered:

Chapter 19. Moving Harry's stuff back to his old room.

"Yes, my lovable and worthy young friend, I would really do that for YOU! Although I cannot promise anything, I will do what I can to help you find Carl. Could you please write down Carl's full name, his last address, and perhaps his old telephone number?"

Together, we went to my desk in my living room, where I handed Jason a piece of paper and a pen. Still looking at me with very much hope and trust in his teary eyes, Jason sat down at my desk and wrote down everything that he remembered from Carl. Then, he went to our kitchen to wash his tear-stained face, while I took my phone...

My lawyer reacted a bit surprised when he heard my voice, and we had some small talk first. Then, I told him about a fifteen-year-old boy, Carl, who suddenly disappeared from our village around a year ago. I also relayed all the information that Jason had written down, and my lawyer promised to try to trace Carl down as soon as possible. He would call me back as soon as he found Carl or had any other news about him or about his disappeared parents, good or bad.

Before we hung up, my lawyer chuckled:

"You are not going to open a shelter for lost boys, at your age?"

"Nah, I'm not THAT old! However, I really think about adopting another young boy, so you will probably hear from me again."

Still chuckling, I put the receiver back onto its cradle and turned around. Jason sat upright in one of our easy chairs and listened to my part of the conversation. From the doorway, both my little soul mate and a dripping wet Nicky stared at me, with questioning eyes and puzzled faces... My little soul came up to me, of course followed by his inseparable friend, and hesitantly asked me:

"Dad, what other young boy do you think about to adopt? It isn't me, because you cannot adopt me twice..."

Of course, my clever little Shaman also tried to page through my thoughts; but he couldn't find any relevant information because I quickly emptied my mind and thought about something different, to mislead my too curious little mind reader...

Teasingly, I asked my surprised looking boy:

"Aren't you a little bit too nosy? Especially you ought to know that too much curiosity tends to kill the cat!"

To read all our famous 'Gypsy Series' books, please visit www.gypsyseries.com   161

Looking disappointed because he still couldn't find any relevant information in my thoughts, my boy wheedled:

"Aw, Dad, you never kept any secrets from me before..."

All the time, Nicky had stared straight into my eyes, while his emerald green orbs burned deep holes into mine, as if he too tried to probe into my very core. Could Nicky be a mind reader too? What could he have read, before I quickly emptied my mind? Obviously, Nicky really had found some information, because he stammered:

"Are YOU going to adopt me, after my Dad dies and Jason and I have to leave our house? I was afraid that my Dad would send Jason and me to an orphanage; because, then, I would lose you and never see Harry and John and Davy again."

At hearing Nicky's stammered words, Jason suddenly jumped up from his chair, now looking pale as a ghost while staring at his younger brother with a severely shocked face. With barely concealed agony in his quivering voice, Jason stuttered:

"Is Dad going to DIE? Is that MY fault, for being only a 'worthless homo'? If so, let ME die instead of him! My life is over anyway."

Looking like some trapped animal that desperately searched for an escape from being a 'worthless homo', Jason stared at his little brother. Obviously, I would have to talk to Jason immediately, before he fled from our house and tried to kill himself! Only, how the heck did Nicky know that his Dad was ill and would die soon? Had he been eavesdropping while BJ talked to me in our kitchen? However, first, I had to reassure Jason, before he really committed suicide...

Quickly turning towards Jason, I reassured him:

"No, Jason, nothing has been YOUR fault! Your Dad has cancer in the last stage and he will probably die in a couple of months, but his illness has nothing to do with you. I know that your Dad tried to talk to you; but he couldn't find the right words and he also was afraid you would still be angry with him for kicking Carl out of the house. But, Nicky, how do YOU know about your father's lethal illness?"

Looking a little bit guilty, Nicky confessed:

"I heard my Dad talking to Davy's mother while I washed my hands in our kitchen. My Dad told her he would probably die from lethal cancer within a few months, but he still didn't know what to do with me and with Jason..."

Chapter 19. Moving Harry's stuff back to his old room.

Slowly, Nicky got tears in his emerald green eyes, while he stared at his bigger brother with very much love in his teary orbs...

Suddenly, Jason rose from his chair, went to his little brother, and pulled him into his arms. He lifted him from the floor and carried him towards his chair, where he sat down and pulled him onto his lap. While Jason started to cry, he told his now sobbing little brother:

"Sorry Nicker, for having been such an asshole. I didn't want to be mean to you, and I still love you very much, but I think I have been jealous of you! After Dad kicked Car out of our house, he only looked after you, but I didn't exist any more. To Dad, I was only a 'filthy fag' and a 'worthless homo', until I just didn't care any more and became a bully because I couldn't cope with my feelings of anger and loneliness. All the time, I have felt so terribly alone..."

In between his own sobs, Nicky told his crying big brother:

"It's okay, Jase, and I now know you couldn't help being a bully. All the time, I've felt terribly alone too, because you didn't play with me any more and I didn't exist to you either. With Carl, we always had lots of fun. Remember how I tried to help you with our tree house but measured everything wrong? Sorry that I couldn't warn you in time when Dad came home early and went upstairs to take a shower. Many times, I've tried to talk to you, but you always told me to piss off, and I didn't know what else to say or what to do to help you out of your misery, so that I could be your little Nicker again..."

At that moment, my little soul mate and I looked at each other, and we had a short conversation without words. Silently, we tiptoed out of our living room, to leave the two brothers alone to reacquaint. Outside, we ambled to our backyard full of happily playing children. Of course, our swimming pool was crowded again! John and Davy had smartly constructed sort of a makeshift slide, from a few boards and a piece of plastic sheet. Now, everybody had very much fun sliding down along the wet plastic and plunging into the water. Clever boys they were, always up to something new!

My boy left me and raced towards our pool, while shouting:

"Attack of the Crazy Gypsy!"

With an enormous splash, he cannonballed into the inviting water. Everybody started to laugh and yell at him, but he only grinned back and quickly swam to John's makeshift slide to try it out.

Davy went to our water tap and turned it on, to refill the pool and have some more fun with the hose. Chuckling, he squirted a water stream at a couple of yelling girls, who tried to escape his torture by swimming under the surface until they had to reemerge for air.

When the girls saw me, they tried to let me help them, by begging:

"Please, sir, tell your naughty boys to leave us alone."

Only, their still happily smiling faces and beaming eyes betrayed them! Obviously, they very much enjoyed all the extra attention they got from my boys. Suddenly, they seized John and tried to dunk him mercilessly, while yelling at Davy:

"Leave us alone, or we will drown your boyfriend!"

While again attacking them with the water stream, Davy chuckled:

"MY boyfriend? Dream on! You are only envious."

To rescue John, my little soul mate tried to distract the girls. Only, John clearly didn't appreciate his help, and curtly told little Harry to leave him alone. Then, he mercilessly dunked his surprised looking little brother. My boy came up spluttering and coughing, and angrily ordered the girls to drown John, to teach him a lesson!

Chuckling about the ageless and immemorial spectacle of young boys and girls always trying to impress each other, I left them alone and returned to my kitchen to brew another cup of coffee. From our living room, I heard Jason and Nicky talking about how much they had missed each other. Obviously, they were now in a new process of reacquainting and reaccepting each other!

Therefore, I just took my coffee to our backyard. Trying to avoid being splashed too much, I sat down at a safe distance, from where I very much enjoyed the happy sight of all the enthusiastically playing and splashing kids. Smilingly, I tried to recognize them...

First, I recognized my two little neighborhood friends who again were having the time of their lives, now clad in tiny swimming trunks. My boys' three girls from yesterday were now clad in colorful bikinis, happily teasing the boys and now and then chasing after them.

I also saw three naked small boys and two naked small girls I was sure I hadn't seen here before. How long would it take, before our entire neighborhood had discovered our enormous swimming pool and John's cleverly fabricated makeshift slide?

Chapter 19. Moving Harry's stuff back to his old room.

Besides, what would my meddlesome neighbors think of me now, now that my boys and I were trying to 'lure' all these innocent neighborhood children into my backyard, clearly not bothered about half of them being clad only in their 'birthday suits'?

A few minutes later, Nicky suddenly appeared from our backdoor, looked around until he saw me, and shouted at me:

"Pop, your lawyer is on the telephone!"

How did Nicky know it was my lawyer? Was my 'sunshine' really a clairvoyant too, just as my little soul mate was one? Quickly, I went inside, put my emptied coffee cup into the sink, and trotted to my living room to answer the call.

Nicky politely handed me the receiver, while he explained:

"Pop, here is your lawyer, and he has GOOD news!"

Happily, I ruffled Nicky's white hair, before I answered my phone.

My lawyer first complimented me for such a polite little operator who had taken his call as a real professional! Then, he told me he had good news about the lost boy, Carl, but unfortunately some sad news as well. The good news was that he had found fifteen-year-old Carl who had been put up for adoption in a nearby orphanage. The sad news was that the boy's parents hadn't survived a nasty car accident, around a year ago, because their car had slipped off the highway and collapsed into the banks. The boy was catapulted out of their car just in time, and that had saved his life. Only, because he didn't have any known relatives, the authorities had put him in an orphanage where all the interested candidates only wanted to adopt younger children. The orphanage turned out to be very strict, and their headmaster didn't allow any children to contact anybody outside their orphanage until they would be at least eighteen years old. To speed things up for me, my lawyer had already told the headmaster that I was both very rich and a trustworthy candidate. Therefore, Mister John Dragon, the orphanage's headmaster, had immediately granted me permission to take Carl home for a couple of days, to get acquainted. Mister Dragon had even hinted at the possibility of an accelerated adoption...

After my lawyer also told me the orphanage's address and phone number, I thanked him abundantly for his invaluable help before I hung up. Surprisingly, Carl's orphanage turned out to be in another small town that was quite nearby!

Immediately after I hung up, I phoned the orphanage, and asked a dull sounding operator to put me through to 'Mister John Dragon'. After a long time of waiting, and waiting some more; finally, a gloomy sounding male voice didn't even bother to introduce itself, but only brusquely inquired what I wanted.

Feeling a little bit affronted, I curtly responded:

"Is this Mister John Dragon? My lawyer just called me and told me I could collect fifteen-year-old Carl at your orphanage, to stay at my house for a couple of days..."

"So, you are that rich parent with a sudden interest in Carl... Well, I suppose you already know how that boy is?"

"Not yet, but his best friend certainly does! Could we please come over and collect Carl this same afternoon?"

"Well... Err... Hmm, I suppose that might be arranged. What time do you have in mind?"

"I would like to collect Carl within half an hour from now."

Very hesitatingly, Mr. Dragon promised to start 'preparing' Carl immediately for our meeting...

Involuntarily feeling very uneasy, I thanked Mr. John Dragon and put the receiver back onto its cradle. What could that gloomy sounding Mister John Dragon be hiding from me, and why did he have to 'prepare' Carl immediately for our meeting?

What the heck could that strange man be up to? My inside already told me, loud and clear, that it did NOT trust that man!

20. Two detached 'soul mates' are reunited.

First, I returned to our crowded swimming pool, where I told the happily playing kids to go home. Of course, a few kids protested, telling me they had too much fun to leave so soon. Then, I told them my boys and I had to go away and that I didn't want to leave them in the water unattended. Reluctantly, they left our pool to collect their clothes, promising to be back as soon as I would be home again.

My two little boys happily cuddled up to me, leaving me with wet stains on my trousers. Feeling surprised by their affection, I lifted them into my arms, from where they offered me two wet kisses. Then, my three girls from yesterday wanted to kiss me as well. Three naked new boys and two naked little girls wanted to kiss me too, with their dry clothes in their hands. Wow! I didn't know that this 'ancient grandpa' would attract so much love and trust from so many neighborhood children! Feeling all mushy inside, I totally forgot to worry about what our nosy neighbors would think of me now. At this moment, they could... Well, you already know what I mean.

Still after-glowing from my happy feelings, I told my own boys to follow me inside, because we had to discuss something important. In rank, they followed me into our living room, looking at me with curious faces. My four boys propped together on our couch, while Jason and I took easy chairs. Inwardly, I chuckled at the thought that I soon would have to buy a bigger couch as well.

Before we went to the orphanage to collect Carl, I wanted to tell my boys a few things I thought they should know in advance about Jason and his lost friend. Therefore, I told them that, around a year ago, Carl suddenly disappeared into nowhere. Today, my lawyer found out that Carl's parents had died in a car accident, and only Carl survived. The authorities had put him in an orphanage, where his headmaster didn't allow him to contact anybody outside their building. The orphanage was less than half an hour's drive from our house.

Suddenly, I again had a lap full of Jason, this time sobbing from sheer happiness, while stuttering:

"Please... sir... are... we... go-hing... to see... Carl... now?"

"Well, Jason, we could go to that orphanage immediately, but only if you REALLY want to see Carl today."

Jason nearly couldn't talk any more from his welling emotions, but he almost lost his head in nodding vigorously! He threw his arms around my neck and tried to suffocate me, while his sobs aggravated and he started to cry earnestly. Both John and Davy stormed towards our kitchen to get a fresh packet of tissues; but they bumped into each other in our doorway and staggered down onto the floor. Looking sheepish, Davy wavered back to our couch while rubbing a lump on his head, while John went to our kitchen to get a packet of tissues, before slumping down next to Davy and rubbing his own lump.

In the meantime, our smallest therapist went to Jason, bent over towards him, and whispered into his ear:

"Let it go, Jason, and don't bottle it up! In a few minutes, you will feel a lot better..."

Suddenly chuckling at hearing my boy's whispered words, Jason started to cry and laugh at the same time. Then, he quickly pulled himself together, while my little soul mate took a few tissues from John's packet and helped Jason dry his eyes and blow his nose. Surprisingly, Jason just let my boy do as he liked. Then, with a bashful smile, he looked around at everybody while he stammered:

"Sorry for being such a worthless homo... err... Oops, sorry, I forgot I am now a wonderful boy with a lot of love in my heart."

Everybody started to laugh at hearing Jason's unexpected change of mind; and that broke our remaining tension. Even Jason himself started to laugh with us, looking more and more happy, and certainly feeling a lot more at ease. Nicky went to his big brother, crawled onto my lap next to him, offered him a wet kiss, and told him:

"Jase, you really are my wonderful older brother with lots of love in your heart; and I still love you very, very much!"

Still sitting on my lap, Jason pulled his little brother even closer against his chest while he assured him:

"My wonderful Nickering Dragon, I love you even more!"

While my old lap nearly started to groan under its added extra weight, I told everybody to get ready because we had to go to Carl's orphanage to collect Carl and take him with us!

Chapter 20. Cooking a salmon, waiting for Christian.

Immediately, Nicky and Jason left my lap and went to our kitchen to wash their tear-stained faces, before they followed the others upstairs to shuck their swimsuits, put on their clothes, and even comb their hair. Clearly, they wanted to make a good first impression on Mister John Dragon, the orphanage's headmaster.

After everybody returned into our living room, I took my keys and my wallet from my desk and put them into my pockets, while my little soul mate took our remote transmitter. He raced outside to unlock our golden van, and everybody followed him, dived inside, and first arranged four seats around a folded table in the middle before they sat down and buckled up. Carefully, I backed our van out of our driveway, and we were on our way to Mister John Dragon's orphanage and hopefully Carl, while Jason sat shotgun.

After a couple of seconds, John instructed Jason to push the red knob to the left on our car stereo. Soon, some nice song reverberated through our van, and all of us started to hum along with its happy tune, as usual. Only Jason remained silent, obviously feeling more and more nervous. Well, I could imagine he felt a bit distracted, after two years of living in hope and fear about his lost friend.

Consolingly, I put my hand on Jason's trembling knee, while I tried to reassure him by telling him:

"Don't be afraid, Jason. Everything will turn out for the best; and, if necessary, all of us will be there for you and for Carl."

"Thank you for all your help, sir, but Carl hasn't seen me for more than a year! Perhaps, he doesn't even recognize me, or he has found another friend and doesn't want to know me any more."

"Of course, only time will tell; but I hope that you are wrong. For now, what are you going to do when you see Carl?"

"I don't know... I feel much more worried about what Carl is going to do when he sees ME! Perhaps, he is still mad at my Dad and at me and tells me to leave him alone. Please, sir, could YOU try to meet Carl first and ask him whether he still wants to be my friend? I'm feeling way too nervous to make a good first impression on him."

"Well... Although your request is a bit unusual, I will try to have a short talk with Carl first, to ask him if he still wants to be your friend. In the meantime, you could best stay in our van with the others, until Carl and I show up and join you. Okay?"

Looking relieved, Jason nodded his consent and even started to look around; until, half an hour later, we entered another town. John directed us to where he thought the orphanage was; and soon a huge monumental building showed up, surrounded by a nasty looking iron fence. This building was Carl's orphanage; but it looked more like a restricted army base, including a bored looking guard! Could this uninvitingly fenced building really be an orphanage for young children? Hesitantly, I stopped at the slowly opening iron gate.

A yawning guard, or was it a lazy gatekeeper, ambled to our car and curiously looked inside. For a second, the man seemed to feel uneasy at seeing so many faces. Then, shaking his head after counting five fidgeting young boys, he asked me:

"Where do you want to go, sir?"

"Good afternoon to you too, sir, and we already have an appointment with Mister John Dragon."

Without answering, the gatekeeper just took his cell phone, spoke a few words, nodded, spoke again, and put his cell phone away into his pocket. For a few seconds, he still seemed to hesitate.

Then, pointing to a small parking lot, he grumbled:

"You may park your car over there, and Mister Dragon will meet you at the main entrance."

While the guard stepped back to let our van through, John leaned into me from behind and shivered:

"Dad, everything around here feels like a prison! No wonder Jason couldn't find Carl for such a long time."

To be ready to drive away immediately, if necessary, I carefully reversed our van into one of the empty parking spots. Sensing a strange mixture of anticipation and dreading, as if I was about to enter a real prison, I promised Jason I would try to be right back, if possibly accompanied by Carl! Then, I ambled towards the huge monumental building and slowly ascended its elevated main entrance, where I would meet Mister John Dragon and, hopefully, Carl.

How would Carl react on seeing Jason back, for the first time after a long year of separation? Had Mister John Dragon already 'prepared' Carl for meeting me; and why had that been necessary? Feeling more and more uneasy, I slowly climbed the huge marble steps, until a monumental wooden door blocked my way.

170 Aad Aandacht is a Dutch psychotherapist who loves writing 'books with a message'

Immediately, I had a very strange feeling; as if inside this building they were still living in the Middle Ages. This enormous door even had an old-fashioned pull bell that looked out of date. Tentatively, I pulled the bell knob, and a couple of loud clangs reverberated through the corridors. At least, the bell worked...

After what felt like a century, the enormous wooden door opened majestically. A sulky looking old man, of around my age or maybe slightly older, showed up and stared at me. For quite some time, he scrutinized me from head to toe, as if I could be some dangerous monster from another planet. Then, disapprovingly shaking his head, he turned around while mumbling:

"You are that foster parent with an interest in Carl? Follow me."

Still feeling uneasy, I followed the strange man into an uninviting darkness. Was I really entering the Middle Ages here? Mr. Dragon shuffled across the dark hallway towards a closed door, and stopped. Slowly, as if hesitating, he opened the door and beckoned me to enter the eerily dark room. He waited until I stepped inside, and immediately closed the door behind. Had he locked me in? Well, I would find out soon enough, but I first needed some time to adjust my eyes to the gloomy darkness. For heaven's sake, where had I landed, and on which strange planet was I now? Or, was I trapped in some time machine that had sent me back to the early Stone Ages?

When finally my eyes adjusted to the darkness, I looked around the gloomy room. Standing next to the only window the room had, I saw a skinny boy of around Jason's age and of about the same height, but looking fragile and extremely thin. Without moving, the boy only stared at me with two dark eyes in a ghostly pale face. For a second, I even wondered whether the orphanage was feeding this young boy properly, as a growing adolescent. Or, was this too skinny boy trying to starve himself, to have at least some sense of control? Nervously playing with his thin fingers, he stared back at me, of course without any sign of recognition. Was this really Jason's friend, Carl?

Hesitantly, I tried to break the ice, by telling the staring boy:

"Hello, Carl, I am happy to finally see you! Of course, you don't know me yet, but my regular friends always call me 'Big Harry'..."

Tentatively, I extended my hand towards the still staring boy, but he only stared at my hand and didn't move.

Well, my first effort to talk to Carl didn't bring me any further. Obviously, this boy didn't trust me at all. Probably, to him, I was just another visitor who was looking for a young child to adopt; and I would soon turn my back to him and go look for a smaller kid. How would this silent boy react to hearing Jason's name?

Deciding to try to wake him from his lethargy first, I told him:

"Shall we sit down first; because I have some good news to tell that probably will make you very happy..."

As if shrugging his shoulders, the boy sauntered to a nearby chair and sat down, with slow and mechanical movements. Feeling happy to get at least some reaction out of him, I took another chair and dragged it in front of him, so that I could see his eyes that were nearly black in an unnaturally pale face. I guessed they had once been beautiful; but, now, they were empty and almost lifeless.

Shuddering from my suddenly welling emotions, I remembered I had seen those empty eyes a few times before, in suicidal patients that had been locked up in solitude... Clearly, this boy had given up all hope, as if he was waiting for his glum life to end. Maybe, he really tried to starve himself to death, figuring it was the only thing he could do to take his fate into his own hands...

Crying inwardly, I opened my heart towards the boy and started to send him as much Universal Love as I was able to muster, hoping it would pull him out of his glum shell. While looking intently for any instinctive reactions, I told him:

"Today, I've met another wonderful boy who told me he still waits for his best friend, Carl. His name is Jason..."

At hearing the name 'Jason', Carl's legs suddenly shifted as if he wanted to stand up, and I saw a glimmer of hope in his nervously blinking eyes. Yes, this depressed boy really was Carl, and he still remembered Jason! Only, very soon, he slumped back on his chair and his dark eyes turned empty again, although he still stared at me with what looked like some more interest. By reading his enveloping aura, I could sense that this skinny boy was terribly afraid of something threatening, but I couldn't find out what it was. Involuntarily, he made me think of some trapped animal, longing to escape from its terrible fate but knowing it would be slaughtered anyway! Again sending Carl as much Universal Love as I could muster, I continued:

Chapter 20. Cooking a salmon, waiting for Christian.

"Jason told me he still loves you and he misses you! He also told me about your tree house, and he still wants you to help him build it."

This time, Carl really rose from his chair, while his eyes seemed to come to life and pierced deeply into mine. For a split second, he let his mask down, and I saw a couple of tears welling in his suddenly radiant eyes that started to glow like bright sunlight shining through heavy thunderclouds. It was now clear to me that Carl still loved Jason dearly, and that he unexpectedly got some more hope!

While I rose from my chair to be at the same height, I told him:

"Jason already waits for you, outside in my car. Shall we join him now, so that you can renew your friendship?"

For several seconds, Carl's dark eyes only pierced into mine, as if searching my soul for sincerity. Could he really trust me? Was I really telling him the truth about Jason still loving him and missing him? Then, he again lowered his head and stared at his feet. With a hoarse sounding voice full of emotion, he mumbled:

"Of course, Jason has already found another friend, after such a long time of not seeing each other..."

Feeling happy to get a few words out of Carl, I responded:

"Carl, you have always been Jason's only friend, and Jason is at least as lonely as you are. Shall we now go outside and join him?"

Much to my disappointment, Carl only shook his head, while he sat down again and mumbled under his breath:

"Mister Dragon will never let me go. He just hates me too much."

What terrible things could have happened to this badly depressed young man who clearly had lost all hope? In Carl's aura, I could still sense a strong spirit that once had been radiant and full of life, until somebody almost killed it. Had really Mister John Dragon something to do with this? Could Mr. Dragon have broken Carl's once powerful spirit, perhaps by locking him up in solitude and starving him?

Involuntarily, I started to feel a bit angry, but quickly suppressed my upcoming emotions. The only thing that would help Carl now was follow me outside and meet Jason. Love is the strongest force in the Universe, and I was convinced that Jason's strong and pure love would help Carl come out of his glum shell in no time...

Therefore, I didn't respond to Carl's statement, but only asked him:

"Please, trust me and follow me outside. Do you remember Nicky, Jason's little brother? Nicky is here too, and he too is very eager to meet you again. Therefore, shall we now leave this too dark room, and go outside to join Jason and Nicky?"

Much to my relief, Carl finally nodded, although very hesitatingly. Before he could change his mind, I just grabbed his hand and quickly dragged him towards the closed door. Immediately, Carl behavior changed considerably; and he suddenly clamped onto my hand with all of his might, as a frightened lamb that headed for its slaughter. Trembling all over, Carl waited until I had opened the closed door, before he shuffled after me into the hallway. Fortunately, Mister John Dragon hadn't locked the door from the outside, as I expected.

In the gloomy hallway, Carl started to look around with frightened eyes, still trembling all over like some hunted deer that tried to escape its hunters. Obviously, Carl still feared that Mister John Dragon would suddenly show up to forbid him to leave the orphanage...

Fortunately, for Mr. Dragon, he didn't show up to block our way, because I was sure I would have raised hell and the devil! Now, I only heaved a deep sigh of relief. Still dragging Carl with me, as some frightened little kid, I had to use a lot of force to push the massive wooden front door open. In a rebellious mood, I decided to leave it wide open, because this building could definitely use some fresh air!

For several seconds, both Carl and I squinted in the bright sunlight, until our eyes got used to the light and we could see some more. Then, we slowly descended the ancient marble steps, still hand in hand, while I pointed Carl to our golden van that waited for us in its parking spot, ready to take off immediately if necessary. To play it safe, I first reinforced my grip onto Carl's trembling hand, before I explained:

"Look, Carl; this is our golden van. Inside our van, both Jason and Nicky are waiting for you to join us..."

Just as I already anticipated, Carl started to tremble even more; because he didn't know how to cope with regaining so much freedom after being locked up in that gloomy orphanage for who knows how long. Almost collapsing from his intense emotions, he tried to pull me back into his 'safe' orphanage; but I didn't let him go and just pulled him downstairs until we had descended all the marble steps and had reached some more solid ground.

Chapter 20. Cooking a salmon, waiting for Christian.

My goodness, what the heck had Mister John Dragon done to this too frightened boy who seemed to be terribly afraid of only stepping outside into some bright sunlight and open air...

Suddenly, one of the doors of our golden van opened; and Jason tumbled outside and stormed at us at lightning speed, as a howling whirlwind, and nearly tripping over his own feet in his tremendous hurry to reach his lost and suddenly re-found friend!

Howling and sobbing at the same time, Jason shouted:

"CARLLLLL..."

Then, he threw himself at his shocked looking friend and forcefully embraced him, kissed him, and again tried to suffocate him.

Being sure that Mother Nature would take over from here, I stepped aside and left Carl to Jason, to use his own powerful love to reunite and reacquaint. For a few seconds, Carl tried to escape from what were now Jason's capturing arms; but then he gave up struggling and just slumped into his friend's ferocious embrace.

Hugging Carl almost to death, Jason kissed his friend, patted his back, turned him around, looked at him, and kissed him again. In the meantime, he started to cry and laugh at the same time, while trying not to squash his re-found friend too much. For a moment, he released Carl, held him at arm's length, looked at him, and then again hugged him, still laughing and sobbing at the same time.

Finally, Carl's dark clouds started to vanish, some life returned into his gloomy eyes, and his built-in sun started to break through. Hesitantly, his eyes started to beam more and more, until they began to look like the beautiful black orbs I was sure they once had been. At last, a faint smile crossed Carl's thin lips, while a hoarse sounding whisper escaped his throat:

"Jase... Is this really you? I've missed you so badly..."

Finally, Carl's resistance broke down, and he started to cry his broken heart out, while Jason kept his arms around his crying friend and tried to comfort him. In the meantime, my happy looking foursome had surrounded our two crying friends, clearly enjoying the beautiful sight of Carl's and Jason's happy reuniting!

"It is really Carl!" Nicky whispered, leaning into my side while getting tears in his emerald green eyes.

To read all our famous 'Gypsy Series' books, please visit www.gypsyseries.com

My little soul mate leaned into my other side without saying a word; but I could feel my little Shaman sending his own powerful waves of Love and Respect towards our two reuniting friends, at the same time cleaning Carl's enveloping aura from its excessive negativity and sending it towards Mother Earth as a small river of dirt.

John and Davy looked at both friends from a small distance, but they too had tears in their eyes and furtively wiped them away. In silence, we waited, until our two reuniting friends had sufficiently reacquainted and would be ready to go HOME.

Unexpectedly, as if coming out of nowhere, Mister John Dragon showed up next to our happily smiling group. Looking at both still hugging boys with barely hidden disdain, he disapprovingly shook his head. Could this strange 'headmaster' also be a 'homo hater'?

Without even trying to be polite, he almost growled at me:

"You will have to sign his papers first!"

Without saying another word, Headmaster John Dragon turned around and disappeared through the still open front door into his dark and gloomy orphanage, without looking back.

Well, I surely wanted to leave this strangely obscure place as soon as possible! Therefore, I just followed Mr. Dragon into his gloomy building. This time, we went straight to his office, where he had already filled in all the paperwork and even signed them. Staring at me as if I could be some dangerous child molester, he growled:

"Do you really want to adopt that boy?"

"Yep! Just tell me what I have to do..."

"Sign his legal papers, and hand the copies to your lawyer."

As quickly as I could, I signed the small bundle of papers, without reading them, and stuffed the copies into my back pocket. Then, I just turned around and left the dark and gloomy building without uttering another word, again leaving its front door wide open!

Outside, I first inhaled deeply, and welcomed the fresh outside air into my lungs, before I trotted back to my own flock and told them:

"Come on, boys, let's go HOME!"

Surprisingly, Carl didn't move at all, but only stared at me with a frightened face, while he hesitatingly asked me:

"Are you now taking me to another home?"

While tentatively ruffling Carl's dark hair, I assured him:

"No, Carl, I am taking you to OUR home. From now on, you are one of my boys, and you are going to live with us!"

Unexpectedly, Carl started to cry from fright and frustration, while he shook his head as in denial and sobbed:

"Mister Dragon will never let me go. He already told me I have to wait until I am at least eighteen years old, and I am only fifteen..."

"Well, take a look at these signed papers in my back pocket. You are now MY boy; and, from now on, you will live in my house!"

Although Carl finally seemed to get some more hope in his teary dark eyes, he still rebutted:

"Mister Dragon will never let me go. Last year, he didn't even let me send a letter to Jason! After he read my letter, he tore it to pieces and told me I was a 'filthy homo' and he would teach me a lesson I would never forget. Then, he threw my papers and pen away, locked me up in a dark room, and gave me only one small meal a day, to root out my abnormalities that were coming from the devil..."

At hearing Carl's sad story, I involuntarily balled my fists from suddenly welling anger and frustration, while I turned around to go back to that orphanage and beat that 'hetero' Mister John Dragon into his own devilish hell! Fortunately, John saw what I wanted to do, and quickly unclenched his own fists. He raced towards me and pulled at my arm, to prevent me from walking away, while my little soul mate quickly stepped in my way to stop me!

Still trembling all over with his own horror, at hearing Carl's unbelievable story, John sternly admonished me:

"Please, Dad, don't do that! Remember what you once taught me: 'Always think first and never judge somebody from the outside'. That hateful man just isn't worth the trouble. Please, take a deep breath, climb into our golden van, and let's go home."

While I unclenched my fists, my inside nearly burst from pride! Here were MY BOYS, my precious little soul mate and my clever young friend, both of them with their enormous hearts of pure gold. I absolutely loved them, with all my heart, my mind, and my soul!

I was sure that, today, my two adopted sons had rescued me from committing first-degree murder! Although they had felt frightened to death at seeing my murderous face, they had stopped me nevertheless.

Okay, let's forget that 'hetero' Mister John Dragon, and go home! Followed by John and my still trembling little soul mate, I slowly turned around and ambled to our already waiting golden van.

In the meantime, Jason had taken Carl's hand and tried to drag him inside. Very hesitatingly, Carl followed his friend, still looking like some forlorn puppy, while moving as on autopilot. Obviously, after being starved and locked into a dark room for such a long time, all these new things were happening way too fast for him!

Jason helped his friend buckle up, and took the seat next to him to keep a close eye on him. I started our golden van, forced myself to smile, and drove past the surprised looking gatekeeper without stopping or saying goodbye. We were on our way HOME!

21. Road restaurant; Carl's beautiful dream.

While Jason tried to get Carl to explain what had happened to him, and John was talking softly to Davy, my little soul mate bent forward and scanned our car stereo until he found some nice background music. Then, he settled back in his front seat, listened to the music, and stared out the car windows. However, I could almost feel my boy pondering about something that seemed to bother him...

A minute later, my boy lowered the stereo volume and asked me:

"Dad? Is Carl really going to live in our house from now on? If so, where will everybody sleep? Our house has only two bedrooms and two folding beds, next to your room and your double bed; but that is not enough when Nicky and Davy want to sleep here again..."

Feeling a bit surprised that such a small boy was trying to help me manage my steadily growing household; I first teased him:

"Sorry, but I haven't thought yet about any sleeping arrangements. However, I know you are a clever deep thinker, therefore, could you please come up with a workable solution?"

"Okay, Dad, let me think it through... Of course, Nicky and I can share my old room, and Jason and Carl can share John's room. Only, then, John still needs another room so that he can invite Davy for sleepovers. Therefore, we seem to need at least three bedrooms, next to yours. Until, within a few years from now, both Nicky and I will need our own rooms when we start studying, and then you will need at least five rooms! Of course, we could rebuild our attic and create three extra rooms in it; or you could buy a bigger house... Yeah, that is it! Dad, I have found a workable solution! Let's look for a bigger house on the Internet, as soon as we get home."

Feeling a little bit affronted, I responded:

"What? You really want me to move again, after I just bought this house? Besides, I hope you don't think I am a millionaire?"

"Nah, you can always buy a bigger house with your credit card!"

Deciding that now would be a good time to let my boy discover the pros and cons of using a credit card, I slyly asked him:

"When I am paying for my purchases with my credit card, where do you think the shop owner gets his money from?"

My little soul mate sat upright, and stared at me with a deep frown on his forehead and a stunned expression in his bright blue eyes. A few times, he opened his mouth to say something, but then hesitated and slowly released his breath. Still thinking, he sank back in his chair and pulled his knees up to his chest, holding them with his arms. I could almost feel his clever brain working overtime; while he stared into empty space, obviously still trying to find out where credit card money comes from to pay a shop owner with...

At last, my boy came to a logical conclusion, and chuckled:

"Sorry Dad, but I didn't think straight. As I'm only eight years old, I've never before thought about money-things like banking, until now. Of course, your credit card can contain only your own money from your own bank account! But, how does your bank know how much money you have paid by using your credit card, so that they can pay the shop owner with your money from your bank account?"

Again, I felt very surprised and extremely proud of my clever little deep thinker, who had found out how banking works all on his own! Happily, I explained to him what I understood about working with credit card numbers, expiration data, and a secret personal pin code.

Of course, my little brainiac had his next question ready:

"Wow, I didn't know that money banks could think out such a clever security system! But, what happens if somebody figures out your pin code by trying out all its possibilities, because a pin code has only four digits and can be tried out in a relatively short time?"

"Well, after three false tries, the bank computer automatically blocks my credit card, so that nobody can use it any more until I contact my bank, explain to them what has happened, and my bank unblocks my card or gives me a new one."

"Now, THAT is a clever solution! Those banking gadjo's have to be really bright, because they seem to have thought of everything."

Obviously, my little deep thinker felt genuinely impressed. For a couple of seconds, he retreated into his own little boy's thoughts, leaning back onto his seat and again listening to the background music. Then, he again sat upright, and told me with an impish grin on his broadly smiling face:

Chapter 21. Astonishing answers to all our questions.

"Dad? We didn't decide where everybody will sleep tonight! That means YOU have to come up with a workable solution. But, my stomach tells me it feels hungry. Could you please stop at some road restaurant and get us something to eat first?"

At hearing the Magic Word for Growing Kids, all five boys in the rear seats immediately perked their ears up, leaned forward, and demonstratively rubbed their empty stomachs, to demonstrate they felt starved, even Carl. Chuckling at seeing my bottomless pits' antics, I told them to hold out until we had found a nice road restaurant.

Two minutes later, Davy's voice echoed through our van:

"OVER THERE, Dad! That looks like a nice road restaurant!"

With suddenly ringing ears, I stopped at a small fast-food restaurant along the road. Of course, my regular foursome immediately bolted out of our van and hurried inside to find an empty table; while I stopped the engine and turned around to look at my remaining boys. Jason tried to pull a fiercely resisting Carl out of his seat, while he admonished his again scared looking friend:

"Come on, Carl, let's follow the others inside and get something to eat. I am sure you are hungry too!"

However, Carl seemed to feel too frightened, and only clamped even more onto his seat. Obviously, he still didn't dare to leave his safe environment, to enter some threatening building he didn't know what he could expect of. After a couple more tries, Jason started to react impatient, and I decided to take over. Therefore, I climbed into the rear and took another seat in front of Carl.

Carl glared at me with suspicious eyes, as if he felt betrayed and didn't trust me any more. What could my new boy be thinking? Trying to help him, I started to assure him:

"Carl? Please remember what I've already told you. You are one of MY boys now, and I will never let you go, unless you want to leave me voluntarily. Now, please, follow us into this restaurant, where we will order a healthy and tasty meal. Are you very hungry?"

Fortunately, Carl's suspicious eyes started to lose their glare, and his hands slowly stopped trembling. Only, his dark orbs still pierced into mine, as if searching my soul for any telltale signs of betrayal. What could have happened to this so fearful and mistrustful young boy, and why didn't he want to leave our safe van?

Finally, Carl whispered, with a slightly trembling voice:

"I am afraid my beautiful dream has come to an end and that you will hand me over to another 'home', as they have done before... Please, sir, I don't want to be locked up again and feel hungry all day, to have my 'homo abnormalities' rooted out..."

Again, I cursed Mister John Dragon for doing such horrible things to such a vulnerable orphan. Didn't that man have a heart? And, when or where had 'they' done those same things to Carl before? However, I decided to ask him my own questions later on. Gently, I put my arms around Carl's trembling shoulders, while I promised:

"Carl, I will NEVER hand you over to another 'home' or to anybody else, unless you ask me for it, and that is a promise. Cross my heart and hope to die! Now, let's go inside this restaurant and join our hungry friends before they start eating the furniture."

My little joke brought a feeble smile to Carl's thin lips. Hesitantly, he left his seat, took my hand, and let himself be dragged out of our van. Jason took his other hand, and we entered the restaurant and looked around for the others. Of course, our foursome had already put two empty tables together and gathered seven chairs around them. All four boys started to cheer loudly when they saw us!

Especially John looked a bit naughty, while he chuckled:

"Here comes our ancient grandpa! A long time has passed, since we had the pleasure of seeing our old man the last time..."

I tried to grab my insolent young monkey, but he dived under a table and popped up at the other side between Davy and Nicky. From there, he laughed at me and teasingly stuck out his tongue. Well, a next time, I will get him for that, if I ever get a chance.

Ignoring my still chuckling teaser, I asked everybody else:

"Are you old enough to order a healthy meal by yourself? Just tell the cashier I will pay afterwards with my credit card."

Four hungry boys immediately stormed towards the service bar, trying to be the first one to order their 'healthy' meal. Only Jason stayed behind, with a trembling Carl who again didn't dare to move and only stared at his feet. His hungry looking friend tried to pull him out of his chair, but Carl just refused to follow him, while looking more and more frustrated... At last, Carl hesitantly looked up at me, and admitted in a low whisper:

Aad Aandacht is a Dutch psychotherapist who loves writing 'books with a message'

"Sorry, sir, but I don't have any money..."

Chuckling from the unexpected anticlimax, I assured Carl:

"Fortunately, I am having more than enough money to pay for you and for all the other meals! Therefore, you may order anything that you want, and I will pay for everybody afterwards, by using my 'inexhaustible' credit card. Okay?"

Looking relieved, Carl slowly rose from his chair. However, he started to look around as if this was the first time in years that he saw a roadside restaurant. Suddenly feeling sad, I thought it probably was!

Trying to help him overcome his hesitancy, I asked him:

"What would you like to eat, Carl? Or, shall we ask Jason to order a healthy meal for you?"

With a grateful look at me, Carl nodded and even started to smile! Still hesitatingly, he followed Jason to the crowded service bar, as a faithful puppy following its master. My other bottomless pits were already ordering their copious meals, while joking and teasing each other as usual. One by one, they returned to our tables, carrying overflowing trays of the most delicious looking junk food. Obviously, this was their boyish idea of ordering a 'healthy' meal.

Chuckling at seeing their over-enthusiastic faces, I left out tables, went to the bar, and ordered a cup of watery looking coffee and a 'healthy' burger 'with all the works' for myself.

In no time, my boys' trays were emptied, and all the boys looked stuffed and rubbed their now nicely filled tummies. Then, they went outside to get some fresh air, letting me pay for everything with my 'inexhaustible' credit card. Feeling in a good mood, I took revenge by ordering another cup of coffee. Sipping slowly, I enjoyed this rare moment of peace and quiet. Through the windows, I saw my boys, teasing each other and impatiently kicking pebbles around.

Everybody started to cheer when I finally showed up, and John muttered under his breath what sounded like 'our too old and too slow ancient grandpa'. Pretending I didn't hear him, I smiled at John and handed little Harry the remote transmitter. With a proud face, my youngest son opened our beautiful golden conveyance from a distance, making her blink twice. We entered our van, quickly buckled up, and drove home with nicely filled tummies.

Soon, I parked our golden van in our own driveway and stopped her softly murmuring engine. Immediately, a happy-looking Thomas and a giggling little Chrissy approached us and looked through the tinted car panes with admiring eyes! Sitting on our porch steps, they had been waiting for us until we finally showed up...

Now, they happily waved to their friends and enthusiastically greeted me. They had returned from their prolonged vacation; and both of them were nicely suntanned and honestly pleased to see us. Thomas peeked again through the tinted side panes of our beautiful golden van, and remarked in awe:

"Wow! This is a really neat car, and it certainly is big enough to take all of us to the beach..."

Chuckling at Thomas' hidden invitation, I ruffled his long yellow hair, emptied my mailbox, and entered our house. All six friends were very happy to see each other and immediately crowded together on our couch to exchange their adventures. Jason took an easy chair and started to listen to their stories, while Carl first looked around in our living room and then hesitantly took the other easy chair after pulling it close to Jason. From there, he started to half-listen to all the enthusiastic vacation stories, still timidly looking at his feet.

In the meantime, I sat down at my desk and sorted my mail. Then, I started to think about my new life. Since today, I had a huge flock of young children around me, and several of them were more or less dependent on me. Little Harry was now my adopted son and had his own room in my house. Oops, sorry... he had his own room in OUR house. John was now in my custody; and he too had his own room here, waiting until his mother returned and claimed him back. Davy had his own room in his own home, but he called me 'Dad' and enjoyed every moment of being here. Nicky was still living in his own home, but his father had already asked me to adopt him and take him into my house. Today, Jason suddenly entered my life, opened up to me, and where would he end? Now, Carl had shown up, and I had already promised to adopt him and take him into my house...

Thomas and Chrissy had their own home, but they liked to be here with their friends. Add three young neighborhood girls and five little neighborhood boys who very much enjoyed playing in our swimming pool... My little soul mate could be right! I really had to buy a bigger house, preferably with an enormous built-in swimming pool!

Chapter 21. Astonishing answers to all our questions.

At that moment, my little soul mate approached me and interrupted my train of thoughts, by complaining:

"Dad? My mask starts itching and my face feels a bit swollen. Will you please help me take it off?"

Trustfully, my boy climbed onto my lap and turned his masked face towards me. Gently, and careful not to tear its edges, I started to peel my boy's sticky mask off his sweaty and a bit puffy face...

Suddenly, I heard a loud groan that clearly came from one of our easy chairs! Looking up, I saw that Carl had turned around in his chair and stared at my boy's loosening mask with bulging eyes full of horror! His meager face looked even paler than it had been before, while he panted for air and almost fainted from sudden distress.

Gawking at my boy's halfway-loosened rubber mask, Carl gasped:

"Why do you peel Harry's SKIN from his face? Are you doing this for punishment? What has Harry done to deserve such sadistic treatment? Sorry Jason, but I don't want to be here any more! Please bring me back to my orphanage immediately..."

Nearly crying from his terrifying thoughts, Carl looked at Jason, who stared back at him with a non-comprehending face. Then, John started to roar with laughter, at seeing Carl's horrified face! Obviously, John's reaction made Carl think he could be my next 'victim', because he suddenly jumped out of his chair and dived for the door.

Fortunately, Jason caught his frightened friend just in time, pushed him back into his chair, and told him to sit down and stop being stupid. Nobody in this house full of love and happiness would ever peel any living skin from their faces, and Carl only had to trust his best friend and listen to Harry's unbelievable story!

Still looking frightened and trembling all over, Carl slumped back on his chair and clamped onto Jason's hand, while I continued to peel my boy's rubber mask from his itching and slightly swollen face.

After I was ready, my little soul mate went to Carl, let him take a good look at his burns, and trustfully started to tell him everything about their caravan on fire and his many skin operations. Vividly, he told how some people had made fun of his burnt face and called him a 'freak' or an 'alien', until his new Dad bought him a rubber mask to hide his so terribly burnt face from any too curious onlookers.

Unfortunately, the sticky rubber started to itch after a couple of hours, and then he had to take his mask off. Fortunately, Dad had already found a skin transplant clinic, where a nice 'face doctor' had peeled some living skin from the insides of his thighs to cultivate it, and soon would give him a new face and new skin on his body!

All the time, Carl had listened to my boy open-mouthed; while he slowly pulled himself together and stopped trembling. At last, he let go of Jason's hand and furtively wiped a few stray tears away.

After heaving a couple of heartfelt sighs, Carl mumbled:

"Did I ever think I had a difficult life? Compared to you with such a burnt face, I am living in paradise!"

Smiling from ear to ear, my little soul mate responded:

"Well, I AM living in paradise, because every day I'm living here feels like it is another birthday!"

From our over-crowded couch, Nicky piped up:

"That yields Harry three-hundred-and-sixty-five birthday presents a year, and one more in a leap year!"

Everybody started to laugh, this time including Carl, while my boy went to our kitchen to clean his mask. Immediately, Nicky wrestled free from our crowded couch and followed his inseparable friend. Teasing each other and bumping into each other as usual, they disappeared into the hallway and closed the door behind.

After they returned, my boy put his cleaned mask onto his green model and put it on my desk in plain sight. In the meantime, John and Davy had told their friends about our new inflatable swimming pool in our backyard. Now, all the boys were in a tremendous hurry! Thomas and Chrissy raced home to put on their swimming trunks, Nicky raced home to get swimming gear for Jason, Carl, and himself; and John went upstairs to get swimming gear for everybody else.

Soon, they returned and hastily changed in our kitchen, piling their clothes onto a chair. Then, they raced into our backyard and plunged into the inviting water. Even skinny Carl went outside, now clad in borrowed trunks and still following Jason as his faithful puppy.

Chuckling at seeing my boys' happiness, I went back to our living room and switched on my computer. First, I sorted the few real emails from all the unsolicited spam. Then, I went on writing my first manuscript about meeting my burnt little Gypsy Prince and giving him his old room back. Soon, I totally disappeared into my remembrances, and forgot everything else around me.

Half an hour later, a dripping wet John entered our living room, came up to me, and asked me:

"Dad, can we... oops... sorry, may we use your water hose again? Our pool is already halfway emptied, but we don't want to use too much water because my father... err, sorry, I mean Eric, always complained about tap water costing too much money..."

"Well, according to your little brother, I am rich, because I can always use my 'inexhaustible' credit card! Therefore, don't worry any more about tap water costing too much money, and just have fun with the spouting water hose."

"Thank you very much, Dad; and also thank you very much for buying such a splendid inflatable swimming pool."

While John hugged me, he also pressed his dripping wet body against mine. Then, he hurried back to our swimming pool, chuckling at leaving me soaking wet... Grrrrr! I still love that boy with all my heart; but, now and then, I could MURDER him!

Then, Carl appeared in the doorway, and timidly asked me:

"Sir? May I use your bathroom, please?"

Chuckling at seeing Carl clamping his wet groin, I teased him:

"What will happen to my floor if I say 'no'?"

Much to my surprise, Carl only stared at me with his dark orbs, looking puzzled. Obviously, this still shy and timid looking young adolescent wasn't used to being teased by grownups like me...

Smiling at seeing Carl's obvious uneasiness, I asked him:

"I suppose you are not used to grownups like me teasing you?"

As if trying to grasp the hidden meaning behind my words, Carl only shook his head, while his hands pressed even more against his groin and he involuntarily started to fidget. A tiny pool of swimming water was already forming under his wet feet...

Therefore, I told my more and more anxious looking new boy:

"Please hurry to the bathroom in our hallway, before you start wetting my floor even more!"

Still looking puzzled, Carl went to our bathroom, where I heard him lock the door first, before he finally let go and sighed in relief. Because I wanted to help Carl get rid of his excessive shyness, I too went to our hallway and waited until Carl showed up again.

Then, I pulled him into an enormous bear hug and assured him:

"Carl, from now on, this is YOUR home, and you never have to ask permission to use the bathroom or anything else in our house."

Slowly, Carl's eyes started to fill with tears, while his wet body trustfully leaned into my stomach and he mumbled:

"I am still afraid this is only a beautiful dream... After I wake up, I will again feel frightened and hungry and sadder than ever..."

"Carl, I assure you this is NOT a dream, and I am not Mister John Dragon! From now on, you will always eat plenty of healthy food; trust me on that! I am also planning to fatten you up some. Now, go back to your new family and have fun in OUR swimming pool."

Carl's eyes showed a glimmer of hope, while he mumbled:

"I really hope you are right, and that my beautiful dream will never come to an end..."

Slowly, Carl sauntered back to our over-crowded swimming pool and his still happily playing and shouting new family.

22. A Moby Dick is a whale; BJ apologizes.

Just before six o'clock, Davy had to go home for dinner, but he promised to return the next morning. Jason and Nicky also went home, because BJ would be waiting for them around this time to eat together. They hugged Carl, told him to be a good boy and always listen to Big Harry, and promised they would be back early in the morning. Thomas and Chrissy followed Jason and Nicky and went home too. One by one, all the neighborhood kids left our pool, hugged and kissed me, and trotted home after promising to be back tomorrow.

My little chef wanted to cook a real healthy dinner, telling us we needed a proper meal after all the junk food that we had eaten earlier. Good boy! While winking at Carl, my little soul mate added:

"Especially skinny Carl needs to grow quite a lot more meat onto his scrawny bones!"

Chuckling at my boy's antics, 'skinny Carl' bumped into him on purpose and ruffled his unruly blond hair, before he followed us into our house. In our kitchen, my little chef explained what he expected from us, to help him prepare our healthy dinner. He climbed onto a folding chair to overlook our preparations, and suddenly turned into a really critical chef, while admonishing us:

"No, Dad, don't slice those potatoes too thin, make fatter slices! Carl, don't smash those lettuce leaves, but be more careful and drape them neatly onto our plates. John, you can now put your frittered onions into a frying pan and add some more butter and a pinch of salt, to brown them. Can I now leave you alone for a few seconds, to get some spicy plants from my own herbs garden?"

After again looking critically at our ministrations, our little chef jumped off his chair and hasted into our backyard. Soon, he returned, carrying a couple of herbs and a few colored pods. First, he washed and sliced them, with the help of my old cutting board and a sharp kitchen knife. Then, he dragged his folding chair towards our electric cook top, and put his herbs mixture into John's sizzling onions.

After tasting his sizzling mixture critically, he ordered:

"John, could you please get me the olive oil from the left cabinet above the sideboard? And, bring the pepper with you. Oh, and I forgot the curry. Dad, could you please hand me your sliced potatoes now? And John, I also want to add a few more drops of hot sauce."

While our little cookie baked the potatoes, a heavenly scent started to fill our kitchen. Soon, he jumped off his folding chair and draped his potatoes next to the already readied lettuce on our plates. Carl added some more frittered herbs and a little bit of mayonnaise onto each plate, while John put some grated cheese onto the baked potatoes and helpfully put all the plates in front of our chairs.

Again, our little cooking magician turned out to be an absolutely superior chef! This time, our dinner tasted slightly outlandish, with a nice aftertaste as if we could be sitting around a glowing campfire. Especially Carl nearly swallowed his own fingers, now that he could eat as much healthy food as he wanted! Chuckling at seeing Carl's over-enthusiastic eating frenzy, our little cookie teased him:

"Carl, even after eating all that healthy food, you still have to grow a LOT more meat onto your scrawny bones!"

A happy looking Carl just smiled back at his teasing little friend, while he gleefully took another helping of heavenly tasting lettuce and baked potato. Fortunately, his former shyness started to disappear. After we had finished our healthy meal, we all licked our fingers clean and scraped our plates for the very last tasty crumbs. Again, we complimented our little chef with his amazing cooking skills.

Our little chef bowed at our compliments, but he also explained:

"I've tried to copy the taste of our regular Gypsy food; but something is missing and I don't know what it is. Dad, do you remember the colored spices they served in that Chinese golden palace; and could you please try to purchase some of their stringy green snot?"

Carl stared at our little cookie with a confused face, and asked:

"You really were in a 'Chinese golden palace', where they served 'stringy green snot'? Didn't that taste yucky?"

At seeing Carl's suddenly disapproving face, all of us started to bellow with laughter; which left Carl even more confused. Nearly hiccupping from the unexpected fun, John started to cough and had to drink a lot of water to free his throat. While John grabbed a tissue to dry his suddenly teary eyes, he snickered:

Chapter 22. I was 'Gypsy Monarch Harold the Great'.

"I suppose that those Chinese cooks purchase their stringy snot from a green dragon with the flu..."

Looking bewildered, Carl uttered from the bottom of his heart:

"Now that I know this, I will never again eat Chinese food!"

Still laughing, we told Carl about our visit to Harry's 'Chinese golden palace', where he first tried out all their different spices, and then cleverly conjured all sorts of nicely tasting flavors for us.

At last, we did the dishes, tidied the kitchen, and went to our couch in our living room. My little soul mate crawled onto my lap as usual, while John pushed his head under my left arm, and Carl sat down at my right side. Heaving a deep sigh of content, Carl cuddled up against my side, while he mumbled:

"I really hope this beautiful dream will NEVER come to an end."

Turning towards Carl, my little soul mate assured him:

"You can be absolutely sure of that; and I really hope you will join us for a looooong time."

Obviously, my 'fifth boy' had found his own place in my steadily growing family! Or, could Carl be my 'sixth boy', if I counted Jason as number five?

Sitting on our couch and basking in each other's close togetherness, we had some small talk; until all three boys started to yawn. Of course, they felt tired after going through such an emotional day and being outside for several hours. Their sleepiness also made me think about our sleeping arrangements! Of course, my little soul mate could sleep next to me in my double waterbed, so that Carl could sleep in my boy's folding bed as a temporary solution. But, what would happen if Jason wanted to sleep here too, to be close to Carl; and both Nicky and Davy wanted to sleep over as well?

Trying to tease my clever deep thinker some more, I asked him:

"Harry, did you already think of some workable solution about where everybody will sleep from now on?"

Immediately, my clever little soul mate responded:

"Of course, Dad! I am only a small boy and therefore can easily sleep next to you in your double bed, and Nicky can join us when he sleeps here. That way, Carl can use my old bedroom and invite Jason for a sleepover if he wishes; and John can keep his own bedroom and invite Davy for a sleepover if he wishes. When are we going to buy double bunk beds, so that everybody can have their own beds? Or, shall we now buy a bigger house? Okay, let's switch on our computer and start looking for a bigger house on the Internet..."

My little soul mate hopped off my lap and raced to our computer, on his way beckoning his friends to follow him. Of course, I had to disappoint them, by telling my boy to wait until our steadily growing household had settled down some more... Reluctantly, my boy returned to our couch, where he punched Carl's arm and told him:

"Come on, Carl, let's go upstairs and prepare my old bedroom for your first night here!"

For several seconds, Carl only stared at my boy and at me, with again some fear in his dark eyes. Obviously, all these new things were still going too fast for my still shy and uneasy new boy. Then, with a guilty sounding voice, Carl mumbled under his breath:

"I don't have any fresh clothes here, so I think I will have to go back to my orphanage and sleep there in my own dark room. Please, sir, may I come back tomorrow, to eat Harry's healthy food and play in your swimming pool again?"

After suddenly forcefully punching Carl's arm, my little soul mate sternly admonished his 'new brother':

"Carl, don't be silly! You are LIVING here now; and I am sure that Dad will take you downtown tomorrow and buy you all the clothes that you need, and he pays for everything with his credit card from his bank. Now, please, try to forget about your abusive past and start living more in the here and now, okay?"

Very hesitatingly and still looking at his feet, Carl responded:

"I am still not sure... Am I REALLY going to live in your house and have my own room here and some new clothes? I still cannot believe that my beautiful dream is really true..."

This time, my little therapist didn't answer any more, but just took Carl's hand and dragged him towards the stairs, while he asked me:

"Dad, may we take our showers now? I want to wash up thoroughly, after swimming in all that diluted sweat and stinky urine..."

Chuckling at seeing my boy's broadly smiling face, I responded:

"Thanks to our electric water filter, I am sure that our swimming water is still crystal clear! And, of course, you may take your showers now. Do I have to help you with the too difficult warm water tap?"

"DAAAD! Again, you are NOT funny! Come on, John and Carl, let's go upstairs and take our showers now."

Chuckling, John left my side, hopped off our couch, and asked me to get them a couple of dry towels. Walking together and bumping into each other on purpose, John and I followed Carl and little Harry up the stairs and straight into our shower room.

Inside our shower enclosure, little Harry first showed Carl the 'too difficult' thermostatic water tap, and then told him:

"John and I wanted to shower together, but Dad didn't want to join us because he was afraid that some people might think he tried to do 'improper sex things' with us. Then, John asked Dad to adjust our 'too difficult' water tap, while I blocked Dad's memory so that he didn't recognize thermostatic taps any more. While Dad looked at the 'strange thing', John and I quickly shucked our clothes and I put the warm water on. Since then, Dad isn't shy any more, and he often washes our hair for us and dries us after we leave our shower."

Suddenly looking baffled, Carl stared at my little Shaman with wide-open mouth, until he exclaimed:

"You blocked your Dad's memory so that he couldn't recognize thermostatic water taps any more? But, then, who the heck are you? Are you sort of a sorcerer, or a powerful magician? A few minutes ago, I suddenly thought I heard your low baritone voice in my inside telling me not to behave silly, but I wasn't sure and thought I could be listening to my own imagination..."

"During several of my past lives, I have been a powerful Shaman and Cosmic Mage, and I can still use my abilities from those lives; although, most of the time, Dad's own Shaman aura is too strong for me to penetrate. However, I am learning fast..."

"Wow, I've never thought you could be a Shaman or a Mage... Are you doing the same things as in those 'Harry Potter' films?"

"Well, 'Harry Potter' is only a product of someone's imagination; but I really am a Shaman and a Cosmic Mage, just like Dad is one!"

In the meantime, I had fetched three dry towels from our hallway closet and put them onto our chest of drawers. While talking to Carl, John and little Harry had already shucked their clothes, stepped into our shower enclosure, and turned the thermostatic water tap on.

With suddenly baited breath, Carl stared at my boy's severely burnt body, now looking even paler than he had been before! While desperately trying not to stare too much, Carl stammered:

"Sorry, Harry, I didn't know you are THAT burnt. It's all over your body, and even the skin on your pee-pee is burnt..."

Smiling at seeing Carl's sudden distress, my boy answered:

"Don't sweat it! Soon, I will get a brand new face, a smooth skin on my body, and a much nicer looking 'pee-pee'! By the way, real boys call it a 'pecker' or a 'dick', and its first name is 'Moby'... Could you now undress a bit faster, or do we have to help you?"

Still looking confused, Carl undressed faster, but he also asked:

"Why are you calling your pee-pee a 'Moby'? I don't understand it. Is it a 'Moby Pecker' or a 'Moby Dick'? Now, wait a moment, wasn't 'Moby Dick' a story about a whale? Yes, of course! Now, that sounds funny, having a pee-pee as a whale..."

At that moment, our melodious doorbell sounded, and I left my bantering boys and hasted downstairs to open our front door.

Outside the door, a huge giant with an enormous mustache waited for me to let him in. Behind the giant's back, two youngsters were trying to hide themselves, while chuckling and pushing each other. Wow, this evening, everybody seemed to be in an excellent mood!

Partaking in their game, I told the broadly smiling giant:

"Come in, BJ! It's nice to see you again, but where are your sons?"

Smilingly, BJ only shrugged his shoulders, while he ducked his head to be able to pass below the doorpost. Teasingly, I started to close the door, pretending not to see Jason and Nicky who still tried to hide behind their broadly smiling Dad...

"Hey!" Nicky shouted, while trying to slip past me.

Trying to tease my little sunshine, I blocked his way and told him:

"Sorry Nicker, you are too late because we are already full!"

"You really are a silly Pop!" Nicky immediately decided, while showing me a big smile on his brightly beaming face. Then, he just ducked under my blocking arm and nimbly slipped inside.

Of course, Jason tried to follow his little brother, but he was too slow and bumped into me. Well, being a 'silly Pop' or not, this 'rude' behavior had to be corrected! Therefore, I grabbed Jason's arm and turned him around to let him face me.

Trying to look as stern as possible, I admonished Jason:

"Little boss, you seem to be extremely exuberant tonight! Please, always remember who the REAL boss is."

"The REAL boss is my Dad, of course! Who else do you think? Dad, Big Harry is trying to harass me..."

Chuckling, BJ turned around and showed me his muscular arms, while trying to look threatening. Pretending to be afraid of the giant, I backed away a few steps and lifted both hands as in surrender.

While BJ started to laugh, Jason threw his arms around my waist, offered me a quick cuddle, and chuckled:

"Now, you know who the REAL boss is! Never forget that!"

"Are you absolutely sure? Just wait, until your Dad is NOT around you to protect you by showing his strong arms."

"Promises, promises..."

Happily, I ruffled Jason's white hair, while Nicky quickly joined his big brother and leaned into me to get his own cuddle. Wow; this evening, both boys certainly were in an excellent mood!

Together, we went to our living room, with Nicky leaning into me and Jason going up front. Immediately when Jason entered the room, he started to look around for his friend. With sudden panic in his eyes, he quickly turned around and stormed to our kitchen. From there, we heard him open the door to our backyard, to look in our now empty swimming pool. Within a few seconds, Jason raced back into our living room, almost crying while shouting:

"Pop, where is Carl? Has Mister John Dragon taken him away?"

Feeling a bit surprised at seeing Jason's sudden panic, I tried to reassure him by quickly telling him:

"Don't panic, Jason; because nobody will take Carl away from you or from me, not even our old friend Mister John Dragon! Your friend is only upstairs and taking a shower with Harry and John. Do you want to join them? Just go upstairs and shuck your clothes."

"Me too!" Nicky shouted, while already undoing his shirt.

Together, both brothers stormed up the stairs, nearly tripping over their own feet in their hurry to be there first. Both BJ and I chuckled at their happy antics, while BJ carefully lowered himself into one of my easy chairs. First, he waited until his pain had subsided. Then, looking at me with tears from happiness in his eyes, he told me:

"Thank you so much, Harry, for helping my sons and me! You gave me my children back, and I am very grateful that my boys and I met you, and that I listened to your advice. For the first time in all those years, Jason and I had a real talk! Normally, I am always too impatient and immediately start shouting; but, this time, I decided to keep my big mouth shut and only listen to what my son has to say. This really worked; and, finally, Jason opened up to me and told me a couple of private things about Carl and himself. He told me how Carl and he met at school and loved each other at first sight. He also told me how they always had to hide their true feelings from me and had to be very careful, because they were afraid of my homo hate and thought I would try to murder them once I knew about their true feelings. I never knew that they could be this afraid of me..."

BJ winced from sudden pain, and first needed a couple of seconds for himself before he went on:

"Now, I know that they were right. I DID think that love between two males could be nothing more than only some sexual aberration that had to be rooted out thoroughly. For the first time in all those years, I looked into Jason's eyes, and I was very surprised to see REAL love in them, instead of only some perverted sexual whim. Then, Nicky stepped next to Jason and told me he loves that burnt little Gypsy boy, Harry, in the same way! Again, I felt very surprised to see the same real love in the eyes of my youngest son. At that moment, I realized that I had to make an important decision. Either I could go on being a homo hater and lose my sons; or I had to accept that I was WRONG in my assumptions. I assure you this was a very difficult decision, probably due to my 'manly' upbringing and to all those contorted stories about 'filthy fags' and 'perverted homos' the 'normal' people around us are dishing up all the time..."

Aad Aandacht is a Dutch psychotherapist who loves writing 'books with a message'

Chapter 22. I was 'Gypsy Monarch Harold the Great'.

Unexpectedly, BJ started to cry, while he buried his face in his enormous hands! Without thinking, I rose from my chair and draped my arms around BJ's shoulders, without thinking about any possible consequences. For a split second, BJ's body went rigid; but then, he let himself go and put his enormous hands onto my hugging arms. He now really started to cry his heart out, while holding onto my arms with all of his might and bruising my arm muscles in the process.

In between his heavy sobs, BJ went on and stuttered:

"Now, I've decided to LOVE my two sons, instead of trying to change them into what they obviously are not. For the first time in all those years, both Nicky and Jason embraced and kissed me; and that felt so good! I never thought they would still love me, after all those years that I bullied them and made their lives a living hell by my condemning behavior... Now, I can see how shortsighted I have been. Without knowing what I did, I have messed up everything for them that was worth living for. I have ruined Jason's life, and I have probably ruined Carl's life as well. Only, it is now too late to change, because I will die within a few months. However, I will still try to make it up to Jason and to Carl as much as I can. I only hope they will forgive me for what I have done to them, eventually..."

Slowly, BJ released my bruised arms, still sobbing and bashfully looking at his feet. While rubbing my sore arms, I went to the kitchen to get him a glass of water and some tissues. With a thankful smile and another heavy sob, BJ accepted the tissues and gulped the water.

This time, I started to tell BJ about my own experiences, both as a psychotherapist and as a human being. I told him about my own conception of real love, love and sexuality, love between two males or between two females, and the so despised 'inter-generational love'. I made him think about loving everybody without any restrictions, which could or could not be followed by sex; and about the bad side of forced sex without mutual consent, which could ruin lives.

I tried to let BJ see that love and sex are totally different things, and the one doesn't necessarily have anything to do with the other. There is 'paid sex', but 'paid love' is impossible! I also asked BJ to think about what would be the difference between one kind of love and the other kind of love, as long as sex isn't involved. Everybody can love a man, a woman, a child, an animal, or Brussels sprouts...

I also asked BJ what might be the difference between playing with yourself, playing with each other, or using a vibrator; because the feelings of relief are the same. When it FEELS good, it IS good! Never listen to other people's social prejudices or crazy beliefs, but only listen to what your Own Heart tells you. Your Own Heart is connected to your Cosmic Inner Knowing and thus to our Supreme Being, and it always tells the truth and only the truth.

After I ended my monologue, BJ looked up at me and sighed:

"I have been so prejudiced... How can I make this up to Jason?"

"Just be yourself, let Jason be himself, and love him with all your heart. All you have to do is listen to what your Own Heart tells you."

"Thank you again, Big Harry, for helping me like this; and, from now on, I will try to better my life! I also want to apologize to Jason's friend and tell him he is still welcome in my house. Is Carl still here? Please, could I meet Carl and talk to him? Or, do you want me to go home now and perhaps come back later?"

"Of course, you can talk to Carl now! I suppose he is still upstairs, in our shower stall, probably having lots of fun with the other boys. Shall we go upstairs and take a look at what they are doing?"

BJ nodded, and dragged himself out of his chair, again groaning from the pain. Walking slowly, we went upstairs, where we opened the door to our shower stall and slowly stepped inside...

23. BJ makes up with Jason and with Carl.

In our shower stall, John had again constructed one of his clever inventions. Using a piece of wire, he had attached our showerhead upside down onto its cradle. Pointing upwards, it now let its warm water form a nice rain shower. All five boys sat in a wide circle and enjoyed the warm rain. Little Harry and Nicky had their arms around each other's shoulders, sitting closely together. Jason and Carl were totally entangled into each other, with blissful smiles on their faces and now and then kissing. John seemed to be totally content with the obvious love of his four happy friends, and looked at them with proud eyes full of bliss and unconditional love.

After a few seconds, Nicky looked up and saw his Dad and me, standing in the doorway while looking at them. Involuntarily, his body stiffened, while he stared at his Dad with sudden fear in his eyes. However, BJ didn't say a word, but only smiled and winked at his suddenly trembling youngest son. Looking relieved, Nicky winked back at his Dad while he slowly relaxed. My little Shaman seemed to feel Nicky's reaction, because he too looked up. He saw BJ winking at Nicky, and started to smile happily while winking back at BJ. Then, he held Nicky even closer, as if demonstrating this was HIS friend and nobody had done anything 'improper'...

Then, Carl looked up; and suddenly saw BJ and me, standing in the open door and looking at him. Immediately, he stumbled upright while desperately trying to untangle from Jason's arms. Pushing Jason against a wall in his sudden hurry to get away, Carl screamed:

"Please, don't throw me down the stairs again! We have done nothing bad. Honestly..."

In his tremendous hurry to get away, Carl stumbled over John's outstretched legs. Desperately, he tried to dive past BJ and me, while holding both arms protectively over his head, as if trying to protect himself from our attacks. Fortunately, I could catch Carl in my arms before he escaped, raced outside, and again alarmed our 'disturbed lady'. For a moment, Carl tried to wrestle free from my arms, still staring at BJ with horror in his eyes. Then, he hesitantly slumped down into my enveloping arms and started to cry his heart out.

Trembling all over and sounding like a small child, Carl wailed:

"I KNEW my beautiful dream would come to an end. Only, please sir, don't let Jason's father kick me down the stairs again..."

Feeling shocked at seeing Carl's frightened reaction, I pulled him even closer to my chest and started to assure him:

"Please Carl, relax, and listen carefully. You are NOT in trouble, and you didn't do anything wrong by loving Jason! Besides, you are now MY boy, and nobody else will ever kick you down MY stairs. Please trust me that you are totally safe with me..."

Despite my reassuring words, Carl kept on shuddering from fear, while glaring at the enormous giant next to us... Looking bewildered, BJ stared at Jason's loudly sobbing friend in my arms as if he didn't comprehend what was happening. Hesitantly, he stuck out his hand towards Carl, as if apologizing and trying to make up for what he had done to Jason's friend... Only, Carl cringed at seeing BJ's enormous shovel, and immediately tried to get away again!

Fighting to get free of my still constricting arms, Carl sobbed:

"Please, sir, don't kick me down the stairs again! Jason and I have done nothing bad and we only sat together. And, please Big Harry, don't let Jason's father send me back to my room in that orphanage. You've already promised I could stay here. Please..."

Obviously, Carl still felt too frightened of the enormous giant next to him to calm down and listen to my reassuring words. How, for heaven's sake, should I go on from here? Again, I tried to reassure a still fighting Carl, by promising:

"Please, Carl, trust me that Jason's father will NOT kick you down the stairs. You are MY boy now, and I will NOT send you back to Mister John Dragon. If necessary, I will protect you with my own life, cross my heart and hope to die! Do you believe me now?"

Still looking very unsure, Carl slowly started to understand that he wasn't in direct danger. Hesitantly, he gave up fighting and slumped down in my still enveloping arms. Tentatively, I tried to release my death grip on him; and, fortunately, Carl didn't try to get away any more. However, he still glared at BJ, and involuntarily shuddered again at any unexpected movement from the enormous giant.

Again, I felt powerless and almost impotent. How could I ever help these two human beings getting to trust each other?

Chapter 22. I was 'Gypsy Monarch Harold the Great'.

Stealthily, I looked at John. At that same moment, my inside was sure I could trust my young friend to do exactly the right things! In him, I could clearly see an already wakening Leader, and I was sure that John would take over from here and talk to Carl and Jason, the very moment BJ would be out of sight. John would be able to reassure Carl, explain what had happened to BJ, and tell Carl he could trust Jason's father from now on! Now feeling much happier, I gently pushed BJ out of our shower room and into our hallway.

Slowly, BJ and I ambled downstairs and into my living room. With some difficulty, BJ sat down in one of my easy chairs, again wincing from the pain; while I slumped down on my regular spot in the middle of our couch. Of course, I still had no idea how I could handle this extremely difficult situation. How would I ever be able to bring BJ and Carl together and help them understand each other?

Although I knew I could rely on John; ultimately, my young friend was only thirteen years old, and I could barely expect such a young boy to do the regular work of a well-trained psychotherapist. Only, what else could I do? Did I have another choice?

BJ stared at me with pain in his eyes, until he asked:

"Is Carl afraid of me because I kicked him down the stairs and threw him his clothes, around a year ago? Up to now, I never realized how much impact my big mouth and my bullying would have on such a vulnerable young boy. Now, I feel terribly ashamed of my rude behavior. What the heck have I done to Carl and to Jason, and how can they ever forgive me for my cruelty..."

Because I couldn't find any reasonable answers, I first went to my kitchen to brew two fresh cups of coffee. Feeling a sudden need to clear my mind and ventilate my entangled thoughts, I opened the backdoor and stepped outside. Happily, I inhaled lots of fresh evening air, while trying to free my inside from its emotional cobwebs. Now feeling much better, I returned into my kitchen, brewed two cups of coffee, and took them to our living room. Fortunately, BJ seemed to have pulled himself together. Looking grateful, he thanked me for all my help and started to sip his coffee.

The door opened, and five timid looking boys hesitatingly entered our living room. As usual, my little soul mate crawled onto my lap, offered me a kiss, and melted into me. Then, Nicky approached us and looked at his friend and me with pleading eyes...

Immediately, my boy scooted to one side, and happily shared my lap with his friend! From under his eyelashes, Nicky peeked at his Dad to gauge his reaction. Fortunately, BJ only smiled at his youngest son, and that seemed to reassure my little sunshine. He winked at his smiling Dad, and his Dad winked back at him.

John sat down at my left side and leaned into me as usual; while Jason slumped down at my right side and beckoned Carl to join him. Only, Carl still looked very uneasy, and involuntarily shuddered again at seeing BJ. Trying to stay as far away from the giant at he could, he wavered towards our couch and sat down next to Jason. Although he still trembled all over, he let himself pull into Jason's embrace...

Much to my relief, BJ did nothing at all, and only smiled at his oldest son and his still trembling 'boyfriend'. Stealthily, I looked at John; and my young friend looked back at me with lots of victory and triumph in his eyes! Again, we understood each other without words. John HAD talked to his friends; but, now, it was MY turn to help Carl with his still remaining fears.

In the meantime, BJ had started to fidget in his chair, obviously wanting to say something. First, he coughed a few times, to get their attention, while looking at Carl and at Jason. Then, he pulled himself together, and bashfully started to explain:

"Carl, I had wanted to talk to you from man to man, but I didn't know how to do that. I suppose I am still too used to swearing and scolding, instead of talking about my feelings. Yet, please, listen to me. I swear that you don't have to be afraid of me any more, because both Big Harry and little Harry have helped me to see everything in a totally different light! Up to now, I thought that homosexuality was a sexual abnormality, and anomalies like those had to be rooted out thoroughly. Therefore, I felt severely shocked when I discovered that one of my own sons could be such a sinner. That is the main reason why I kicked you out of my house and Jason into a hospital. Now that I have changed my mind, I feel very sorry for having ruined both your life and the life of my oldest son, and I am utterly ashamed of my rude behavior and my way too big mouth..."

BJ first dried his again teary eyes, before he went on:

"Yesterday, Nicky's new friend, Harry, showed up in my house; and I felt very surprised at hearing how that small boy talked about his adopted Dad with so much love and reverence. Then, I found out that my own son, Nicky, already adores Big Harry and even wants

Aad Aandacht is a Dutch psychotherapist who loves writing 'books with a message'

him to be his second Dad or his Grandpa! At first, I felt a bit jealous, because my own sons never talk to me about their feelings or kiss me. However, after I had another talk with Big Harry, I realized this is my own fault, because I never showed my own love to my sons. Now, I realize how terribly wrong I have been. I have ruined your friendship with Jason, and I don't know how to make it up to you. For a moment, I thought that apologizing for my behavior would be enough; but, of course, I was wrong again, because I simply cannot wipe out a full year of misery and loneliness. I can only hope that, eventually, you will forgive me for what I did to you and to Jason... From now on, I will do everything I can to make you feel more comfortable around me. As you probably know, I will die within a few months, so I don't have much time left. Therefore, I only ask you to have consideration with me; and I want to ask Jason to let me try to be a real Daddy from now on. In the meantime, feel free to be together and love each other, whenever you want and as often as you wish..."

Silence fell over our living room, while BJ slumped back in his chair with a contorted face, obviously from both too much pain and too much shame. John left his cozy place next to me and went to our kitchen, probably to fetch a glass of water for BJ.

Suddenly, Jason jumped up and threw himself onto his Dad's lap! While desperately embracing his Dad, Jason cried:

"Please Dad; forgive me for causing you so much pain! I still love you very much, and I don't want you to die now that both Carl and I need you again. Please Daddy, could you try to live a bit longer for me? Only, don't ask me to abandon Carl, because I need both you and him, and I want you to see me grow up together with Carl and be happy with our mutual love and friendship."

Awkwardly, BJ draped his muscled arms around his still sobbing oldest son and pulled him closer to his chest. Father and son started to mingle their tears, while, at the same time, trying to comfort and support each other. Then, Nicky left my lap and worked himself into their embrace, while Jason made some more room for his little brother, and BJ folded his muscular arms around his two sons.

Nicky started to cry too, while he sobbingly asked his Dad:

"Please Daddy, I need you too, and I want you to live longer for me too! Please, don't abandon Jason and me, by dying too soon..."

For several seconds, I enjoyed the lovable sight of BJ starting to reconnect to his two sons. Again, everything had turned out for the best, and it was now clear to me that BJ had really changed!

Soon, my little Shaman started to help them, and I could clearly feel my boy's powerful love and happiness radiating towards BJ and his sons. John leaned into my left side while heaving deep sighs of happiness and furtively wiping his teary eyes. Fortunately, Carl had stopped trembling. He even scooted a bit closer and leaned into my right side, while he mumbled, loud enough for us to hear it:

"This new dream is even more beautiful; and I really hope I will never wake up from it."

From my lap, my little soul mate teasingly told Carl:

"Carl, you are a real sleepyhead; and that at your age..."

Suddenly, BJ tried to put in a little joke, and grinned:

"By the looks of it, we are one big family of crybaby's!"

Trying to joke back at BJ, my little soul mate declared:

"We've bought a fresh packet of tissues, so be our guest!"

All of us started to laugh; and that broke our remaining tension, while my chuckling boy hopped off my lap, took our packet from the table, and dealt tissues round at everybody who wanted one.

Suddenly, BJ turned towards Carl, and asked him:

"Carl, I know that your parents died in a car accident, so that you now are an orphan without any relatives. Therefore, I would like to take you into my house as my third son, and I also want to try to be your new Dad. That is, if you are willing to give me a chance..."

Looking very surprised, Carl didn't seem to know what to think of BJ's unexpected request... Again, things were going way too fast for this wary young boy who still needed a lot more time before he really could trust other grownups, and especially BJ! For a long time, Carl only looked at his wiggling feet, until he finally sat more upright.

Still thinking and pondering, Carl hesitatingly asked me:

"Big Harry? I thought that YOU would take me into your house and adopt me, so that I can be with you and Jason all the time?"

Chapter 22. I was 'Gypsy Monarch Harold the Great'.

Oh my... What should I do now, to help Carl with his dilemma? Trying to sound as reassuringly as possible, I responded:

"Of course, I was only suggesting it; and it is still up to you to decide where you are going to live from now on. Please, give yourself lots of time to make up your mind; and remember that nobody will ever resent your decision, because we all love you very much and we want you to do only what feels best for you!"

While Carl still pondered, BJ slowly rose from his chair, groaning with pain. For a couple of seconds, he stared at my boys and me who were again sitting together on our couch, and a faint smile crossed his lips as if he very much enjoyed the happy sight. While extending his enormous shovel towards my boys and me, he smiled:

"Big Harry, I am jealous of you and your happy family! Thank you very much for listening to me and helping me again. Now, I want to go home to take my medicine. Could both Jason and Nicky spend the night here; and could you please send them home tomorrow to do a couple of necessary chores for me? That is, if they want to..."

Of course, both Jason and Nicky wanted to spend the night at my house, and they immediately nodded enthusiastically! Together, they walked their Dad to our front door and waved him out. After they returned into our living room, we sat together on our couch and had a long and deep talk, because we felt very surprised about this sudden and absolutely positive change in BJ's attitude!

Jason thanked me for giving him his Dad back, and told me:

"From when I was still little, I remember having a real Daddy who always cuddled little Nicky and me and often played with us, until Mom suddenly died and Dad started to drink. Then, things became hell, after Dad caught Carl and me in our shower stall and went berserk. Fortunately, Dad has now stopped drinking, and he also tries to better his life. Thank you very much again, Pop, for helping us and giving my old Dad back to Nicky and me. Tonight was the first time I could sense that happy feeling again, of having a real Daddy..."

Carl leaned into his friend for support, while he confessed:

"I never had a real Daddy; and I always was afraid of my father because he tried to make a 'real man' out of me. He never cuddled or pampered me, but only pushed me to be a sportsman. After Jason's father kicked me down his stairs and phoned us, my father started to ignore me, and that hurt even more! A few days later, he sold our house and drove to another town. Because my father was still angry and drove too fast in the rain, our car slipped and hit the banks..."

Carl took a tissue and wiped his teary eyes, before he went on:

"Both my father and my mother died in our wrecked car, but I was catapulted out of a window and that saved my life. After being in a foster home for a few months, they betrayed me and took me to that orphanage. I wrote a letter to Jason, but Mister John Dragon found it and tore it apart. From then on, my life was worse than hell! Mister Dragon separated me from the other kids and locked me up in a dark room, because I might infect the others with my 'sick homosexuality'. Many times, I thought about committing suicide, but I was too scared and couldn't do it. Now, my hell seems to be over; but I still have to get accustomed to my new life, and that is difficult for me! I think I will need a lot more time to get used to my sudden freedom, and to all the healthy food that you and Harry are trying to pump into me."

Everybody started to laugh, even Carl himself who clearly felt a bit surprised about his own radiant plea! Sitting together on our couch, we had some more small talk, until it was time to go to bed and we had to decide about our sleeping arrangements. Of course, Jason and Carl wanted to sleep together in Carl's new room, and they assured me that one single bed would be enough for them. Teasingly, John told them not to wear out their love in one night. Of course, my little soul mate and his inseparable friend wanted to sleep together in John's bed, so that John had no choice but to sleep next to me in my double waterbed. Feeling satisfied with our arrangements, we went upstairs, shucked our clothes, showered, and dived into our appointed beds.

The next morning, I woke up, turned around, and stared in silence at my softly snoring thirteen-year-old friend next to me. In his sleep, John looked peaceful and totally at ease, with an expression of pure bliss on his serene face. Yes, I absolutely loved my young friend with all my heart, mind and soul! Careful not to wake him up, I put my nose in his curly hair and inhaled the by now well-known scent of my dear friend. His bodily aroma differed quite a lot from my little soul mate's, being much stronger and more 'pubertal'. Clearly, John was lingering on the verge of becoming a young adolescent.

Then, I heard two muffled voices that came from our hallway. The door handle moved slowly, and the door opened just a little bit. Two pairs of mischievous eyes peeked through the small crack, obviously trying to find out if John and I were still sleeping. When they saw I was awake, two very happy looking little savages stormed into my bedroom and shouted at the tops of their lungs:

"Attack of the Dangerous Gypsy!"

"Attack of the Nickering Dragon!"

Chuckling, both boys launched themselves onto my waterbed, making it wobble vigorously. John woke up to the commotion; but he immediately dived back under our blankets, pulled them over his head, and groaned with a frustrated voice:

"Here are our toddlers! Couldn't you just leave us alone? Dad and I want to get some more beauty sleep..."

Of course, our 'toddlers' didn't listen to John's complaints. They only crawled under out blankets, pushed John aside, and started to compete for the best place on my stomach! I got a big smack on my left cheek and a wet kiss on my right cheek, while two pairs of boyish arms tried to strangle my neck and two pairs of small legs tried to play octopus with my much taller and certainly hairier legs. A happy sounding baritone voice and an utterly boyish voice told me:

"Morning, Dad! I thought you would never wake up."

"Morning, Pop, what do you have for breakfast?"

Trying to tease my two cuddling imps, I complained:

"I thought you would make me breakfast in bed?"

My complaint made my little soul mate explain to Nicky:

"Today it's John's turn to go downstairs and bring us breakfast in bed; because, last time, I did it!"

Still groaning, John tried to disappear completely, by pulling our blankets around his body and over his head, in a futile attempt to get some more sleep. However, my two inseparable friends only laughed at John's groaned complaints, while tickling his ribs in their combined attempts to make him wake up completely.

Then, my door opened again, and two other pairs of hesitant eyes peeked through the crack. When they saw that I already had a lot of company, the door opened all the way, and John and Carl hesitatingly entered our bedroom. Chuckling at seeing the unexpected commotion in my double waterbed, they happily greeted us:

"Good morning, everybody! Pop, may we please come in?"

Both boys hesitantly approached our double waterbed, until I decided to tease them and asked them:

"Please, Jason and Carl, could you help me fight these 'Dangerous Gypsies' and 'Nickering Dragons'?"

Jason started to laugh at seeing my exaggerating face. Then, he jumped onto our wobbling waterbed and tried to pull Nicky and little Harry off my stomach, while telling them:

"Come on, boys; leave this ancient grandpa alone. He is too old to fight for himself!"

Feeling a bit affronted at being called 'old', I first pushed little Harry and Nicky towards John, before I pulled a shocked looking Jason onto my stomach, planning to teach him a lesson. While I tried to tickly Jason's sensitive spots, I admonished him:

"WHAT did you say? Am I too old to fight for myself? That earns you a morning tickle torture!"

Immediately, Jason started to squirm, while he squealed:

"Please, Pop, stop, don't do that, because I am too ticklish! Carl, come on, DO something! You are my best friend, so you have to help me fight this dangerous ancient grandpa!"

Hesitatingly, Carl climbed onto our bed and started to help Jason. Only, now, all five boys started to tickle me wherever they could! Soon, their combined attacks became too much for me, and I panted:

"Okay, I give up! You are too strong for this 'ancient grandpa'."

"Then, say 'uncle'!"

"Uncle..."

"What? This is too easy... Dad, you really are getting old!"

Still laughing, all five boys left my stomach, to take their morning shower before they raced downstairs to fill their empty tummies.

24. A new tree house; and BJ will survive.

After we went downstairs, my little cookie quickly created another tasty and healthy breakfast. Then, Nicky and Jason had to go home to do their chores, as BJ had requested. Surprisingly, Carl suddenly decided to accompany the two brothers and help them with their chores! They put on their shoes, hugged me, and promised to be back as soon as possible, to start working on their tree house.

My house felt empty now that Jason, Carl and Nicky had left and only John and my little soul mate remained. Together, we went into our backyard, to take a breath of fresh morning air. We also looked at our still empty swimming pool. When would we have to clean it out, for the first time since we bought it? Some litter was floating on its surface, mostly fallen leaves from the surrounding trees.

Would our electric water filter really be big enough to intercept all the diluted sweat and pee? The water looked clean and didn't smell nasty, yet... Soon, the first neighborhood children would show up and shuck their clothes, again without paying at the entrance. Chuckling, I again thought about setting up a cash register in our driveway...

Then, Davy showed up in our backyard, looking relieved when he saw us. He raced towards us and jumped up at me, to let me catch his heavy frame in midair and give me a big morning kiss. Still panting from his running, my 'third son' told me:

"Morning, Dad! I was a bit afraid you could have left without me, because I rang your doorbell a couple of times but nobody answered. Then, I saw our golden van in your driveway, went to our backyard, and found you here. What are you doing?"

"Well, if we had planned to leave, we would have warned you in advance; because you are one of my boys now, and I hope I can still reckon on you to help us if necessary and whenever you can."

"Of course you can always reckon on me, Dad; and I also love you very much for treating me as if I am your own son. Shall I make your doorbell a little bit louder, so that you can hear it better?"

"No, please NOT! Since you've repaired it, I am way too happy with my decent sounding doorbell as it is now."

Chuckling at seeing my mock-shocked face, Davy let himself slide down to the ground, where he enthusiastically joined little Harry and John at Jason's stacked pile of used wood and lumber. Soon, all three boys were again discussing their tree house plans and deliberating about making another preliminary design. A couple minutes later, my three musketeers surrounded me, and John asked:

"Dad? Do you please have a tape measure and another sheet of paper? We want to make a new provisional design for a really big tree house in those three birches over there."

"I suppose you can find my old tape measure in our garage, and sheets of paper are on my desk in our living room."

Little Harry disappeared into our living room, and soon returned with a few sheets of paper and a new pencil; while John and Davy returned from our garage with my old but still usable tape measure. Enthusiastically, they started to draw the outlines of a brand new and much more complicated tree house.

Suddenly, Thomas showed up in our backyard, already clad in swimming trunks. For a few minutes, he joined his enthusiastically drawing friends, until they disagreed on something technical and started to quarrel. Showing them a long face, Thomas left his friends and went home, while complaining:

"I came here to swim, and not to build stupid tree houses."

"Okay, see you later. Bye!"

Looking disappointed, Thomas sauntered home, while my three technicians just went on with their newest tree house design as if nothing had happened. Soon, my boy raced inside again, to get more sheets of paper, a ruler, and a couple of colored pencils.

My two little neighborhood boys showed up, already clad in tiny swimming trunks, and immediately embraced me. However, my three heavily designing boys told them that, for today, they were too busy to baby-sit any young kids! With disappointed faces, both little boys sauntered home, on their way telling a couple of approaching others that our swimming pool would be closed for today...

Chuckling, I went to our kitchen to brew a fresh cup of coffee, on my way thinking I really should do something about my obvious coffee addiction, before I turned into a coffee bean...

While sipping my heavenly tasting coffee, I thought about helping my boys with their complicated tree house design, but then decided to let them work it out for themselves and make their own errors. Of course, I would always be there for them, in case they had any questions or wanted my help. However, I also relied on their technical insights, especially John and Davy with their clever inventions.

Finally, I went to our living room and resumed working on my manuscript. Soon, I disappeared into the story and again relived our adventures, while typing them into my computer. Now and then, one of my boys showed up for a quick cuddle or a hug. It felt good to be in the center of their existence, even when they were extremely busy.

Davy told me they had abandoned their too complicated tree house and now designed a much simpler version. Little Harry told me John had some very good ideas, and he was trying to draw them into his umpteenth design. John told me they were still looking for the best place in between our three birches, to support its wooden floor. Could I please start an Internet search for 'tree houses', to give them a few building hints or some more workable ideas?

Of course, I happily obliged. While my three enthusiastic boys surrounded me and looked over my shoulders, we stared in awe at all sorts of enormous wooden buildings, huge platforms, and entire castles, all of them built in between huge trees, on tropical islands, or across enormous cultivated gardens.

Staring at all those beautiful tree houses, with longing eyes, Davy thought aloud with a suddenly saddening voice:

"We will never be able to build such a beautiful castle, because we are only young kids and don't have enough allowances to purchase all that expensive wood and special equipment..."

With a naughty face, my little soul mate mused aloud:

"Perhaps Dad could lend us his 'inexhaustible' credit card, to let us buy all the necessary things that we need?"

Smiling at seeing my boy's naughty face, I rebutted:

"Well, I am sure that designing your own tree house will be a lot more satisfying than copying such a beautiful one from the Internet, even if I really would be rich enough!"

Albeit reluctantly, all three boys agreed. Soon, they offered me a quick kiss and a cuddle, and returned to our backyard to resume their planning. Feeling happy with my enthusiastic threesome, I returned to my computer and went on with my manuscript.

Around noon, three hungry looking boys surrounded me, now swaying with a colored piece of paper while telling me:

"Look Dad; Harry has made a really nice design, and we cannot wait until Jason, Carl, and Nicky are here to help us! What are they doing for so long? And, what do we eat for lunch? We are almost famished after all that heavy designing..."

Feeling impressed, I praised the much simpler design my little soul mate had sketched in many different colors. Then, we went to our kitchen, where our cookie created a pile of healthy sandwiches. In no time, all the heavenly tasting food had disappeared into my three bottomless pits and into one more sophisticated one. After drinking fresh orange juice, we burped loudly to thank our food spirits for their healthy sustenance. Again, it felt good to act a bit naughty...

After my boys had cleared the table and cleaned the dishes, little Harry first got his mask from his green model in our living room and glued it to his face. Then, my three musketeers marched off to BJ's house, to try to free their three friends from their chores, and to ask them to come over and help them with their newest design. In the meantime, I returned to my computer and again disappeared into my manuscript. Slowly, a nice first manuscript started to develop.

An hour later, my three musketeers returned, and John told me:

"Dad, we've helped Jason's Dad clean up his garage and throw his old garbage away, because he wanted to sell his house before he died. However, Harry started to talk to him, and convinced him to wait until Jason will be eighteen years old and can live on his own in their house! Now, both Jason and Nicky will inherit their house after their Dad dies, but their Dad wants to talk to you first."

Before I could answer, my little Shaman raced to our front door and opened it. Soon, he returned, followed by BJ, Jason, Carl, and Nicky. Again, I wondered how my boy always knew that somebody would show up, at least ten seconds before our doorbell sounded...

BJ immediately came up to me and asked me:

"Please, Big Harry, could I talk in private with you first?"

Chapter 22. I was 'Gypsy Monarch Harold the Great'.

"Yes, of course! Only, let me brew fresh coffee first. Boys, could you please leave BJ and me alone until we are ready?"

Helpfully, all six boys nodded, while John responded:

"Of course, Dad! You can take your time, while we show Jason and Carl our newest tree house design. Oops, sorry, I forgot our best original tree house sketcher, Nicky..."

First, I brewed fresh coffee for BJ and for myself. Then, we went to our living room with, where BJ started to tell:

"Firstly, I want to compliment you with such an extremely clever son, your burnt Gypsy boy Harry. My goodness, that boy can talk the nits out of your hair and make the louses shrivel from fear, with his piercing blue eyes! This morning, I had planned to clean my house, to sell it before I died, and to set up a fund, so that Nicky could study and Jason and Carl could rent a room if they wanted. Then, your three boys showed up. Within five minutes, Harry totally convinced me that it would be cruel to sell my house to a stranger and saddle Jason and Carl up with a lousy rented room somewhere else. It would be far better for my sons and for me to set up a will, so that Jason and Nicky can inherit our house after I die! Thus, they will keep their own home and Carl can stay with them. Harry even promised that both you and he can look after my three boys until they will be old enough to fend for themselves. He also told me you know a good lawyer who can set up everything legally... Harry has totally convinced me, and I still feel very impressed. Boy, can that little Gypsy kid argue!"

BJ took a quick sip of his coffee, and then went on:

"Now, I also want to ask you for something else. My doctors want to give me some treatment that might be able to cure my cancer, but it also implies hospitalization for a long time, and the outcome is unsure. Up to today, I've always refused to undergo that treatment, because I didn't want to go on with my life as it was. I was sure I had nothing left to live for, and that everybody would be better off when I died. Only, since yesterday, all my feelings have changed! Jason loves me again and, at least every ten minutes, he and Nicky want a quick kiss and a cuddle. For the first time after all those years, I feel totally and completely alive! Now, I want to undergo that cancer treatment; because I want to be there for my sons and to see them grow up, for as long as will be possible... Big Harry, could you please look after my boys, and perhaps take them into your house during the day, while

I am in that hospital to undergo my treatment? I even want to pay for your invaluable help, but I don't have much money..."

Feeling a bit surprised, but also very happy to find out that BJ had changed his mind this much, I responded:

"Don't worry, BJ! While you are in that hospital for your cancer treatment, I will look after your boys and help them with everything that I can. Of course, you don't have to pay me, because the spontaneous love from Nicky and Jason will be more than enough payment! I will give you my lawyer's address and telephone number; and I will call him in advance and ask him to help you set everything up legally, next to adding the costs to my bill without any further questions..."

"Oh, WOW! Big Harry, how can I ever thank you? Thank you very much again for all your invaluable help, Big Harry, and... err... from now on, I would like us to be good friends."

For a brief moment, I fell silent and didn't know how to react... Then, my Own Heart told me, loud and clear, what I had to do. Yes, I certainly wanted to be BJ's friend! Without using any words, BJ and I rose from our chairs and spontaneously embraced. We looked into each other's eyes, and clearly saw each other's trust and determination. From this very moment on, BJ and I were good friends!

BJ almost crushed me between his strong arms, while he sighed:

"This is the first time in my life that I'm embracing a real friend. Up to now, I always was only a big bully, and nobody ever liked me. Fortunately, both you and your little son have made me see, just in time, that it's never too late to change."

"Yes, BJ, and you certainly DID change; quite a lot more than any of us ever expected! Now, I feel honored to be your friend."

After we sat down again, we talked about what would happen during the time BJ was in a hospital to undergo his cancer treatment. He would first phone my lawyer, to explain his situation and ask for his legal advice and all the necessary papers. He also wanted to grant me temporary custody of his two sons during the time he would be in that hospital; and grant me full custody of them in case his cancer treatment failed and he died after all. If BJ died, Jason and Nicky would inherit their house and continue to live in their own home, probably accompanied by Carl; while little Harry and I would 'keep a close eye on them' until they would be at least eighteen years old, as my little soul mate already had promised in advance.

Feeling satisfied with our mutual agreement, we rose from our chairs and went to the kitchen; where we started to laugh at seeing the kitchen table littered with all sorts of futuristic tree house designs!

All six boys sat or stood around our littered kitchen table, obviously involved in a heated discussion about their newest plan, because John was afraid our three birches would be too far away from each other to support the wooden floor sufficiently. Fiercely defending his own point of view, he deliberated all the pros and cons of too long supporting beams and too small iron clamps.

My little soul mate had drawn a picture with all the measurements on it, and used it to clarify why long wooden beams wouldn't be safe enough. John was responding more with his hands than with his mouth, while depicting what kind of a clever solution he had in mind.

Nicky agreed with his inseparable friend, and told Jason to shut up because he didn't know what he was talking about. Jason reacted a bit angrily, but had to admit little Harry could be right and that they should work out John's clever solution. Nicky looked around triumphantly; while Carl and Davy only listened to their heated discussion but clearly had their own thoughts about everything. In the long run, they might turn out to be the most sensible ones...

Slowly and carefully, BJ lowered himself onto one of our folding chairs. With a contorted face, he waited until his back pain subsided. Then, he coughed a few times, to get everybody's attention.

While everybody turned towards BJ, the giant started to explain:

"Boys, I want to explain a couple of important things to you; so, please, listen carefully to what I have to say! Since yesterday, a lot of important things around Jason, Nicky, and me have changed. I suppose you already know that I have cancer in the last stage and will probably die soon. However, I didn't tell you that my doctors also offered me a long-term treatment that perhaps might cure me. Up to now, I just didn't want to live any more, because I still thought that nobody ever loved me or would miss me, with my angry tantrums and my too big mouth... Then, I suddenly met Big Harry and little Harry, and both Jason and Nicky started to love me again, which made me think about my earlier decision. Today, my young friend over here, little Harry, thoroughly changed my mind. Within five minutes, he convinced me it would be cruel to sell my house to some stranger and let Jason and Carl rent a lousy room somewhere else..."

BJ started to cough, and took another sip of his coffee before he wiped his teary eyes, blew his nose, and finally went on:

"Since today, I've decided to stay alive for my own sons and for Carl, for as long as I can. Therefore, I now want to undergo that cancer treatment. I also want to adopt Carl as my third son, so that he too inherits my house in case I will die after all. Perhaps I'm again rushing things too much, but I'm still afraid that I don't have much time left... Please, Carl, do you want to be my adopted son, start living in my house, and get the same rights as Jason and Nicky?"

For about ten seconds, nothing happened, while everybody looked around at each other with surprised faces. Especially Carl looked at Jason and Nicky, swallowed a few times, looked at me, and still hesitated. Then, totally unexpectedly, a living cannonball jumped up from his folding chair and launched himself at BJ, with a loud Indian howl and a face full of tears and happiness!

Clamping himself onto his new Dad, Carl started to cry and laugh at the same time, while he exclaimed:

"Yes, sir, I certainly want you to be my new Dad, and I also want to become your adopted son! Since this morning, I've already started to love you more and more, and I am now very happy to know that you want to stay alive. I am also still feeling a bit sorry, because I've been waiting for such a long time with my decision..."

This time, we all started to cheer, at seeing Carl's happy looks and BJ's proudly beaming face. Then, we all crowded around Carl and BJ, and congratulated them with their spontaneous decision.

Finally, for the first time since I met him, BJ's face beamed! Spontaneously, he folded his enormous arms around Carl's thin frame and pulled him even closer to his broad chest, while desperately trying not to squash his new son too much. Only, Carl didn't seem to mind at all.

A few seconds later, Carl suddenly looked up at me with a hint of fear in his sparkling eyes, while he stuttered:

"Pop, I know that YOU wanted to adopt me, but..."

Before Carl could go on, I interrupted him and explained:

"No, Carl, I've only wanted to adopt you because I wanted to try to free you from Mister John Dragon's prison! Of course, this important decision has to be yours and only yours. Now that you have decided for yourself, I am sure that BJ will be a wonderful Dad to you!"

Spontaneously, all of us rose from our chairs, even BJ, and folded our arms around each other's waists or shoulders. Then, we embraced as one big happy family! Bear-hugging each other like this felt wonderful, and we all basked in our powerful feelings of mutual love and sheer happiness. Again, everything had turned out for the best!

I also heard Jack's warm and soulful voice in my inside:

"My dear brother; thank you very much for again listening to your Own Heart, this time without doubting any more. Therefore, we will help your new friend to get rid of his cancer, and to be there for his own two sons and for his adopted third son. Be blessed!"

At exactly that same moment, my little soul mate looked up and smiled at me, to let me know he too had heard Jack's happy message! We only had to keep it a secret until BJ's cancer had healed...

After a long time of bear-hugging and feeling happy, BJ wanted to go home, because he started to feel too tired and had to take his medicine for his more and more upcoming pain. Of course, BJ's three sons wanted to accompany their Dad to their house, to help him with his undressing and to set up Carl's new room. Tomorrow, BJ would take Carl downtown, to buy him lots of new clothes and all the other necessary things that his young adolescent needed, and I would assist BJ with my 'inexhaustible' credit card if necessary.

Before BJ's new happy family went to their own house to set up Carl's new room and to make plans for their upcoming future, Jason hesitantly asked me:

"Pop? Now that Carl has started living with us, could we please take our wood home and build our tree house in our own backyard?"

Of course, my own boys immediately agreed, although my clever little soul mate came up with an important stipulation:

"That is okay with me, but only if you allow us to help you!"

Chuckling, Jason ruffled my boy's unruly blond hair, draped his arms around my boy's tiny shoulders, and sincerely promised:

"Harry, we wouldn't dare build our tree house without your help as our best technical designer and Gypsy brainiac!"

Immediately, my little soul mate fished Nicky's first design out of his back pocket and gave it to Jason and Carl, while smiling:

"Now, you can build your own tree house exactly as Carl and you originally designed it, but with our help!"

Still laughing, my happy threesome and I waved BJ's new family out until they disappeared around a corner. Tomorrow, we would first drive Jason's stack of used wood and lumber back to their backyard. Then, my boys would help them build their tree house in their own backyard, by using Carl's original design.

Soon, my three boys disappeared upstairs, to put on their own or borrowed swim gear. They went outside and immediately plunged into our still empty swimming pool. However, within two minutes, the first neighborhood children showed up in our backyard and politely asked if our swimming pool would be open again...

# # #

---. You've reached the end of our third book.

Although you've reached the end of this third book, it is NOT the end of our ongoing adventures! In the FOURTH book of our 'Gypsy Series', which is called *'a Man loves a Boy -4- my boy gets a new face'*, my little soul mate and I are surviving many more funny, sad, nasty, and powerful adventures. First, we visit his parent's graveyard and buy them a beautiful marble gravestone. Then, BJ heals from his lethal cancer. Our youngest little neighborhood boy turns out to be a very powerful upcoming Shaman. Finally, my so badly burnt little Gypsy Crown Prince gets a brand new face and new skin on his body; but, after he returns home, nobody recognizes him any more!

#

In the meantime, my little soul mate has started writing his OWN 'Gypsy Series' of books, about his growing up as a little Gypsy Crown Prince until he meets me! In the first book of his OWN series, which is called *'a Boy loves a Man -1- Gypsy Heir to the Throne'*, our little Prince grows up in a secluded site in the Rumanian mountains, surrounded by steep ravines and dangerous forests. He is a 'wise old soul', an upcoming Shaman, and way too intelligent for his own good. His Inner Wisdom already knows he has to fulfill an Important Task on Earth, assisted by all his Cosmic Friends, Beloved Ancestors, and Spirit Guides; but his too witty brain is always in the way and confusing him with its many questions and annoying 'buts' and 'ifs'.

#

Please visit our own Internet site ***www.gypsyseries.com*** ; to stay informed about our newest 'Gypsy Series' books; and please send us a stimulating email. I am a retired Dutch psychotherapist, living in The Netherlands, and still writing powerful 'books with a message'. May our Supreme Being always be with you, bless you, and send you lots of Pure Love and Happiness in your life!

Aad Aandacht, retired Dutch psychotherapist and writer.

#

Aad Aandacht is a retired Dutch psychotherapist, living in a small country called The Netherlands. Just like in all his beautiful Gypsy stories, he has been married but divorced, and he has two lovable grown-up daughters but no grandchildren to spoil.

After writing many books in his own language, Dutch; he decided to write his next series of books in a to him foreign language, hoping that writing them in the International Language would spread their important messages all over the world more easily.

Aad still loves writing 'emotional roller coasters' and 'books with a message'; and he plans to go on writing them for a very long time! Next to being a psychotherapist, he studied several 'alternative' and 'paranormal' treatments and remedies; for example 'aura reading and healing', 'contacts with Spirit Guides and Helpers', 'past lives' or 'reincarnations', and the 'Laws of Karma'. He always interweaves his lifetime of vast knowledge and experiences into his stories, so that his readers can pick up his important lessons easily.

Although Aad retired in 2004, he is still very active; helping many so-called 'sensitive children', 'new-age children', 'indigo children', 'crystal children', or 'Aquarius children' get a better life; with more understanding from their parents and surrounding grown-ups.

Enjoy Aad's powerful books, by visiting his Internet site:

www.aadaandacht.com
aad@aadaandacht.com

# # #

CPSIA information can be obtained at www.ICGtesting.com
Printed in the USA
LVOW081816120712

289841LV00021B/158/P